"It isn't necessary for you to carry me inside."

Avery spoke with as much dignity as she could muster under the circumstances. She was aware of what a woebegone sight she presented to his hard, unsympathetic gaze, her face tearstained as well as wan and pale. Never had she felt more defenseless in her life.

"Carrying you is easier and faster." Clark's grim tone ruled out any argument.

His gentleness in transporting her totally belied his voice and his demeanor. Avery helped as much as she could to prevent herself from being a deadweight by putting her arms around his neck. She kept her eyes closed, her only means of screening her emotions at such close quarters.

His strength infused her with much-needed comfort. It also awoke an aching need to be held. With her self-control so battered and bruised, like her body, Avery couldn't close out the realization of how wonderful it would be to have this strong man hug her tight.

Dear Reader,

Last year, I requested that you send me your opinions on the books that we publish—and on romances in general. Thank you so much for the many thoughtful comments. For the next couple of months, I'd like to share with you quotes from those letters. This seems very appropriate now, while we are in the midst of the THAT SPECIAL WOMAN! promotion. Each one of our readers is a special woman, as heroic as the heroines in our books.

This August has some wonderful books coming your way. *More Than He Bargained For* by Carole Halston, a warm, poignant story, is the THAT SPECIAL WOMAN! selection. Debbie Macomber also brings us the first book in her FROM THIS DAY FORWARD series—*Groom Wanted*. MORGAN'S MERCENARIES, Lindsay McKenna's action-packed trio concludes this month with *Commando*. And don't miss books from other favorite authors: Marie Ferrarella, Susan Mallery and Christine Rimmer.

I hope you enjoy this book, and all of the stories to come! Have a wonderful August!

Sincerely,

Tara Gavin
Senior Editor
Silhouette Books

Quote of the Month: ''Romance books provide the escape that is needed from the sometimes crazy and hard-to-live-in world. It takes me away for that three or four hours a day to a place no one else can come into. That is why I read romances. Because sometimes there is not a happy ending, and going to a place where there is can uplift the spirit that really needs it.''

—J. Majeski
New Jersey

CAROLE HALSTON

MORE THAN HE BARGAINED FOR

Silhouette®

SPECIAL EDITION®

Published by Silhouette Books New York

America's Publisher of Contemporary Romance

SILHOUETTE BOOKS
300 East 42nd St., New York, N.Y. 10017

MORE THAN HE BARGAINED FOR

ISBN: 0-373-09829-4

First Silhouette Books printing August 1993

CAROLE HALSTON

is a Louisiana native residing on the north shore of Lake Ponchartrain, near New Orleans. She enjoys traveling with her husband to research less familiar locations for settings but is always happy to return home to her own unique region, a rich source in itself for romantic stories about warm, wonderful people.

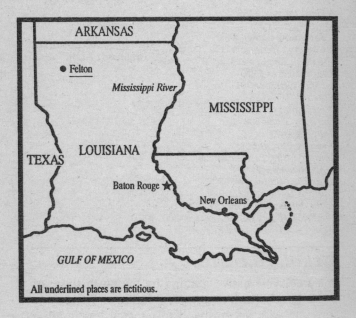

ARKANSAS

● Felton

Mississippi River

MISSISSIPPI

TEXAS   LOUISIANA

Baton Rouge ★

New Orleans ●

GULF OF MEXICO

All underlined places are fictitious.

Chapter One

I would make the boys French toast for breakfast as a special treat except that I don't know whether I have the ingredients. . . .

Avery's vague sense of worry became painful sadness as she awakened in the strange bedroom. No, she didn't have the ingredients for French toast, the twins' favorite breakfast, downstairs in the unfamiliar kitchen.

Even if she did, she couldn't cook breakfast for them. They weren't with her. They were with their father. And not just for a visit. Perhaps permanently.

It was that *perhaps* that provided Avery with the necessary optimism to get up each morning and face a new day.

The lusty crowing of a rooster came through the open window, drowning out the cheery twitter of birds. Avery sat up in bed as the rooster crowed again, this time joined by assorted squawking and bleating sounds. Even to her uneducated city ear, there was no panic in the barnyard concert. Larry Wade's feathered flock and lone goat, Avery's charges, were probably getting impatient for their breakfast.

"Okay, I hear you guys," she said aloud. "Do you mind if I grab a cup of coffee first? Then I'll be out to tend to you."

The cacophony rose up again, and Avery smiled, imagining that she detected a note of indignation. The smile grew wistful as she thought about how much fun her move to the country might have been if the twins were sharing the novel experiences with her.

They would visit her during the summer, Avery reminded herself. Being unemployed had its compensations. She could spend every minute of the time with them.

Downstairs Larry's elderly black Labrador retriever whined a patient reminder of his presence. "I'll be right down to let you out, Sam," Avery called, climbing out of bed. It seemed there would be little opportunity for wallowing in self-pity on awakening in the country. That was good. Avery was so used to being needed.

After a hurried cup of coffee, she went outside, amused by her own faint apprehension. This was her first day as resident caretaker. Mentally she rehearsed Larry's instructions as she approached the pump house, where the chicken feed and goat feed were stored. The little building was painted a putty color with dark green trim like the Acadian-style house with its steep-pitched galvanized tin roof.

Avery filled two containers from the large sacks. A plastic ice-cream bucket held chicken fare, cracked corn, and a coffee can held goat fare, some sort of oats. *Be sure and keep the pump-house door closed,* Larry had cautioned. She would close the door on her return when she replaced the emptied containers, Avery decided, both hands occupied.

At the gate to the pen, she had to set down the feed to deal with the latch, which stubbornly wouldn't release. *There's probably a trick to it,* she thought. Meanwhile, the dozen or so chickens and the rooster and the goat, who shared the pen with the poultry, all crowded near the gate with anxious clucking and bleating.

"Just relax, girls and boys," she chided, trying to sound calm and in control. Animals were supposed to sense human nervousness, weren't they? "Breakfast is only seconds away."

Finally the latch responded with a rusty click, and the gate started to swing open of its own accord. Avery hastily shoved it closed to keep the animals from escaping. The containers of feed were behind her. Some acrobatics were required to pick them up. A farmer obviously had to be in good shape, she reflected ruefully, balancing on one foot and turning and bending while she kept her other foot aloft and braced against the gate.

With a container in each arm, she managed to maneuver herself through a narrow opening. Once inside the pen, though, she was loath to pull the gate closed. What if she couldn't operate the troublesome latch from inside? Then she'd be penned up with the chickens and goat. What a predicament that would be.

Avery gambled on letting the gate swing open, trusting that hunger would keep the inhabitants of the pen inside. After a nervous moment or two, she saw that her judgment had been good. The danger was in being knocked to the ground and trampled.

"Shoo! Shoo!" The farm vocabulary had little noticeable effect. "Out of my way, you silly things! Where are your manners?" Using her sternest no-nonsense tone—the one that alerted the boys she really meant business—Avery waded into the fray, opening up a path to a pail attached to the fence, the goat's feeding bin. *Feed Billy first,* Larry had said.

With the animal occupied greedily munching his oats, she scattered the chicken feed by handfuls, feeling foolishly inept. Apparently her technique worked well enough, though, because the chickens scurried from around her ankles and commenced pecking up the kernels with frantic bobbing motions.

Avery drew in a deep breath, her tension easing with a budding sense of competence. In a few days, she would be an old hand at this.

"Eat up, girls and boys." The rooster raised his head and eyed her doubtfully. Avery grinned and addressed him. "You might as well get used to my conversation. Your owner is going to be away for a whole year, and he's left all of you in my care. Admittedly I'm inexperienced, but I'll get better with practice. All of you can help by showing some patience and developing a few manners."

The rooster made a throaty sound as though in answer and resumed pecking the ground with vigor.

"Let me put any rumors to rest," Avery went on. Talking to poultry and a goat was surely healthier than talking to herself. "Your owner and I were employed by the same major oil company until a few months ago, when the whole New Orleans office was closed down and we lost our jobs, along with everyone else except high-ranking management people who got transferred. He and I were friendly acquaintances, but we were never romantically involved. He needs someone to live here and take care of his place while he's working in the Persian Gulf for a year. Being his caretaker seemed a better alternative for me than moving to a cheaper apartment in a worse neighborhood. I've been job searching without any success," she explained.

The goat withdrew his head from the pail and gave Avery a glance as though to say, *Go on. I'm listening, but keep it brief*. Then he burrowed his head again, his stubby tail twitching.

"I would just appreciate it if you'd pass the word to the neighbors' animals that my living in your owner's house is on the up and up," Avery concluded, taking his hint. She sighed. "It's not for myself that I'm concerned about my reputation, but I'm the mother of two sons, eleven-year-olds. Their names are Bret and Bart. They'll be coming for a visit from California during the summer so you'll get to know them well. They're wonderful boys, even if I am rather biased. Excuse me, but I get choked up like this when I talk about them. . . ."

Blinded by tears of lonely, sad emotion, she left the pen. Again the gate latch was uncooperative, and she pinched a finger as she was securing it.

"Darned thing," she muttered and sucked on the injured finger as she waited a moment to make sure that the gate was secure.

Her chore finished, she returned the empty containers to the pump house, closed the door and retraced her steps to the back porch of the house, where Sam, the Labrador, waited to be let back in. In the kitchen she refilled her coffee mug and took it outside, exiting through the front door this time. The house faced east, and the front porch, which afforded a view of the pond, was bathed in bright sunshine.

Larry hadn't exaggerated. This country place of his offered all the pleasures of a private park, all hers to be enjoyed. Tall pine trees were reflected in the mirrorlike surface of the pond. In her estimation it qualified as a small lake, fringed with reeds and purple and yellow irises in bloom.

While she watched, a fish splashed out in the center, creating a circle of widening ripples.

All hers to enjoy—if only her heart weren't so heavy.

Avery stepped off the porch with a determined air and walked across the grass to the edge of the pond. According to Larry, there were bass and catfish large enough for eating just waiting to be caught. He'd generously given her permission to use his fishing paraphernalia. Scooping a goldfish out of a glass bowl of tap water was Avery's entire experience with catching fish.

She could imagine herself perhaps hooking and landing a fish, but she couldn't bear to think of dealing with the gory stages between live, squirming fish and baked or broiled filet. No, thank you.

Fishing in the pond would be fun for the twins, though. A vision of them sitting cross-legged on the bank a short distance apart, holding cane fishing poles, brought a rush of warm mother's love to her breast. But the vision triggered the wrenching pain of separation, too.

Don't you tear up, she threatened herself, turning away from the pond. *Crying your eyes out isn't going to help one bit, as you well know by now.*

Past the house back in a far corner was Larry's large vegetable garden that she'd inherited. Gulping the last swallow of coffee in her mug, Avery headed for the garden.

On the perimeter of the garden plot, she surveyed orderly rows of thriving plants. He'd mentioned that he had corn, tomatoes, okra, squash, several varieties of beans, green peppers, cucumbers. Avery, whose familiarity with vegetables was restricted to produce departments in supermarkets and vegetable stands, could identify the tall corn stalks and the tomato bushes. She would simply have to see what grew on the great variety of other plants and vines, some of which looked quite exotic.

A garden full of vegetables, unlike a pond teeming with fish, was a challenge Avery thought she *could* manage. Picking vegetables couldn't be all that much of a specialized skill. She would learn the proper methods for preparing the surplus for freezing. Larry had an upright freezer the size of a refrigerator that was at her disposal. If she could find a book on the subject, she might even try her hand at canning.

It could be such fun if only the twins were here to lend a hand and get in the way—

Avery cut off that futile line of thought and went to the house to get her purse and the keys to Larry's small economy pickup, her means of transportation now that she'd sold her car. This morning she would go to the village and do her grocery shopping.

Sam, the Lab, wasn't interested in accompanying her. He thumped his tail in apologetic refusal to her invitation, "Want to go for a ride, Sam?" Avery left him in the house. Before driving away, she glanced to see that the pump-house door was closed and that all seemed well with her charges in the pen.

The sight of the gate brought to mind the ornery latch and she made a mental note to purchase some sort of lubricant.

Larry's house was set near the back of his five acres of property. His long gravel driveway measured at least a couple of city blocks. *I'll get my exercise walking to and from the mailbox,* Avery thought wryly, checking for traffic and pulling out onto the two-lane highway with not a vehicle in sight.

The next mailbox wasn't that far from hers. She read the name, C. STRONG, lettered in white paint against the black metal, as she drove past. Larry had forewarned her that his nearest neighbor was antisocial and hard to get along with.

C. Strong's house, like Larry's, wasn't visible from the road. Nor had Avery glimpsed it through the woods from Larry's yard. Did he have a wife and family? she wondered. It hadn't occurred to her to ask Larry at the time. If there were a Mrs. Strong, she might be as sweet and nice as her husband was crabby.

Avery would certainly welcome having another woman close, whatever her age. Larry hadn't indicated how old C. Strong was. She had a hunch that he was probably in his fifties or sixties, old enough to be set in his ways and inflexible.

The highway dipped and curved. Off to her left was rolling pastureland with cows grazing. Avery was more interested in a sign on her right, Pleasant Hollow Nursery. It was impossible to tell whether the owners lived on the premises because the asphalt road to the nursery wound through a pine forest and out of sight. But maybe they did. And maybe they were neighborly people, unlike grumpy old C. Strong.

Passing the sign again a couple of hours later on her return, Avery sighed in discouragement. She'd learned in the village why Larry hadn't mentioned the owners of Pleasant Hollow Nursery. There was only one owner, singular. C. Strong himself, who apparently was a retired man who'd bought the nursery and the house and property adjacent to Larry's from the Dorseys, a well-liked couple with five children. The Dorseys had moved to Florida. They sounded like the neighbors she would have loved to have next door.

C. Strong— Avery still didn't know what the initial stood for—didn't have a wife. He was either a crusty old bachelor or a widower, probably the former. Without ever seeing the man or meeting him, she was forming an impression of him as a reclusive type, an old sourpuss.

Darn, what bad luck that someone like him had to turn out to be her only close neighbor.

However, all was not lost. The good news was that Avery had visited the tiny public library branch in the village and found a book on canning and freezing food. Also a thick manual on raising livestock, with sections on poultry and one on goats. She planned to become better informed about the requirements and characteristics of her feathered and hooved charges.

With that thought in mind, Avery turned into Larry's driveway. Already it seemed a little more like *her* driveway.

All appeared tranquil when the house came into sight. The surface of the pond was calm without a ripple. There was no activity in the pen. Were the chickens all inside their house, laying eggs, and the goat taking a midday siesta in his house? Avery wondered. The rooster wasn't in evidence, either.

Anyone might think the pen was empty—

Dear God, it was empty!

The appalling realization dawned when she got closer and saw the gate standing wide open. *Had some thief come in her absence and stolen all the poultry and the goat?* What other explanation could there be?

Avery got out of the pickup, dismayed and uncertain about what she should do next. Was there a rural police department? Should she call the state troopers and report the theft?

A movement in the garden caught her attention. She looked and was flooded with emotion akin to joy when she saw two chickens busily scratching. Another movement at the edge of Larry's property made her turn her head just in time to see a chicken disappearing into the woods—C. Strong's woods.

"Come back!" Avery called, a new possibility occurring. Maybe the gate had come open, allowing the chickens and goats to wander out.

A loud sound like a gunshot made her jump. The shock to her eardrums seemed to make her ears sensitive. She heard a dog barking and a man shouting.

Avery's blood turned to ice. That irate man could be none other than C. Strong. The sound like a gunshot *was* a gunshot. He was shooting at Larry's poor escaped chickens! He might even have shot Billy, Larry's goat!

Another loud booming report released her from a state of horrified paralysis. Avery took off for the woods at a run. She had to stop the murderer!

There was a letter from his little girl, Elizabeth, in the mail.

Clark held the pink envelope in his big hand, studying the childish handwriting while his mixture of emotions subsided to a manageable level. Protective love and fatherly pleasure held in check the anger and bitterness that otherwise might have destroyed him.

Clark couldn't turn into a raging maniac because he had to keep his sanity and be as good a father for Elizabeth, as *much* a father, as the biased courts and judges allowed him to be. Still, the anger ate at him, even here in this quiet, peaceful locale where he'd come to escape all confrontation.

It was lunchtime. On his way home from the nursery, he'd stopped out on the highway beside his mailbox. There was no traffic coming from either direction, so he gently tore open the envelope and scanned the single page of pink paper. His daughter's favorite color was pink.

"Dear Daddy," she had written. "I miss you very much. Mommy has been sick a lot. Grandma and Grandpa Laird take me to their house. I helped Grandma make cookies. They were delicious. I drew you a picture. Love, Elizabeth.''

Her block printing blurred. Clark blinked away a burning haze of tears, his jaw set so hard that it ached. Marilyn was doping herself up on prescription drugs again. That was Mommy's illness. Her parents were taking care of their grandchild, supportive of their daughter as always, a part of her problem because they covered up for her.

The Lairds were good, upstanding people. Clark at least had the reassurance that Elizabeth wasn't being neglected. But he was her parent. She should be in his care, not theirs. But tell that to a court. God knows Clark had tried to get custody.

The unsuccessful battle had turned him into a cynical, bitter man, and he knew that. He didn't vent his bitterness on anyone else. He didn't ask for sympathy. He coped alone. All he asked was to be treated with similar consideration.

Isolation and privacy were the balm to Clark's spiritual rawness. He'd quit a successful career as a landscape architect to gain the seclusion he needed. Owning and operating a small nursery was no cherished dream of his. It came more under the category of a therapeutic endeavor.

Today of all days, he was in no mood to arrive at his house and have to deal with the scene of mayhem awaiting him.

His backyard was strewn with chicken feathers, and a maimed, bloody chicken was fluttering on the ground. Shep, his German shepherd, was in savage pursuit of several more chickens. He brought one down as Clark leapt from his van, shouting the dog's name.

Shep reluctantly, but promptly released his prey and trotted over to Clark, but the chicken flopped helplessly, in sad condition.

Clark cursed. He would have to put the poor thing out of its misery and the other one, too. "Stay!" he ordered as half a dozen more chickens wandered into the yard from the woods and Shep tensed for attack, barking. The obedient and normally gentle dog sat on his haunches.

The only place the chickens could be coming from was next door. Clark had heard through the grapevine that the fellow over there, Wade, was going overseas for a year to work. Had he turned his chickens loose to fend for themselves? Clark just hoped he hadn't turned that damned goat loose.

He and Wade had had a couple of run-ins over the goat, which originally Wade had allowed to roam free. The pesky animal had made several destructive visits, on one occasion not contenting himself with grazing on Clark's flower beds and shrubbery, but butting in the screen door to the porch and entering Clark's house in his absence and wreaking havoc inside.

"You stay, Shep." Clark's voice was fierce as he reiterated the command, his gaze seeking out a bed of tender young lilies, hybrid daylilies that he'd painstakingly cultivated as a pet project as well as a possible commercial venture. Trust that damned goat to head straight to those lilies if he were on the loose, Clark thought as he went to fetch the pistol that was his only firearm.

His sole reason for owning it was for a situation like this. Clark had no fondness for guns despite the fact he was good at handling them. His skill with guns came naturally to a young boy who grew up in Texas. Bringing down a deer by the age of twelve had been a rite of manhood, one that had given him no thrill.

The pistol was unloaded. He had to take time to load it. A fresh bout of barking from Shep made him hurry. More chickens must be arriving, oblivious to the danger. Clark would never raise chickens. They were such incredibly stupid creatures.

Shep's barking reached a new pitch. The realization had barely sunk in when Clark heard a goat bleating. The damned goat was outside! Shoving the last bullet into place, he took off at a run through the house. Emerging onto the back porch, he flung open the screened door, letting out a roar of pure rage.

The goat was munching on his bed of daylilies, eating them down to the roots. Clark waved his arms, the pistol held aloft in one hand, and rushed at the goat, yelling a string of curses and violent threats. The perverse animal munched faster.

One of the fatally wounded chickens lay in Clark's path. As furious as he was and intent on rescuing his lilies, he was stirred by pity. He paused to lower the pistol and shoot the chicken in an act of mercy.

Stepping over the carcass, he took long, running strides to the lily bed and bodily picked up the smelly goat, carrying him over to where the second chicken lay flopping weakly. Grimacing, Clark performed his repugnant deed, aiming the pistol with accuracy.

He was carrying the goat under one arm toward a shed to get a length of rope when a woman's shouts coming from the woods brought him to a standstill. With the pistol dangling, Clark turned around, still holding the goat. He made out the woman's words as she came nearer, thrashing her way through the underbrush.

"Stop! Stop! You murderer! Don't you dare kill Billy! I swear, I'll have you put in jail!"

Clark recovered from his initial surprise and he waited grimly. Wade must have rented his place to a couple. They were the ones responsible for this mayhem and annoyance. Through carelessness or thoughtlessness they'd let the chickens and goat out and were going to answer to Clark's wrath.

The overwrought woman burst from a dense thicket into his yard, her forward momentum almost sending her sprawling. Seeing him, she stopped and stared, her screams dying in her throat. Her eyes widened and she went pale at the sight of the dead chickens.

"You . . . you *shot* Larry's chickens," she accused in a horrified tone, clasping her midriff.

Clark suspected that she was weak in the knees. Undoubtedly she was finding the gory scene nauseating. He had to admire her gutsiness when she took a step forward, going against what was probably her true instinct, to back away. This scene was her and her husband's fault, he reminded himself.

"Yes, I shot them," he confirmed harshly. "Would you rather I let them suffer?"

"Let them suffer?"

He gestured with the butt of the pistol at the feathers covering the ground. "Hell, lady, don't you see what's happened here? It's lucky I got home when I did and called off my dog, or you wouldn't have had any survivors."

Her gaze went to Shep, who'd come over to station himself beside Clark.

"You're telling me that your guard dog attacked the chickens?" she demanded, a quavery note betraying her. "You let him run free in your yard?"

"He isn't a guard dog."

"He looks like a German shepherd."

"All German shepherds aren't guard dogs, lady. This one lets rabbits hop around unharmed. He's never been around chickens. I suggest that in the future you keep yours penned up if you value them. Now get them out of my yard and take this damned goat, too." Clark set the goat down and gave his rump a push toward her. "If he gets loose and comes over on my property again, I just might shoot him."

It was nothing but a bluff, meant to intimidate her into keeping the goat confined, but she obviously believed him quite capable of the violent act.

"Come here, Billy," she urged protectively, holding out her hand.

The goat bleated and headed straight for Clark's bed of daylilies. Clark roared a warning at the woman, "You'd better stop that sonofabitch!"

"Don't you dare shoot him!" she blazed back, and rushed to the goat, getting down on her haunches and protecting his body with her own. "You'll have to shoot me, and it'll be murder. You'll go to prison."

"For heaven's sake, lady, I'm not going to hurt you or him. Just get him the hell out of here before he does any more damage. I'll take Shep inside." Clark snapped his fingers and walked toward his house, the docile German shepherd at his heels.

"Come on, Billy. Let's go home. Come with Avery." The relief in her voice turned to frustration as she cajoled and pleaded, obviously to no avail. "Er, Mr. Strong—"

Clark had reached the back porch. He stopped and turned around, taken aback that she'd addressed him by his name.

"Could I possibly borrow a leash?" she asked.

"A leash?" he repeated skeptically.

"Yes, you must have a leash for your dog. Could I use it? Obviously this goat hasn't been to obedience classes."

Clark frowned, not about to be humored into making light of the situation. This was no laughing matter, and she needed to have that fact impressed upon her. He'd been able to conclude by now that she didn't know beans about chickens or goats.

"I'll get you some rope," he said curtly.

Without any further conversation, he shut Shep in the house and, leaving the gun on the porch, got the rope from the shed. It irritated him that he wanted to unbend and play the chivalrous male. Acting friendly would only result in encouraging these new people next door to make nuisances of themselves.

He liked this woman on sight, though. In her mid-thirties, she wasn't beautiful by any means, but she was attractive. Taller than average, she had a lanky, full-breasted figure, tawny-colored hair and pretty blue eyes. Her attire was simple, a denim skirt and print blouse.

Clark hadn't noticed a wedding ring, but she was definitely a married woman with a family. She had *Mom* written all over her, unlike his ex-wife, Marilyn.

"Thank you," she said with dignity, reaching out her right hand as he approached, holding a coiled length of lightweight rope.

"Let him go and I'll tie a lead on him for you," Clark offered brusquely.

"I can manage," she replied, refusing his aid.

Clark handed her the rope, turned on his heel and headed once again for his house. At the screen door he paused and looked around. She had tied one end of the rope around the goat's neck, forming a slack noose, and was on her feet, tugging gently.

"Come on, Billy," she scolded in a maternal tone. "I've had enough of this stubborn behavior of yours." The goat planted his feet. She pulled harder, her lips compressed. The recalcitrant animal lowered his head and freed himself of the noose. Frantically she grabbed him again with both arms and looked in desperation at Clark, whom she'd been ignoring. "Is there a local fire department that you could call for me?" she implored.

"Lady, fire departments in the country put out fires. They don't rescue kittens from trees or deal with other such minor crises."

"My name is Avery," she informed him. "Avery Payton. I'm trying to deal with what isn't a minor crisis for me. I happen to be responsible for this dumb animal and for a flock of poultry scattered all over creation. Not to mention those two poor chickens lying dead on the ground that I'll have on my conscience. Surely there's someone around here you could call to help me, some person who knows the meaning of the word *neighbor*."

"What about your husband?"

The inquiry was more grudging curiosity than anything else. Clark was resigned by this point to coming to her aid himself.

"I'm not married."

Her answer came as a surprise. He hadn't figured her to be living with a man. Obviously the guy was at work. Otherwise she would have suggested summoning him.

"Is there an older kid at home who might give you a hand?"

Mutely she shook her head. Unless Clark was imagining things, his question caused her pain. After a second's pause, during which she must have tapped new resources, she began retying the rope around the goat's neck, embarking on another attempt to lead the rascal to safety.

"I'll take the goat over," he stated brusquely. "You worry about the chickens."

She stopped immediately, but didn't rise when he reached her. "You won't be rough with him?"

"Not nearly as rough as he deserves. I'd like to give him a bad case of indigestion for eating my hybrid daylilies. Now do you want me to take him over or not?"

She stood up and backed away.

Clark hefted the goat up under one arm and strode toward the woods. A chicken was pecking in his herb garden. Swearing under his breath, he veered toward it, scooped it up and tucked it under his other arm. The chicken squawked a protest.

"Should I follow your example?" she asked hesitantly. "Pick the chickens up bodily like that?"

"Unless you can figure out some better method," he replied.

The damned goat was a deadweight and stunk to high heaven. Once Clark got him penned up, he would have to spend another hour searching for chickens and carrying them, two at a time.

Let her carry one or two, he thought. *It wouldn't hurt her, and in the future she would be mindful of preventing this kind of thing from happening again.* Clark steeled himself against any sympathy for Avery Payton, who hadn't asked for sympathy.

Avery stood there, gazing after him. His faded yellow cotton knit shirt pulled across broad shoulders and a taut, muscular back. He'd picked the goat up without so much as a grunt. *He was well named,* she thought.

It had made this whole disaster that much more unsettling, discovering that Larry's antisocial neighbor wasn't an older retired man, as she'd assumed, but a man in his prime, tall and well built and physically fit. In addition to her surprise, she'd grasped at once that his wasn't an irascible, peevish nature.

C. Strong wasn't just a grouch. He seethed with anger and controlled violence. At the sight of the gun in his hand and the poor chickens on the ground, Avery had experienced an elemental terror. If her knees hadn't failed her, she might have turned tail and fled back through the woods during those first seconds.

She had soon realized, though, that she probably wasn't in danger of being murdered herself. C. Strong wasn't a maniac or a sadist or a psychopathic killer. He was, however, possibly the most hardened individual she'd ever encountered. An iron man with enormous restraint, thank heaven, but lacking any hint of gentleness or kindness. His emotions were like a blast furnace heating him to the core without softening the iron.

How fitting that he owned a German shepherd rather than a Labrador retriever or a collie or some other gentle-natured breed. Not one sign of affection had he shown toward the vicious dog, nor had the dog licked his hand.

Avery had sensed almost immediately that she would be wasting her breath to offer C. Strong excuses or explanations or apologies. He wasn't interested in hearing reasons. He probably wasn't even capable of sympathy or understanding. Any intrusion by animal or human was inexcusable in his book.

What did the initial C. stand for? she found herself wondering, watching him disappear into the woods. It hardly mattered because she was never likely to be on a first-name basis with him.

What did matter was that he wasn't going to be pleased to return and find her standing there, like a statue, doing nothing. The thought stirred Avery into nervous action.

She tracked down a chicken and with gingerly inexpertise lifted it and bore it in both hands along the fresh path that C. Strong trampled down between his backyard and hers.

The path wouldn't be used again after today. The crushed underbrush would straighten. Avery wouldn't be making any trips over to C. Strong's place. She was absolutely sure of that.

Chapter Two

Clark shut the gate to the pen with a vigorous motion. Frowning, he manipulated the latch several times.

"You should oil this latch."

Avery Payton brushed a feather from her denim skirt and replied with dignity, "I had every intention of doing that when I got back from my shopping trip today. I purchased some machine oil expressly for the purpose."

He glanced with her at the small pickup. The door on the driver's side stood open. She'd evidently returned from her shopping trip and found the pen empty. Her purchases must still be inside the truck.

Had she gone shopping by herself? Clark wondered. Where were her children? There wasn't a tricycle or toy in evidence. He hadn't changed his initial perception that she was a mother. In fact, he was more certain after overhearing her conversations with the chickens and the goat as she assisted Clark in retrieving the escaped poultry, making not the first attempt at conversation with him.

Did she have a tragic story to tell that would explain the absence of her children?

He hoped not.

Clark liked Avery Payton. Or he liked the side of her that she'd shown him. This had been a trying experience for her, and not one whining, complaining remark had she made to him to arouse his sympathy.

"If you'll get the oil, I'll take care of the latch for you," he stated.

"No, thank you." She lifted her chin proudly. "I can handle that myself. You've done more than enough already. I'm very grateful for your help."

Clark gave the gate a pull, testing the latch to make sure that it held. He wanted to insist and make sure the job was done. But there was also an urge to prolong the time in her company. He couldn't remember when he'd last felt so inclined with anyone, male or female, certainly not during the past eight months since he'd moved here.

"You needn't worry," she said. "I won't even rely on that latch in the future. I plan to go immediately to a hardware store and buy a length of chain and a padlock."

"The latch should be adequate," Clark objected. "A chain and padlock aren't necessary."

"They're necessary for my peace of mind. Thank you for your help, Mr. Strong. I apologize for causing you this terrible unpleasantness and putting you to all this trouble. It won't happen again. I promise you."

Now if you would please leave, she added with her body language, turning slightly toward the house.

"People here in the country aren't formal. I'm Clark Strong." Clark introduced himself tersely, tightening his right hand into a fist. He wanted to shake hands with her merely as an excuse to step closer and make the physical contact. "I own Pleasant Hollow Nursery, which is down the highway about a mile. For the most part I'm either there or at my house. You can call upon me in an emergency."

"That's kind of you," she murmured skeptically.

"My home number isn't listed." He stated the seven digits, disclosing them for the first time to a person who lived in the area.

She repeated the last four digits and commented politely, "That's easy to remember. With any luck I won't be having any more emergencies."

Clark had no further excuse to delay leaving. He nodded farewell and, giving the gate one last testing pull, strode toward the woods that were a part of his property. Her voice stopped him when he'd gone about twenty yards.

"Mr Strong—er—Clark." She got his first name out as though she were pronouncing an unfamiliar word that felt strange on her tongue.

He turned around. She stood in the same spot. She'd been watching him walk away. The knowledge sent a surge of disturbing sensation through his body, which hadn't reacted to a woman's gaze in a hell of a long time.

"What about—" She wet her lips, breathing deeply.

"Yes?" he prompted.

"The dead chickens. I'll need to get them from your backyard and bury them."

Clark didn't answer. He frowned, annoyed with himself because he was damned disappointed that she had nothing but dead chickens on her mind.

"I'll dispose of the chickens," he said curtly.

She sighed. "I shouldn't leave it to you. I should deal with it myself. Could I get your permission to drive Larry's pickup down your driveway to your house? I'd rather not carry the poor things." Her voice was full of guilt and revulsion.

The reference to the pickup reminded Clark that she was living there with a man. He lifted his hand in an abrupt gesture, settling the debate.

"You take care of oiling the latch. Leave the other to me."

She nodded, obviously relieved and yet troubled. "If that's what you prefer. But how will you 'dispose' of them?"

"Bury them deep enough so that their bodies won't be dug up by animals."

"Oh. I hadn't even thought of that. A shallow grave wouldn't do. It requires more muscle than I had realized."

A job *he* wouldn't have any trouble handling, her tone implied. Presumably the owner of the pickup truck, Larry, could also handle it if he were around, Clark reflected.

"Time's wasting," he said brusquely. "I was due back at the nursery an hour ago."

"Goodbye. I'm terribly sorry to have caused you all this trouble. Not that being sorry does any good."

Clark clamped his mouth into a firm line to keep from uttering his own apology. His sense of regret was complex and best left unexpressed.

He was sorry that she'd been put through this unpleasantness today. Sorry that their meeting had had to be like this. It was too bad that they couldn't have gotten to know one another under different, better circumstances.

But being sorry didn't do any good. It didn't change him from being the bitter man he was. It didn't change the fact that she was another man's woman, with her own emotional baggage.

Something wasn't right that Avery Payton was living with Larry, the fellow she'd mentioned. Something wasn't right that her children hadn't been with her today.

Because she *was* a mother. Or *had been* one.

Clark was certain that one or the other was the case. He couldn't bear to think that a warm-hearted woman like her might be a victim of one of life's worst tragedies, losing a child.

Avery didn't trust herself yet to call the twins and talk to them on the phone. She was certain to break down and cry, hearing their voices. That would upset them and possibly cause them to feel guilty about going to live with their father.

A letter was a safer communication and more economical, even counting the box of tissues close at hand. Writing a newsy, upbeat account of the past few days served another purpose, too. It helped her get through the lonely evening with only Sam the dog as company.

Her pen stopped when she came to the point where Clark Strong entered her narrative. How to describe him in broad simple terms? Certainly not "the nice man who lives next door." But adjectives like *mean* and *awful* and *horrible* weren't apt, either.

Certainly *ugly* wasn't apt. Clark Strong wasn't an unattractive man, even with a frown on his face. He was good-looking, in fact, with strong, rugged features, neatly cut dark brown hair and dark brown eyes.

Masculine was definitely a keynote description, if Avery were typecasting him for the benefit of another woman. Also, *virile,* she was forced to admit, visualizing him in his jeans and cotton-knit shirt. There wasn't an ounce of flab on his tall, rangy body. Touch him anywhere, and her fingertips would encounter hard male flesh.

Embarrassed by the drift of her thoughts—not to mention by the little stir of feminine excitement—in the midst of composing a letter to her sons, Avery wrote, ... *the man next door, a rather unfriendly, ill-natured person*...

After she'd finished the letter, she watched the ten o'clock news and then bade Sam good-night, interrupting his dozing.

"Now you be a good watchdog," she admonished him fondly. "Don't let any rapists or murderers inside the house." He yawned, thumping his tail, and rested his big black satiny head back on his paws again.

His presence did help to prevent her from being uneasy. If he hadn't been in the house, she would probably have been more bothered by the fact that there wasn't a door at the head of the stairs that she could close and lock. Evidently Larry hadn't seen the need for one.

Tonight she was so emotionally exhausted that she could probably have slept without locks on the doors downstairs. It had been a wearing day. Combating depression and keeping one's spirits up took its toll, she reflected as she switched off the overhead light in Larry's spare bedroom and made her way to the bed in the pitch darkness.

His bedroom was at the opposite end of the short hall. In between was a bathroom. Both bedrooms being about the same size, it had made more sense to take this one and leave Larry's intact for now. When the twins visited, Avery would make room for their things in his closet and turn the bedroom temporarily into their quarters.

When the twins visited ...

She hugged the thought to her, like a pillow hugged for comfort, and fell deeply asleep, a wistful smile on her lips.

Avery's only moments of deep contentment and happiness now were in her dreams. In her good dreams, she still had her boys with her and felt *whole* and complete. More often, though, she had vivid, troubled dreams that made waking a relief, despite the fact that consciousness brought wrenching sadness.

Rarely did Avery have dreams that couldn't be categorized as either good or bad, dreams that she hated to have end and yet was loath to have continue, at one and the same time. Never in her life had she awakened, as she awoke in the middle of the night on this night following her first day in the country, *embarrassed* as well as disturbed over a dream.

It was a highly sensual dream involving her and her hostile neighbor, Clark Strong. A dream in which his anger and restrained violence turned to heated passion, and he reached for her, taking her down on the ground with him on a soft carpet of pine needles in the midst of the woods. And she had posed no resistance!

Lying in the darkness, Avery could feel her cheeks burning with shame. She could also feel the heaviness of her breasts and the tingling of her nipples.

Thank heavens, I woke up when I did, she thought groggily. *Before the dream went any further and I actually had sex with him.*

But a voice that wasn't her conscience suggested, *Go back to sleep. It's only a dream.*

Avery threw off the sheet. A trip to the bathroom in the darkness would settle her body without bringing her wide-awake. There wasn't a clock in the bedroom, but she knew that it must be still the dead of night.

Sitting up on the side of the bed, she blinked, waiting in vain for her eyes to adjust. It was pitch-black. Evidently there was no bright moonlight outside to shed any illumination. In her apartment she'd had night lights plugged into the sockets. They would have come in handy here in the country, but she'd forgotten them, she realized drowsily, standing. Either she would have to feel her way to and from the bathroom or else turn on an overhead light.

At the doorway, Avery found the wall light switch with her hand, but in her semiawake state decided against flipping the switch and flooding the bedroom with blinding brightness. The bathroom was just down the hall. If she went too far, she would only end in Larry's bedroom.

Inching her way along the hall with her eyes closed, Avery sleepily reviewed the layout of the bathroom. As she entered, the sink would be on her left, the bathtub enclosure on her right and beyond the tub, the toilet, located in a little alcove.

By now she had surely passed the stairwell, she judged. Sliding her hand along the wall, she encountered a doorframe. The doorway into the bathroom. A right turn would take over the threshold. Eyes still closed, Avery stepped through the void. Her foot came down and didn't encounter the bathroom floor.

There was a second of startled confusion before her foot finally rested on a solid foundation. But she had lost her balance and was pitching forward. The panicky realization hit her—*she was falling down the stairs! She'd turned into the stairwell, not the bathroom!*

Her main sensation was sheer helplessness laced with petrifying fear. Those loud, thudding sounds were her body hitting the hard, wooden treads, her head bumping against the wall. Rather than slowing her descent, the bruising, painful impacts seemed to speed her downward momentum, hurling her faster and faster toward the bottom.

Yet there was time for despairing thoughts to fly through Avery's mind. *What if I'm seriously hurt when I reach the bottom! What if I'm disabled! I won't be able to be a mother to the twins!*

The floor, like the stairs, was uncarpeted, unyielding, hard as stone. Avery landed on her back with a force that knocked the breath from her lungs. Dimly she realized that the cracking noise she heard was the back of her head striking a pine plank. Sharp, throbbing pain filled her skull. Moaning, she slowly turned on her side and curled up sideways into the fetal position, all the bones and muscles and joints of her body coming achingly to life.

Nausea welled up in the pit of her stomach. *Please don't let me be sick,* Avery prayed. Time passed. She lay inert in a haze of pain and distress, the coolness of the hard, bare floor seeping through her skin. Blessedly the nausea subsided, and Avery slipped willingly into semiconsciousness.

Her pain and discomfort formed a cruel cushion on which she floated, sapped of all strength. The only course of action seemed no movement at all, just patient endurance.

Dimly she heard and felt brittle, clicking sounds, first from a distance and then nearer. A plaintive whine accompanied a rush of smelly heat on her face. Then a warm, wet, abrasive wiping across her cheek and another whine, conveying concern.

Avery moaned and, comprehending the meaning of the sounds and sensations dragging her back toward consciousness, murmured, "Sam." The effort of speaking made hammers pound in her head. She had to wait a few seconds before mumbling weak words of reassurance to the anxious old Labrador, "It's all right, boy. I'm alive."

Sam administered more licks.

"You're right, Sam," Avery murmured. "I can't just lie here."

She gathered strength and pushed up on her elbow. But dull pain and dizziness made her lay her head down again. *I might have a concussion. I need to get to the telephone.*

There were two phones downstairs, one a wall phone in the kitchen. Standing upright didn't seem a remote possibility. Avery focused her thoughts on reaching the more accessible phone, located on a table in the living room area.

Even if she couldn't raise her head, maybe she could scoot her body along the floor. With the first maneuver, Avery cried out sharply with a pain in her left ankle. It was either broken or badly sprained. When the shock waves had subsided to a throbbing level that she could withstand, she crooked her left leg under her, abandoning any effort to use that foot. She would have to propel herself with her right foot.

Without the whining encouragement from Sam, Avery might have been tempted to give up, but the old dog accompanied her on her slow, arduous journey. When she'd finally reached the table, she was clammy with perspiration. Expending one last spurt of strength, she stretched her arm upward, groped, found the phone, clasped the receiver in her hand and brought it down.

The buzz of the dial tone confronted Avery with the question she hadn't considered yet: *Who could she call for help?*

Clark Strong's telephone number surfaced clearly from her memory.

The electronic beeps pulsed painfully in her head as she pressed each button on the lighted pad. Never had punching out the digits of a telephone number been such a laborious process. Moaning with the completion of her task, Avery squeezed her eyes closed again and held the receiver against her face with weak, unsteady fingers. The phone felt heavy. The noise of the call being put through on the other end was cruelly loud and harsh.

The second ring was blessedly cut short. Clark Strong barked into Avery's ear. "Hello."

His voice was deep and stern, bringing his presence across the line. Tears suddenly came to Avery's eyes. Tears of overwhelming relief. Everything would be all right. Clark Strong would come over immediately. He would know exactly what to do, take quick, decisive action.

"Hello. Who is this?" he demanded, his grim note as wonderfully reassuring as it was intimidating.

Avery wet her lips, trying to find her voice. It came out weak and wispy and halting, "I'm terribly sorry—to wake you. This is Avery Payton—next door. I'm hurt. Could you please—get me to a doctor?"

A shocked silence.

"Avery, what the hell is going on over there? What's wrong?"

His reaction was in line with his personality. Alarm was mixed with steely accusation. Avery mumbled an explanation. "I fell down the stairs. It was stupid of me—not to turn on the light."

"You *fell* down the stairs? Accidentally?"

Avery moaned, her confusion making her head pain worse. Why would he think that she would fall down the stairs deliberately?

"Avery, are you alone in the house now?"

"Sam's here—but he can't help much. Sam is Larry's dog—poor old guy..."

"I'll be right over to get you to a hospital."

"Thank you, Clark," Avery breathed. "Doors are locked. Key outside—a nail in the pump house."

"So Larry's gone? I'm not likely to have a run-in with him?" The inquiry was murderous. The mention of Larry's name had been like a dirty word.

"Larry's out of the country—working in the Persian Gulf. I assumed you knew that...." Like everyone else in the village she'd talked to today had seemed to know.

"You're living by yourself?"

"All by myself," Avery whispered sadly.

"Don't move. Stay where you are. I won't be five minutes." The order was harsh and concerned.

A decisive click signaled that he'd hung up. Avery let the phone fall to the floor and drifted off into semiconsciousness again, secure in the knowledge that Clark Strong would look after her.

There wasn't a single qualm about trusting herself to the angry, hostile man she'd seen with a recently fired gun in his hand less than twenty-four hours earlier.

In what seemed no time at all she heard an automobile driving up. Soon the rasping of a key in the lock of the back door. Sudden brightness as he switched on the kitchen light. Avery closed her eyes tighter and said as loudly and distinctly as she could manage, "Over here, Clark."

His quick footsteps were surprisingly light for a tall, big man. Then he was kneeling beside her, hanging up the phone.

"Where are you hurt, Avery? Any broken bones?"

For a man made of iron, not flesh and blood, he had wonderfully gentle hands. Avery sighed, letting him turn her on her back. His touch comforted her, but disturbed her, too. Why did she have an odd sense of déjà vu? Surely he'd never touched her before. Had he? Some elusive memory chased through bruised passages in her aching head. What was it?

The sexy dream...

Avery pushed weakly at one of his hands to stop his cautious exploration of her body. For the first time it occurred to her that she was clad in nothing but her cotton knit nightshirt, which fell about midthigh when she was standing. It was pulled up around her hips, exposing her to him.

She tugged at it while she gave him her diagnosis of her worst injuries.

"My left ankle may be broken. And I might have a concussion."

"It's hardly the time to worry about modesty," Clark said harshly, pulling the nightshirt down for her.

Her eyes closed, Avery murmured, "Thank you." Then she added contritely, "Such a stupid accident. So sorry to bother you like this."

"Don't apologize," he ordered her roughly. "We need to get you to the nearest hospital emergency room. I'm going to carry you out to my van."

"I'm too big and heavy," she protested feebly. "Help me stand up. Maybe I can walk."

But he was picking her up in his arms ever so gently, then rising without a grunt of strain. Avery sighed, trusting utterly in his strength.

"I'm a lucky woman to have a Superhero living next door," she mumbled in a lame attempt at humor. "Have to see you without your shirt."

"Hush," he ordered in his rough voice that was so at variance with the careful manner in which he was bearing her in his arms. Arms of iron that despite their hardness absorbed any jarring motion.

Avery dispensed with talking. The least she could do was respect his wishes. He preferred playing Good Samaritan without any conversation.

Clark Strong wouldn't be any less antisocial after coming to her rescue tonight. He didn't want to be friends with her. It was probably nothing personal. Despite the fogged condition of her mind, Avery understood that. Later she would puzzle over the reason. For now she could only manage deep gratitude.

* * *

"It's none of my business, but I think you were foolish for refusing to be admitted into the hospital."

"I don't have any hospitalization insurance," Avery explained. She avoided meeting his sharp questioning gaze, mainly out of embarrassment and not over her lack of insurance.

It was full daylight by now, and they were back in Clark's van, returning to the country. Lying semireclined in the bucket seat on the passenger's side, she was aware of being very skimpily attired in her rumpled nightshirt. With her hair uncombed, Avery knew she looked awful, pale and shaky. She wished she had a sheet to cover herself from head to toe.

"Wade must have home insurance with coverage that would pay for your hospital stay."

"We didn't discuss it before he left for the Persian Gulf. My injuries aren't that serious anyway. Thank heaven, my ankle is only sprained, not broken, and I just have a slight concussion."

His disapproving gaze raked her again. "What do you have in mind? Are you going to notify some relative or friend to come and get you?"

"I can't leave. I'm responsible for feeding Larry's goat and chickens and picking up the eggs."

"You aren't physically able. Is there someone who can come and stay and look after you?"

"No, no one. I don't have any relatives in Louisiana. Originally I'm from Florida. I have friends in New Orleans, but they're women with jobs and families. By this afternoon, I should be capable of getting around on crutches."

Avery kept her answer brief, knowing that he wasn't interested in hearing her background. She could have gone into more detail, telling him how she'd married John Payton when she was twenty, having completed two years of junior college, and moved with him to New Orleans, where she'd lived ever since. She could have explained that her parents had divorced when she graduated from high school, that both were remarried and had their assorted health and financial problems.

If Avery called either her mother or her father with news of her accident, the conversation wouldn't stay on her very long. She knew that she would end up listening to accounts of their ailments and their spouses' ailments and all the recent daily trials and tribulations. Eight years ago when John had left her, Avery might have moved back to Florida if she could have counted on her parents being supportive. She could definitely have used some help with twin three-year-olds. That not being the case, she'd stayed in New Orleans, worked at a full-time job and devoted herself to being the best mother she could be.

Clark Strong wasn't interested in hearing any of that. To show her appreciation for all he'd done, Avery spared him any portion of her life story.

"I'll be able to manage without any trouble," she said. "Don't think that I have any thought in my mind of bothering you. And I did oil that latch yesterday, you'll be glad to know."

His dissatisfaction emanated from him in waves of silence. Avery sneaked a glance at his profile. His squared jaw, shadowed with dark beard stubble, was tight. A muscle twitched in his cheek.

"How long is Wade going to be out of the country?" he asked.

"A year."

"It's your intention to live on his place for that entire period of time?"

"That was our agreement."

Clark was shaking his head disgustedly, his jaw clamped tight again.

"After today, you won't even know I'm next door," Avery promised humbly. "I know you've gotten a bad impression of me, but I'm actually a very independent, self-sufficient person. Normally I'm not a disaster waiting to happen."

He shot her one of his frowning glances, rebuking her for her attempt at levity. "Normally I don't give advice, but you should pack your things and go back to New Orleans where you belong. Let Wade make some other arrangement for a caretaker."

"If I were to pack my things and renege on my agreement, I wouldn't go back to New Orleans," she replied tiredly. "I would go somewhere safer where children can play without the threat of violence."

He didn't answer. If he had, Avery might have confided that she had eleven-year-old twin boys who had been beaten up by a gang of thugs and had their bicycles stolen in broad daylight, the incident occurring in what wasn't considered a bad neighborhood. After that, her sons had been afraid to venture out of the apartment. Then the apartment had been broken into, wrecking the illusion that it was a sanctuary.

Probably it was just as well that Clark Strong's lack of interest kept her from mentioning her boys. In her present vulnerable state, Avery would have started to cry in front of him. Just thinking about the twins had caused a big lump to form in her throat. She closed her eyes tightly, but tears of sorrow welled up anyway. Try as she might, there was no preventing them from leaking through her eyelids, down her cheeks.

Avery turned her head sideways, away from him, and wept soundlessly.

Chapter Three

"I can walk with your help. It isn't necessary for you to carry me inside."

Avery spoke with as much dignity as she could muster under the circumstances. She was aware of what a woebegone sight she presented to his hard, unsympathetic gaze, her face tear-stained as well as wan and pale. Never had she felt more defenseless in her life.

"Carrying you is easier and faster." His grim tone ruled out any argument.

"I guess it would be faster," she conceded, immediately contrite. He wanted to wash his hands of her as quickly as possible. "I'm sorry. I hadn't considered that aspect."

"Don't apologize," he said harshly.

"But I feel terribly apologetic. Wouldn't you in my place? Imposing like this on a total stranger?"

"Accidents happen."

Once again his gentleness in transporting her totally belied his voice and his demeanor. Avery helped as much as she could to prevent herself from being a deadweight by putting her arms around his neck. She kept her eyes closed, her only means of screening her emotions at such close quarters.

His strength infused her with much-needed comfort. It also awoke an aching need to be held. With her self-control so battered and bruised, like her body, Avery couldn't close out the realization of how wonderful it would be to have this strong man hug her tight.

Her voice held an embarrassing wistfulness as she instructed him, "Please put me on the sofa, if you don't mind."

"Isn't your bedroom upstairs?"

"Yes, but I'll just nap down here today."

Avery figured that she would sleep on the sofa temporarily until she was able to negotiate the stairs again. Her toothbrush and toiletries and clothes were all upstairs. Until she was strong enough to manage a trip up to get the basic necessities, she would just have to manage without them.

"Thank you," she murmured as Clark eased her down on the sofa as she'd requested.

He turned away. "I'm going into the village to get your prescription for pain medication filled," he stated over his shoulder. "You just lie there and don't try to get up while I'm gone."

"That's very kind, but don't bother. I have some aspirin to take for pain. There is one favor I'll ask of you," she added. "Could you feed Larry's chickens and goat for me? Poor things. Since he left, they're completely off their regular schedule."

"I intended to feed them," he replied.

"Thank you again for...everything." The door had closed in the middle of her statement of gratitude.

Sam had gone out with him. A short time later, Avery roused up to the sound of the door opening and closing. Clark had let the old dog back into the house, but not bothered to stick his head inside and speak a word of farewell to her. Hearing him start up his van and drive away, Avery felt utterly alone and abandoned.

She thought of her letter to the twins. It would be several days at least before she could walk that long distance to the mailbox.

Please, God, protect my boys. Keep them safe and let them be happy. Without me. With that most unselfish of prayers that a mother could offer up, Avery welcomed the oblivion of sleep.

This unfortunate accident reinforced that she'd done the right thing, sending her twin sons to live with their father. It hadn't been the best thing for her, but for them.

The bruises of Avery's body that she'd sustained falling down the stairs were nothing compared to the emotional trauma she'd suffered, making a heart-rending decision to relinquish the upbringing of her children for their benefit. Her body might heal, but she doubted that her heart and soul would ever mend as long as she lived.

Someone had entered through the back door and was making no effort to be quiet. Sam whined over in his corner. Avery heard water running.

"Who's there?" she inquired groggily and groaned with the effort of trying to get up. Her whole body ached and her ankle throbbed painfully.

"I had to drive to Covington. The pharmacy in the village couldn't fill your prescription." Clark made the terse explanation from the kitchen.

"You came back," Avery murmured, marveling.

"Of course, I came back. Did you think I meant to leave you here, helpless?" He came and knelt down by the sofa. "Here. Take one of these pain capsules. That shot you got at the hospital must be wearing off by now."

"I never take pain killers," she demurred. "They knock me out and make it impossible to function. With children, you can't afford to be zonked..." Her voice drifted off with the poignant realization that her long aversion to pain-killing drugs wasn't necessary anymore.

"You don't need to function. All you need to do is rest and sleep. Open your mouth." He inserted the capsule between her lips and raised her, supporting her with his arm and shoulder, enough so that she could drink from a glass of water that he held.

"Thank you. You've very kind."

He lowered her gently and stood abruptly. "A woman who works for me at the nursery, Billie Hano, will be arriving within an hour to look after you. She'll knock on the back door and let herself in."

Apparently he'd contacted his employee and made the arrangements. Avery sighed. "How can I ever repay you?"

He didn't answer. After a frowning inspection of the room, his gaze halting several times, he shook his head slowly and departed without a word.

She puzzled a moment over what had caught his attention. Then suddenly she knew almost without doubt that he'd been looking at pictures of the twins that she had put out on prominent display.

Did he view them as potential nuisances who might show up on the scene eventually? Judging from his reaction, that was a likely guess. Like mother, like sons, he'd probably thought to himself.

What had caused such a decent man to turn so hard? For Clark Strong was unquestionably decent and humane. His seething anger and hostility weren't allied with any cruel instincts. The answer was surely in his background.

Avery felt a sense of dread in having her curiosity satisfied. Something told her that his story was one she wouldn't want to hear. Possibly it was a tragic story.

She doubted that there was any reversing the change in him from the man he must have been when he was capable of smiling. What a terrible shame, she thought. What a terrible loss. All that powerful negative emotion in him must have once been positive emotion. Hope. Enthusiasm. *Passion.*

Avery shivered, her erotic dream coming back to her with disconcerting immediacy.

The pain capsule he'd given her was starting to take effect. She felt deliciously comfortable and surprisingly clearheaded and analytical. Why she'd had the dream last night was suddenly no mystery, but completely understandable. Her subconscious had perceived that Clark Strong's brooding intensity indicated a passionate nature. His anger was hot, not cold and calculating.

It had not been lost on her that if he channeled the turbulent, masculine force of his personality into making love to a woman, he would be a masterful lover. He could well give credence to terms such as *rapture* and *ecstasy*.

Those terms had little or no relevance in Avery's life since she didn't have a sex life. Being a single working mother took all her time and energy.

Had taken all her time and energy. The bleak correction brought the inevitable sadness and pain that couldn't be eased by medication.

Billie Hano was a black woman of indeterminate age. Avery's guess was that she was in her fifties. She wore men's khaki trousers and a man's long-sleeved shirt. A bandanna was tied to form a cap on her head. Apparently she was dressed in her normal working attire as a laborer at Clark's nursery.

Avery attempted to engage her in friendly conversation and found Billie to be about as laconic as her employer and nearly as authoritative in her own quiet, capable way. With no superfluous expressions of sympathy and no signs of curiosity, Billie entered and took charge.

"We give you a sponge bath and get you changed into clean clothes. You feel better," she stated.

"Please bring down several outfits and a supply of clean underwear," Avery requested. "Also my toothbrush and hairbrush out of the upstairs bathroom."

Billie ignored the part of the instructions about the additional clothing. And she didn't bring down daytime wear, but a nightgown and peignoir set that Avery never wore. It had been a present from the boys, purchased at a discount store. Both garments were a bright pink, flimsy nylon trimmed with lace. Avery had kept the set purely out of sentiment.

"Billie, I think slacks or a skirt would be better, don't you?" she objected, not wanting to hurt the woman's feelings by outright rejecting her selection.

"You be able to rest more comfortable in bed clothes," was Billie's answer.

"But I'll be getting up and hobbling around, hopefully by this afternoon."

"You able to hobble around this afternoon, we worry about it then," Billie replied.

"Aren't you going to report to work at the nursery?"

"Mr. Clark didn't mention nothing about that. We see what he say."

After her sponge bath, Avery found herself settled on the sofa, wearing the nightgown and peignoir, which at least was longer in length than her cotton nightshirt. The thin silky nylon felt cool against her skin. She had to admit that Billie had been right. The flimsy ensemble was comfortable.

"Thank you, Billie," Avery said gratefully. "Now why don't you call Clark and tell him you're on your way to work. I'll be fine. Although I would appreciate it if you would bring down some extra clothes before you go."

Billie ignored the recommendation. "You take a nap," she said. "I see if I can pick us something out of your garden to fix for our dinner. Maybe some squash and string beans and new potatoes."

"That sounds delicious, but I don't think I could eat anything," Avery murmured drowsily, her brain suddenly fuzzy again. It was such a good feeling just to turn off responsibility for a change and do what she was told, take a nap.

She awoke to appetizing scents of food and Billie's voice. Evidently she was conversing with someone, perhaps with Clark over the phone, Avery deduced.

"She been sleeping like a baby. I was just wondering whether I should wake her up and get some nourishment in her. She ain't got no weight to lose. She on the skinny side."

Avery had dropped ten pounds during the past six months, not from dieting but from worry that turned into anxiety and then from depression.

"No, don't wake her. Let her rest."

That was Clark's deep, authoritative voice. Billie wasn't speaking to him on the phone; she was speaking to him in person. *He was here.* The realization put Avery in a panic.

If she'd had any inkling that he was coming back, she wouldn't have let Billie dress her in the nightgown and peignoir. What would he think? That she'd wanted to put on her sexiest nightwear for him?

Avery was lying on her side. Slowly she eased on her back, surreptitiously smoothing down the thin garments covering her body. Until now she'd liked the design of Larry's house, the kitchen and dining room and living room all combined into one large open room. At this present moment, she would have given anything to have a wall between her and the kitchen.

"She stirring around now," Billie noted.

Together they came to stand at the end of the sofa. Avery could feel herself blushing.

"Whatever you're cooking smells wonderful, Billie," she declared. "A little later I'll get up and serve myself." After both of them had gone.

"It's done cooked," the other woman replied. "It's ready to eat." She glanced at Clark. "They's plenty of it, too."

Sniffing, he glanced back over his shoulder. "Don't tempt me, Billie. I don't get any home cooking except my own."

His tone was terse and humorless, but it was still the nearest he had come to making an unguarded human response.

"Both of you please go ahead and eat," Avery urged hospitably. "Make yourselves at home. Then Billie can report to work. I can take care of myself now."

"Do you feel up to sitting?" Clark asked.

"I think so."

"I dish up our dinner," Billie stated, turning away.

Apparently some plan had been formulated with a minimum of words. Instead of returning to the kitchen himself, Clark came around to the front of the sofa. Before Avery could figure out his intention, he was picking her up in his arms.

"Wh-what are you doing?" She gulped in surprise.

"Carrying you to the table. You can't walk. You aren't supposed to put any weight on that ankle."

"I could walk with a crutch or a cane."

"You don't have a crutch or a cane," he pointed out brusquely. "I've arranged for some crutches, but you won't get them until later this afternoon."

Avery thanked him with gratitude.

After he'd set her into a chair, he stood behind her, his strong hands clasping her shoulders. She closed her eyes, yielding for a moment to a sense of being supported and protected.

"Are you holding up all right?" he asked.

"Yes, I'm fine."

"She look mighty pale," Billie observed. "Maybe we rushing her to sit up to the table."

"Really! I can sit here," Avery insisted. "I'm a little light-headed, but that will pass." She sat straighter.

Clark removed his hands from her shoulders. Instead of taking a place at the table, as she was expecting, he backed off and stood behind her out of sight while Billie finished ladling the steaming contents of a pot into a serving bowl.

"Fresh string beans cooked with new potatoes," she announced with satisfaction, setting the bowl onto the table. "We got smothered squash and stewed chicken. And a pan of biscuits be coming out of the oven in a minute. They's plenty, like I said."

These last words were directed toward Clark.

"Please, won't you join us?" Avery invited.

"There does seem to be enough food," he replied.

"Enough for a small army. I could never consume the leftovers."

"Day after tomorrow you'll have more squash to pick and more string beans," Billie stated as she pulled open the oven door.

The sight and aroma of the golden-brown homemade biscuits must have overridden Clark's reservations about having his meal with Avery. Without a word, he took the vacant place at the head of the table. After Billie had stacked the biscuits onto a plate and poured iced tea, she sat down across from Avery.

Clark heaped his plate and ate hungrily. Billie applied herself to her meal with almost as much appetite. The only conversation, if it could be called that, consisted of appreciative comments about the delicious country fare.

"You'll have to give me your recipes, Billie," Avery said. With food in her stomach, she felt stronger and also more able to cope. "How do you 'smother' squash?"

"Like you smother most anything," Billie replied. "You cook it in a pot with a lid and stir it to keep it from sticking to the bottom and burning."

Clark spoke up. "Isn't this diced ham in the squash and the green beans, Billie?"

The other woman nodded. "Ham was all I could find in the refrigerator for seasoning. Wasn't no bacon or salt pork. Wasn't much groceries," she observed.

"It doesn't take a lot of groceries for one person," Avery pointed out. "That ham steak, for example, would have made the main course for two or three evening meals for me. I'm glad I had bought it," she added, lest she sound ungracious. "How did you prepare the stewed chicken?"

Billie explained that she'd dredged the pieces in flour, browned them in a small amount of hot oil, returned the chicken to the pot, added water, put the lid on and cooked on a low setting.

"I like cooking a whole chicken better," she stated. "Then you got different pieces, dark meat and light meat."

"I'm sorry. I only buy packages of breasts now." Her intention had been to separate and freeze individually the four chicken breasts that Billie had located in the meat drawer in the refrigerator and cooked. "Until recently I bought packages of chicken legs. My sons, Bret and Bart—"

"Would you pass me the biscuits," Clark interrupted tersely.

"Certainly."

He'd cut her off before she could divulge any personal information about herself. All he wanted was to satisfy his hunger, not be burdened with any insights into her background. Avery couldn't help feeling offended. But as indebted as she was to him, she had to respect his wishes.

There were a few facts, though, that she was determined that he and Billie both should know.

"Were you acquainted with the owner of this house, Larry Wade?" she asked, addressing the other woman.

"I seen him now and then and knowed who he was."

"I've known Larry for a number of years. We both worked for the same major oil company, but in different departments." Avery named the nationally known company. "Then four months ago when the New Orleans office was closed down, he and I were laid off, along with everyone else except high-ranking management."

Billie nodded. "That was on the news about that oil company closing down. Can't you eat some more dinner?" She pushed the bowls of vegetables closer.

Avery obligingly spooned small second helpings on her plate and persevered in her explanation of how she happened to be there. "I haven't had any success in finding another job. I don't have a college degree, just two years of junior college, and good-paying office jobs are scarce. On unemployment I couldn't afford to keep my apartment. To make a long story short, I ran into Larry a couple of weeks ago. We shared our problems and worked out an arrangement that solved both of our most pressing worries. While he's out of the country, I've agreed to stay here on his place, look after things and take care of his animals."

She looked at Clark, who had put down his fork. "So you can see that I'm obligated to live up to my end of the bargain, in spite of having had this accident."

"It's a foolhardy arrangement, a city woman living by herself in the country," he pronounced sternly. "Wade didn't use good judgment. There're a hundred and one problems that can crop up that you're not equipped to handle."

"Like what?" she inquired worriedly.

"Like the water pump on the well malfunctioning. If that happens, your water supply stops at the source. You're not hooked up to city water. You did realize that?"

"I hadn't given the matter any thought," Avery admitted.

"This house has its own septic system. Any plumbing problems that occur are yours to solve, not the community's responsibility."

"I'll just have to keep my fingers crossed and not borrow trouble. Whatever happens, I won't bother you," she promised.

Billie spoke up. "Everybody gonna have their share of headaches, wherever they live. Me, I'd rather have country problems than city problems. You got more room to suffer."

Clark shot his employee a keen, frowning glance and compressed his mouth, silenced by her sage wisdom, which applied to his situation, Avery divined. He had moved to the country, she suspected, to have more space to wrestle with his own demons. Clearly he was an educated man. His speech indicated that.

"Where are you from originally, Clark?" she asked, mustering her nerve to express some curiosity.

"Texas."

"Did you own a nursery there?"

"No, I worked as a landscape architect."

"I see. Your former career was related to growing plants and trees. Was it a long-time ambition to own your own nursery?"

"No, it wasn't." The denial was curt. "Are you finished eating?"

"Yes." Avery took a final bite and put down her fork. "Thank you, Billie. That was a wonderful meal."

"You more than welcome," Billie said. "Now you need to lay back down and take another rest."

"I think I will lie down a little while. If you would be so kind as to store the leftovers in the refrigerator, I'll clean up later."

Clark had pulled out her chair. He scooped her up into his arms without so much as a word. En route to the sofa, he glanced at the fireplace mantel, where two picture frames hinged together displayed eight-by-ten photographs of her children. His rigid jaw tightened.

Avery wanted to reassure him. "Those are my sons. They aren't going to turn up one day and be a nuisance—"

"It's time for you to take another pain capsule," he stated tersely, cutting her off.

"I would rather not take another one unless the pain gets unbearable. I don't like the feeling of being out in space."

"Don't wait until the pain is more than you can stand. Before it gets to that stage, have Billie give you a capsule."

With that grim order, he deposited her on the sofa with the gentleness she'd come to expect. For all the emotion he showed, though, she might have been a rare, valuable sack of potatoes that shouldn't be bruised.

"But Billie isn't going to stay here through the afternoon, is she?" Avery's protest was directed to his back. "Isn't she returning to her job at your nursery?"

He spoke over his shoulder. "You need someone here with you."

"Clark!"

He stopped and half turned, radiating impatience. But there was also reluctance in the sideways movement of his head and in his glance at her. It occurred to Avery suddenly that he might have been making a hasty retreat rather than just hurriedly leaving to go about his business. She was mortified anew to be wearing sleeping apparel designed to be alluring.

"You've been a good neighbor," she said with all the dignity that she could muster with a hot blush burning her cheeks. "I'm extremely grateful for all you've done. Please, just send someone with those crutches and don't give me another thought. If Billie will bring down some clothes and personal items from upstairs, I can manage."

"What you should do is have Billie pack your things," he replied. "Arrangements can be made for taking care of Wade's goat and chickens and for keeping an eye on his place while he's gone. I'll assume the responsibility myself and relieve you of it. You make other, more sensible plans for yourself." He hesitated, then nodded in the direction of the fireplace mantel. "Life goes on after a tragic loss."

With those final harsh words, he departed, leaving Avery to recover from her surprise and puzzlement over his meaning.

The obvious explanation soon dawned on her. Clark assumed that her sons weren't with her because something terrible had happened to them. It was a natural kind of mistake. Mothers usually had custody of their children.

To come to his wrong conclusion, he must have tuned in on her psychological state and sensed her despair. That was the part that rather amazed Avery. And yet why should it amaze her that a man with a gentle side to his nature might not also be perceptive?

He impressed her as a man of sound judgment, too. Avery didn't doubt that his reservations about her decision to live alone in the country were well-founded. He wasn't just wanting to be rid of her, though that was undoubtedly a factor.

She would like him to know that she didn't misinterpret his impersonal kindness. She understood and accepted that he wasn't interested in her in any capacity, friend, woman, neighbor.

Avery was just as glad that Clark Strong wouldn't want to be friends with her. His raw masculinity brought to life long-repressed female urges and needs. In a way he had even been responsible for her accident. That dream had woken her up, and then she'd gotten up to go to the bathroom.

The last thing she needed in her life right now was to become involved with a man—and certainly not with a man like Clark Strong. Fortunately, there wasn't any danger.

Billie stayed through the afternoon. Despite her objections, Avery was glad for the other woman's presence as well as for her capable performance of the duties of a practical nurse, including helping Avery to the bathroom.

Avery napped, secure in the knowledge that the taciturn woman was there, in charge. Billie didn't insist when Avery awoke, moaning with the throbbing discomfort of her injuries, and refused the offer of a pain pill, asking for aspirin instead.

"Me, I don't like being all doped up, either," she remarked.

"Turn on the TV, Billie, if you want to watch any programs. It won't bother me," Avery assured her. "You've done nothing but work. Sit down and rest."

"I get paid to work, not rest. They got things to do out in the garden. Them tomato plants need tying, and the suckers need to be pinched off or you ain't gonna have nothin' but tomato bush."

Billie might have been speaking a foreign language for all the sense the words made. Avery sighed, swept by deep discouragement. There was too much she needed to learn for her to cope with the challenges of her country environment.

"I should stick to buying my tomatoes from the grocery store," she said tiredly. "Clark is right. I've bitten off more than I can chew, moving out of the city."

Billie grunted. "Them men. They don't know it all. And you ain't never tasted a tomato until you pick one fresh out of the garden."

To have female support coming from such an unexpected quarter was heartening. "Men do underestimate women, don't they?"

"They don't give us credit for having much sense. I stuck my head in the pump house just now when I went out to pick up the eggs. That pump look almost brand-new to me."

"You think there might still be a warranty on it?"

"I 'spect there might be. Another thing. This house ain't been built but about five or six years. A septic tank don't give trouble in that short amount of time. Besides which, the rules on putting in septic tanks has got strict in this modern age. You got to have a permit and a government inspector comes out to make sure everything's up to par."

"You think Larry had to comply with the more strict regulations?"

"I 'spect he did."

"I'm so ignorant that I didn't know any of that. Thank you for easing my mind."

"Ignorant ain't stupid," Billie said. "We wasn't none of us born knowing everything. Now you take another nap."

Avery gratefully did as she was told.

At four o'clock, Billie announced that she was leaving and added, "I 'spect I be back tomorrow."

"By all means, please come and visit me." Avery was replying to what she thought Billie was saying after her own laconic fashion: *I can come back tomorrow if I'm needed.* "By then I should be more alert. We can talk and get acquainted."

"I ain't much for talking," was the other woman's response.

An hour passed, the only noises Sam's breathing and the quiet creaking sounds of the house. The silence seemed filled with suspense as Avery wondered whether Clark would deliver the crutches himself or send someone with them as she'd suggested.

There wasn't any fear that he would forget about her and leave her to her own devices. She'd known him only a short time, but she knew that she could depend on him to keep his word.

I hope he comes himself.

I hope he sends someone else.

Impatient with herself that it seemed to matter so much, Avery focused her thoughts on her boys and remembered the letter to them. Whoever delivered her crutches, Clark or a stranger, she would ask that person to mail the letter for her.

The sound of an automobile approaching the house brought a ridiculous sense of panic. *Thank goodness,* Avery told herself, pushing into an upright position on the sofa. Someone was delivering her crutches.

All her ambivalence was back full force. What a relief it would be if a stranger knocked on the door.

And what a disappointment.

Chapter Four

"Come in, Clark," Avery called. She jerked down her hands, realizing that she was combing her fingers through her hair.

As she spoke, he was pushing the door open. The top half of the door was glass panes, so that she'd been able to see that he'd come on the mission himself.

He was wearing the same clothes he'd worn at lunchtime, she noted, jeans and a navy-and-maroon-striped knit shirt, neither garment new. Evidently jeans and a short-sleeved knit shirt were his regular working uniform at the nursery this time of year.

"You brought the crutches," Avery stated when she saw that he held a pair of crutches in one hand. "Now I can get around and stop feeling like an invalid. Thank you so much."

Closing the door, he advanced into the kitchen, halting when he had a full view of her on the sofa. "Have you ever walked with crutches?" he asked.

It didn't escape his notice, Avery was certain, that Billie had spread sheets on the sofa, making it more comfortable for use as a bed. At Avery's insistence, Billie had also brought her a clean nightshirt into which she'd changed. Written across the chest in bold letters was Mom.

Another detail that he didn't miss was the neat pile of folded clothes on the coffee table, a fresh outfit for her to change into tomorrow morning, including bra and panties. Avery suddenly wished that she'd had Billie put the clothes out of sight in some less accessible place.

Until now the stack of apparel had seemed inconspicuous, but not so under his piercing, though indifferent, gaze. She might have been less embarrassed if her underwear had been lacy and sexy, apt to provoke lust in a man. Instead it was the plain, serviceable variety, not to mention slightly dingy from many launderings.

"If you'll just lean the crutches on the end of the sofa here, I shouldn't have any problem reaching them," she said, her cheeks warm.

"The height may need to be adjusted. I adjusted them some, using guesswork," he informed her.

"I'm five-seven." Avery blushed hotter at her own irrelevant remark. He made her feel self-conscious. "If they need more adjusting, I'm sure Larry must have a screwdriver in the house. I'm quite handy with tools."

He pulled a screwdriver from his rear pocket, brandished it and then stuck it back in his pocket, indicating wordlessly that he had come prepared. Then he advanced into the living room area with a grim, businesslike air, a crutch in each hand, plainly intending for her to get up and walk while he was there.

Avery tucked her top sheet more firmly around her waist.

"At the risk of seeming prudish, I would rather not parade around in front of you wearing my nightshirt," she protested. "It was embarrassing enough to expose myself to you this morning when I was half-conscious."

"I wasn't suggesting that you parade in front of me," he replied curtly, his slight, habitual frown becoming a scowl of irritation. He propped the crutches near her feet and then backed away abruptly.

"I didn't think you were suggesting that," Avery hastened to assure him. "Please don't be offended. Believe me, I'm very appreciative of your good intentions."

"I'll leave this," he said shortly, jerking out the screwdriver.

"Would you, please? I'll be sure to return it."

Avery held out her hand. He approached the sofa and gave the tool to her, coming no closer than was absolutely necessary. Immediately he turned to leave.

She spoke quickly to detain him. "Wait! Don't rush off before I have a chance to thank you for assigning Billie to take care of me today."

"I don't want you to thank me," he said over his shoulder, having almost reached the kitchen door.

"Wait! Please, Clark! I have a small favor to ask!"

He finally paused, his hand on the doorknob. "What is it?"

"Could you mail a letter for me?"

"A letter? I guess so."

Avery could sense his surprise that mailing a letter was the favor. She talked fast to get in her explanation, which included information she wanted him to know, namely that her sons were alive and well. "Last night I wrote a letter to my eleven-year-old boys, Bret and Bart, who are in Califor-

nia with their father. I meant to get it in the mail today..."
Her voice died in her throat at his reaction.

He'd wheeled around, his expression not only disbeliev-
ing, but accusing, as though she'd just divulged incriminat-
ing details.

Avery went on with an air of apology. "Earlier today
when you made a reference to tragedy, I was too mystified
to comprehend your meaning. Then I put two and two together and realized that you probably thought something
terrible had happened to my children. Actually they were the
victims of violence on two occasions during the last year, but
they're healthy, except for the psychological damage. Their
father thinks that he can help them overcome being frightened. He insists that he's better qualified than I am to deal
with their problems."

Clark had taken several steps into the kitchen. His grim
expression made Avery want to cower. It mirrored accusation. Before he could speak, she quickly continued her explanation, which sounded more like a defense.

"You see, my ex-husband has been pressuring me for a
number of years to give him custody of the twins. He's
bombarded me with articles by child psychologists who
support the view that a man's influence in the home is critical for developing self-esteem in boys. John is a sales rep-
resentative for a company that sells athletic equipment. He
visits schools and has contact with coaches. Some of his cli-
ents are directors of boys' camps. In his spare time he helps
with the youth sports program in his community. He's con-
vinced that athletic prowess is important. And he may be
right." Avery's voice died in her throat.

"You voluntarily *gave* your ex-husband custody of your
two children?" Clark demanded. The question was a
scathing denunciation rather than an inquiry.

"I haven't signed any documents or legally relinquished custody, but, yes, I sent my sons to live with their father. It was a heartbreaking decision, one that I made after much soul-searching and counseling with the twins' teachers and the principal of their school and the minister of the church we attended—and after discussions with my sons over what was best for them."

"Your sons *wanted* to leave you and go live with their father?" His tone clearly conveyed the other question in his mind: *What kind of mother was she?*

"No, they didn't *want* to leave me. I'm their mother." Avery struggled for composure. This wasn't a subject she could discuss calmly. "What they really wanted was for me to go along with them to California. Do you have any idea how devastating it is to have failed in giving your children a secure home?" Her voice broke on the last word, *home.*

Clark shook his head, his lip curling cynically. "No, I'm afraid I don't empathize," he said harshly. "My sympathies are more with your ex-husband. I can well imagine how he felt."

"I did my best," Avery cried. "I was the best possible mother I could be to my boys! They came first with me."

"Where's the letter?" he asked brusquely, unmoved and unconvinced by her impassioned defense of herself. He obviously didn't care to discuss the matter further and see her side of it.

"Forget about the letter! I've changed my mind! I don't want you to do any more favors for me!" Avery was trembling. The urge to hurt him as he'd hurt her made her continue her tirade. "There's one thing you can be sure of. If my ex-husband were at all like you, hard-shelled and bitter and mad at the whole world, I wouldn't even have considered letting him take care of our children."

Immediately she regretted her truthful, but spiteful words. They had found a vulnerable spot in his tough armor and had inflicted pain, although he didn't visibly flinch. Nor would he retaliate, she sensed immediately.

"I don't doubt you tried to be a good mother," he said with a harsh kindness. "If my ex-wife had been a more maternal woman, like you, I might have turned over custody of our daughter without a court battle and not ended up becoming bitter and mad at the world."

"You lost?" Avery posed the question tentatively, apologetically. This was the first semblance of a conversational exchange between them.

"I lost. And so did my little girl."

"How old is she?" she asked, fearful of finding out that he was the one who had suffered a tragic death of a child.

"She's seven."

"That young?" Avery's voice expressed her relief. "Is she being neglected by her mother?"

"Yes, she's neglected. Her mother is mentally unstable and hooked on prescription drugs."

"That's appalling! No wonder you're so angry. Clark, I'm sorry." Avery put all of her compassion into the apology. "I shouldn't have attacked you the way I did. You made me angry and hurt my feelings."

"Don't be sorry," he said brusquely. "It doesn't matter. Do you want me to mail the letter or not?"

Enough sharing of confidences was his message. He wanted to be on his way. Avery felt rebuffed.

"Only if it's not too much trouble," she said.

"If it were too much trouble, don't you think I would have told you that it was?" he demanded angrily. "Where's the damned letter?"

"It's there on the middle shelf of the hutch."

He found the letter and, gripping it in one large hand, he strode for the door.

"Who should I return the crutches to?" Avery inquired, her pride losing out to a desperate desire to prevent him from leaving so abruptly. It didn't take a psychology degree to know that talking about his embittering experiences and opening up could only help him heal. She had never wanted to reach out to any human being more than she wanted to reach out to Clark. He was a good person inside, capable of sympathy for others. His actions showed that, belying all his gruffness of manner. "I could drop them off at your nursery," she suggested.

"I don't want them back," he said without a backward glance. "Keep them or give them away." The door closed on the last word.

Evidently the crutches weren't on loan. He must have purchased them or else someone had given them to him.

Whichever was the case, his attitude was unmistakably clear: he didn't want anything more to do with her.

Avery leaned her head tiredly on the back of the sofa, conscious of a dull headache and throbbing pain in her injured ankle. Eyes closed, she listened to the sound of Clark driving off. After she could no longer hear the engine noise or tires, she sighed, depression and loneliness settling over her like a dark shroud. The world seemed a place of hopeless struggle and unfulfilled needs and disillusionment.

Raising her head with an effort, she looked down at the screwdriver she'd forgotten she was still holding. It symbolized the kindness and thoughtfulness Clark hadn't communicated by his curt tone and his brusque demeanor.

He was a kind, compassionate man despite all his efforts to appear otherwise. Awakened during the night by a virtual stranger he'd met only hours earlier, he'd come immediately in response to Avery's plea for help. He'd driven miles to take her to the nearest hospital and hadn't dumped her there, as he would have been justified in doing. Instead he'd waited more than an hour and had transported her back to Felton.

For all his angry reaction to Avery's rejecting his advice that she should return to the city to convalesce, still he hadn't washed his hands of her. He'd gone to more trouble getting her prescription for pain medicine filled. In effect he'd paid for a practical nurse, since Billie was in his employ. Whatever work Billie would have performed at his nursery that day had gone undone.

Finally he'd located and personally delivered a pair of crutches. And had the forethought to bring a screwdriver in case the crutches weren't adjusted to her height. Apparently he'd taken the time to make some adjustment in advance, using guesswork.

Those weren't the actions of a man indifferent to the feelings and needs of others.

Perhaps deep down, Clark craved friendship. Certainly he needed friendship. He needed sympathy and understanding.

Avery would have to return the screwdriver to him. There was a legitimate reason to see him again. On that occasion, she would express her gratitude to him and not take any offense, no matter how gruff he was toward her.

Maybe she could be a good neighbor to Clark Strong, in her own way. She would like to repay him and help him somehow.

Her depression gone, Avery used the crutches to make a trip to the bathroom. Clark had adjusted them to a comfortable height. It wasn't necessary to use his screwdriver.

Her accident hadn't been for naught, she reflected, settling back down on the sofa. When she could walk again, she would *appreciate* walking, not take it for granted.

Pain and inconvenience were a small price to pay for regaining the belief that the world wasn't such a bad place, not as long as people helped one another, like she'd been helped by Clark and by Billie Hano.

Life wasn't purposeless, a meaningless maze. It was up to Avery to discover purpose, to make meaning out of her day-to-day existence. Maybe she could do some good for others while she was surviving this difficult chapter of her life, and in the process become a stronger, better person.

Avery perceived the irony. She largely owed her new-found lease on life to meeting Clark Strong, a bitter, angry man. If only she could help him somehow to get a new lease on life himself during her stay in the country.

When she moved again, she would be moving across the country to California to live near enough to her sons to be a part of their lives. The plan formed full-blown and definite in her mind. She knew it was the right thing for her to do.

Avery let Sam out and, while he was gone, made her way laboriously over to the sink, where the bottle of prescription pain capsules stood beside a bottle of aspirin. She ran water into a glass and swallowed two aspirin, the thought occurring to her, *I need to reimburse Clark for the capsules.*

Here was another reason to make contact with him.

Billie showed up the next morning, a welcome sight in her rather bizarre attire. Once again she wore men's trousers and a man's shirt and today a red bandanna tied snugly into a skullcap. After she'd fed the goat and chickens, she came inside and proceeded to prepare a hearty breakfast of bacon, eggs and toast for the two of them. She'd brought a pound of bacon and a pint jar of homemade strawberry jam. Afterward she cleaned up the kitchen with no particular haste and announced, "Now I better help you take a shower before I go."

"Won't you be late for work?" Avery asked worriedly. "I don't want to get you in trouble with Clark."

"He knows where I'm at," Billie replied without concern.

"But you'll lose wages."

"No, I won't. My paycheck be the same. Mr. Clark, he say to come here and do for you." The reference to her employer was respectful, but not in the least servile. It didn't strike Avery as strange that Billie called him Mr. Clark rather than Mr. Strong because the usage was common in the south.

"You're here today at his instructions?"

"He telephone last night."

Avery digested the information that he'd departed yesterday afternoon without so much as a goodbye and later made arrangements to dispatch Billie, his employee, to return today and see to Avery's needs.

"What time, Billie?" Curiosity made her ask.

"'Bout six or six-thirty."

Within an hour of leaving her.

"I be coming back to warm up some dinner for you," Billie said as she was about to go.

"That's not necessary. Though it would be nice," Avery added honestly. She would welcome the woman's company, more than her help. For all her unsmiling demeanor, Billie's personality wasn't dour, but stoic and unflappable.

To Avery's delight, she detected a humorous twinkle in Billie's dark brown eyes and Billie actually chuckled, a deep, rich sound, and divulged with her own candor. "I got my mouth all set for some of that warmed-over dinner I cooked up yesterday."

"Then by all means, please come and eat with me, Billie."

Some barrier had been passed.

Sitting down at lunch a few hours later, Avery was reminded of the midday meal the previous day. Today she was getting to the table under her own power, not being carried by Clark. The memory brought a flush of warmth. Briefly she relived the moment he'd stood close behind her chair, his strong fingers clasping her shoulders. The remembered sensation of being safe and protected swept through her.

I wish he were here today, too, Avery was surprised to find herself thinking.

She realized as she asked Billie questions about her work at the nursery that in addition to genuine interest, she wanted to have Clark's name come up in conversation and to get Billie's view of him. The picture that emerged was of a fair, but exacting and very hardworking employer with impressive expertise and scientific knowledge who did his share of manual labor. He didn't just supervise.

None of that came as a particular surprise, nor did the insight that Billie volunteered. "That man do love plants. He treat 'em like they got feelings."

For all his outward callousness, he treated people as though they had feelings, too, Avery knew firsthand. With hindsight she doubted that Larry's goat had been in any danger two days ago. She even had to wonder if a part of Clark's rage that day hadn't been distress over the fate of the poor chickens his dog had maimed.

Billie came again that afternoon to perform her own schedule of chores, including gathering the eggs, which Avery insisted that she take home with her.

"I be here bright and early tomorrow morning," the woman announced with her calm certitude. "You just take it easy when you wake up. You gonna have plenty to do before the day's over, snapping green beans.''

"Tomorrow we're going to pick green beans out of the garden?" Avery's voice had an eager note.

Billie's voice was dry and indulgent. "I don't know about 'we.' ''

"Tomorrow's the last day that I can impose on you and take advantage of Clark's generosity in keeping you on his regular payroll while you're dividing your time between working for him and helping me out.''

"Reckon Mr. Clark got some say. Reckon I got some say,'' Billie pointed out equably.

The truth was that Avery was glad to be outvoted for at least one more day, as humbling and strange as it was for someone so used to being independent to find herself the recipient of neighborly charitableness.

When she was back on her feet, literally and figuratively, she would reciprocate somehow and repay Clark and Billie in deeds of helpfulness, she resolved.

Tomorrow she intended to take a crash course from Billie and learn as much as she could about freezing and canning and garden maintenance. Of course, she didn't have to learn everything in one day. Billie wasn't going anywhere, and neither was Avery, not for a year.

"Does Clark ask you about how I'm recovering?" Avery had managed not to ask that question for a week. Finally gnawing curiosity conquered reluctance. He hadn't telephoned or visited or sent any message to her via Billie.

Avery had to *know* whether he was personally concerned about her.

"It ain't exactly necessary for him to ask,'' Billie replied in her laconic fashion. "I tell him how you getting some color in your cheeks and putting on a pound or two and walking on them crutches like you growed two extra legs.''

In other words, he hadn't made the first inquiry.

It was time for Avery's pride to take over and for her to assert her independence.

''This afternoon you can tell him that I'm able to take care of myself now, Billie,'' she said pleasantly, but firmly.

The two of them were seated at the kitchen table, having just finished the midday meal that Billie called dinner. Avery rose and admonished, ''Now you just sit there and finish your iced tea. I can handle clearing the table.''

Billie didn't argue. ''I tell Mr. Clark,'' she said, referring to Avery's instructions.

Avery resolved suddenly that she was going to tell him herself tonight over the telephone.

She hugged the woman when she left and got a fond pat on her cheek in return.

''This doesn't mean that I won't be expecting you to visit me, Billie. And I'm going to insist on supplying you with eggs, you know.''

''You'll see plenty of me. And you won't have to insist about them yard eggs.''

Billie cracked one of her rare smiles, transforming her face and revealing porcelain-white teeth and a gold cap.

Avery stood out in the yard and watched her drive away at a crawling pace in her automobile, an ancient gas-guzzler. She thought about the Japanese concept of a human national treasure and reflected that Billie Hano was a human rural treasure, if ever there was one.

Thank you, Clark, for sending Billie when I so badly needed a friend here in the country.

That was one of the things Avery would like to say to him when she called him this evening.

* * *

A dozen irrelevant questions crowded Avery's mind as she built up the necessary nerve to phone Clark. Where would he be sitting when the phone rang? In his living room or a den? Would he be watching television? Reading? If the latter, what would he be reading? A trade magazine? A book? What sort of book? A biography of someone famous? A novel?

What sort of novel? A thriller perhaps?

What were his tastes? His habits?

It occurred to her that thanking Clark and assuring him of her restored self-sufficiency weren't her only reasons for wanting to talk to him. She wanted to know more *about* him.

Such intense curiosity about a man was out of the ordinary for Avery. Information, though, would satisfy her curiosity, she expected. Everyday banal details would kill what amounted to a kind of fascination.

Underneath his aloofness, Clark Strong was probably just an ordinary man no more or no less compelling than the men she'd known the past eight years, since her divorce, and easily kept at arm's length. She'd built him up to mythic proportions, a modern Samson, for heaven's sake.

The key was for Avery to establish a new basis for a casual, nonthreatening neighborly relationship. That was her assignment as she punched out the digits of his telephone number, forever emblazoned in her memory, she was certain.

He didn't pick up until the third ring.

"Yes?"

"Don't you ever answer the phone with a hello?" Avery inquired lightly.

Intimidating silence.

"I can tell from your reaction that you recognized my voice," she said. "Don't worry. There isn't any disaster in progress next door. This is just a brief, friendly call."

Continued silence.

"It really wouldn't hurt you to carry on a normal conversation, now would it?" Avery demanded, irritated that he was making her feel like an utter fool. Let him hang up on her, if he wasn't going to cooperate at all. "I realize you're out of practice, but it's not that hard. You say something simple like 'How are you?' and I answer with something like, 'Oh, I'm fine.' Then I get down to the point of my call, wasting as little of your time as possible."

"I can guess the reason you called. You want to thank me," he stated tersely.

"Well, humor me and let me say the words anyway."

He said nothing, his silence unreadable. Since he didn't hang up, evidently he was humoring her.

Was he sitting? Standing? What had he been doing when she interrupted him? Avery wondered. She decided to press her luck and try to find out.

"I hope I didn't call at a bad time. Were you just walking into the house? When you didn't answer by the second ring, I was half expecting an answering machine."

"I don't have an answering machine." A pause. "I had just stepped out of the shower when the phone started to ring."

He was standing naked talking to her or else wrapped in a towel. Avery found either possibility shamefully titillating. She hoped she was conveying only embarrassment as she apologized and hastily concluded the call.

"I'm sorry. I won't keep you. Thanks a million for sending Billie to take care of me. She's a real jewel of a person."

"You aren't walking on that ankle yet, are you?" he inquired before she could lower the phone from her ear.

"I'm not putting my full weight on it. But I am hobbling around some without the crutches," she admitted meekly.

"Have you made an appointment with an orthopedist?"

Avery confessed that she hadn't.

"You should have a checkup." *If she had any sense,* he might as well have added. "That was a dangerous fall you had."

She'd had about enough of being lectured as though she were an imbecile. "A trip to an orthopedist would be quite expensive by the time I had to pay for X rays. If I don't develop any complications, there's no real need for seeing a doctor."

"The reason you should see a doctor is to prevent any complications from developing," he persisted. "I can drive you into Covington myself if you're worried about transportation."

"Thank you for offering, but fortunately Larry's truck has automatic transmission. I can drive myself. I appreciate the advice about seeing a doctor," she said, tactfully closing the subject and bringing the call to an unsatisfactory end for the second time.

"Have you contacted Wade?"

Prepared for him to hang up on her in disgust, Avery stuttered in her reply. "C-contacted him? Why, no, I haven't. It's not as easy as placing a long-distance call. I saw no need."

"You're planning to stay and live in his house." *A decision that was pure idiocy,* he grimly implied.

"Yes, I am," she confirmed with dignity. Only her gratitude kept her from informing him that what she'd decided was none of his business. "I think that spending a year in the country is just what I needed to do at this point in my life. I'll get along fine. I'm not a stupid person, and I've got my share of backbone. I've dealt with much worse problems than rural survival, believe me."

No answer.

Avery's pride joined with stubbornness. *She'd be damned if she would let this man intimidate her and quell her spirit.*

"At the risk of bragging, I'm catching on fast," she declared defiantly. "Just ask Billie, if you're interested, which, it goes without saying, you aren't. Not many women on crutches have mastered the art of blanching vegetables, I'll bet. At last count, I have a dozen packages of green beans in the freezer. Tomorrow I'm canning squash. Before this is over, I may end up winning a blue ribbon at the county fair."

"Blanching vegetables involves immersing them in boiling water, doesn't it? Don't you think you would be wise to wait until you can stand on two feet?"

"If I wait, the green beans would be too tough to chew," she retorted. "When vegetables in a garden are ready to be picked, they have to be picked." A quote from Billie, her gardening authority. "You of all people should know that."

"Are you canning, using a pressure cooker? They're dangerous, especially in the hands of a novice."

"For your information, I'm *not* using a pressure cooker because I don't have one and I can't afford to invest in one! Do you know what you are, Clark Strong?" she demanded, losing her temper. "You're a wet blanket! You get no joy out of life yourself and you can't stand for someone else to look on the bright side! If your ex-wife should suddenly die, giving you custody of your little girl, I would hate the thought of the sour influence you would be on her. A father should be able to smile, at least."

"There was actually a period when I prayed that my ex-wife would die."

His grave revelation caused chills to chase down Avery's spine. Her anger evaporated to make way for horror.

"What a terrible thing, Clark!" she murmured. "To pray to God for another human being's death!"

"Yes, it is a terrible thing. Hate is a terrible, destructive emotion, especially allied with helplessness."

"You should get psychiatric help, Clark! You should deal with your anger!"

"I am dealing with it, Avery. I avoid conflict with other people and I stay to myself. I don't wish to hurt anyone, involve anyone."

Leave me alone. That was his somber, clear message.

"But you need friendship, Clark! It's not healthy to put a wall around yourself and be completely isolated!"

"Friendship at my age entails sharing another's pain, another's problems and disappointments. I don't have any leftover emotion to invest."

"That's a totally negative point of view," Avery argued. "The other side of friendship is sharing another's joy, another's successes. There are different levels of friendship. There's the simple pleasure in enjoying another person's company. I experienced that this week with Billie."

"The only relationship that I would be interested in with you is physical," he said bluntly. "Is that what you're offering?"

After a moment of sheer speechlessness, she gasped, "No, I'm *not* offering that! I certainly hope you don't think that my gratitude would go that far!"

"If you want anything more or anything less from me, keep your distance, Avery."

"Don't worry!" She slammed down the phone, trembling with her outrage. "The *gall* of him!" she blazed, knowing that a strong element of her humiliation was that some shameless feminine part of her was more pleased than insulted.

Clark held the phone to his ear, listening to the buzz of the broken connection. Then he cradled the receiver and looked down at his naked body, noting what he already knew.

He was partially aroused. In a matter of seconds he could be ready to make love to Avery Payton.

Clark could have told her that she'd awakened his long-dead sex drive. She'd stirred to life his long-unexercised faculty for erotic fantasy. Glancing at his bed, he could visualize her lying there wearing nothing, her thighs enticingly open and her arms lifted, ready to enfold him when he lowered himself on top of her, buried himself inside her.

It wasn't necessary to rely totally on imagination. Hell, he'd seen her unclothed almost from the waist down. At the time he hadn't felt lust, but the sight had been registered in his male memory.

He could sink so deep in her. She could accommodate a big man like him. Rock-hard now, Clark closed his eyes, imagined getting into the bed with her, positioning himself for entry, the tip of his manhood probing her wet softness. A vigorous movement of his hips, a thrust—

No.

Clark gave his head a hard shake. He didn't want to take Avery Payton even in fantasy.

Chapter Five

When the phone rang almost immediately, Avery jerked back, startled. *Did Clark Strong actually have the nerve to call her back?* was her first thought, a thought that made her agitation worsen.

Composing herself, she grasped the receiver as though it were a bomb that might explode in her hand.

"Hello," she said with cool dignity.

"Mom!" Her sons' young voices, dear and familiar and high-pitched with excitement, sounded in her ear.

Clark Strong was forgotten. Anger and insult and ambiguous female emotions were swept away by a torrent of mother's love that filled Avery's heart to brimming capacity.

Both boys, each on a separate phone, talked at once, hardly giving her a chance to speak, a circumstance for which she was grateful the first minute or two. Poignant emotion made it difficult for her to speak in a tone they would expect to hear, loving, but calm and in control.

Their father had enrolled them in karate class. That was their first item of big news. The lessons would cure them of being sissies. That was the reason behind taking the lessons—not just to have fun.

Avery didn't like what she was hearing. "You aren't sissies," she objected.

Before she could build a case in their defense, they overruled her. Yes, they *were* sissies. Their father said they were, and they subscribed to his view. He'd been a sissy himself when he was a little boy and had overcome it, they explained. His problem, too, had been that he was a mamma's boy.

John's father had died when he was a baby, and he'd been raised by his mother and doting aunts. Avery couldn't refute his description of himself as a mamma's boy. Worst of all, she couldn't deny that Bret and Bart were timid boys. Maybe the karate lessons would be good for them. Certainly they sounded happy, and that was what was important, that they grow up well adjusted and happy.

"Just don't turn into bullies," she admonished. "Remember how it feels to be pushed around."

The second big item of news was an in-ground swimming pool that their father could afford now with the money he'd been sending every month for child support. Avery bit her lip and managed not to remark that John's child support payments hadn't been a huge amount, certainly not enough to provide even his sons' basic needs of food, clothing, and lodging. She surmised that he must be taking out a loan for the swimming pool, probably a second mortgage on his house.

She hadn't given him custody of the twins. The understanding was that they would live with him permanently if the change in home environment proved to be better for them. Here John was taking on financial debt as though there were no element of doubt and his days of writing out a check for child support were forever ended.

Avery wouldn't have been human if she hadn't felt some jealous resentment. For all her joy in the enthusiasm she heard in her children's voices, it hurt that she wasn't the parent who could give them a swimming pool in their backyard. It hurt that her prayers seemed to have been answered and the twins were apparently thriving without her.

Thank you, God, was the heartfelt sentiment she had to offer up, when despair weighed down her soul.

"We miss you a lot, Mom. Do you miss us a lot?" her two sons wanted to know.

"I miss both of you every minute of every day," Avery said, her voice husky with the effort to hold back tears.

She didn't cry and feel sad all the time, did she? they inquired anxiously.

"I have lots of things to do to keep me busy," she answered evasively. "When I start feeling sad, I make plans for things we can do when you visit me."

Mom is all right. There's no need for you to feel guilty because you don't miss me constantly. That was the reassurance they were seeking, and Avery gave it to them like she'd tried to give them every reassurance they'd ever needed since she'd held them as newborn infants, one in either arm.

Tried, but hadn't succeeded.

Avery had done her very best, and yet her boys were no longer living with her.

How to live with such a devastating hurt was the question she was having to answer for herself one day at a time.

"It's Sunday morning. Give me a break," Avery grumbled, throwing off the sheet.

The chorus of clucking and crowing and bleating coming through her bedroom window didn't abate as she sat up on the side of the bed. Larry's goat and rooster and flock of chickens were giving her her wake-up call, she reflected with sleepy amusement.

They set up a ruckus this time every morning. Lying abed past seven o' clock wasn't allowed here in the country, weekend or no.

"Coming, Sam," she called in response to whining down below. "Hold it a couple of minutes more, old guy."

Avery got dressed quickly, putting on a pair of everyday shorts and sleeveless cotton blouse. She didn't bother with a bra. After splashing cold water on her face and giving her hair a hasty combing, she descended the stairs, holding on to the handrail, conscious of being careful. Walking without crutches was still new enough to be appreciated.

Three weeks had passed since her accident. She could place her weight on the ankle that had been injured and not feel any painful twinges. Bruises had lost their soreness and stiff joints and muscles were operating smoothly again. Avery was back to feeling thirty-five instead of seventy-five, or the way she imagined seventy-five might feel.

The late-June morning was cool and dewy fresh. Out on the small back porch, she sucked in a lungful of pine-scented air as she worked her bare feet into her yard shoes, old red canvas espadrilles.

She thought, *I could be very happy at this moment if I had my boys with me. This could be the most contented summer of my life.*

Avery was fast coming to feel at home here in the country. She loved the simple routine of her days, the absence of tension, the peace and quiet, the sense of unhurried purposefulness and accomplishment. It amazed her that a gardening chore like digging a pail of new potatoes from the earth could bring such satisfaction.

Always at the fringes of her mind, though, even at moments that verged on contentment, was the awareness of being separated from her children.

At least sadness didn't sap her energy now and sink her into apathy. Physical activity wasn't an enormous effort and didn't seem totally futile. Avery was able to experience simple enjoyment. She rested her mind, thinking as little as possible and concentrating on what needed doing. She employed her senses and was becoming more and more attuned to nature.

Avery was coping. She was adapting.

The faintly musty smell of the pump house, a combination of the scent of oats and the scent of cracked corn, had become familiar and rather pleasant. What continued not to be pleasant was the sight of the pump, which had unpleasant associations, always bringing to mind the man next door, Clark Strong.

Avery inevitably got indignant all over again, remembering that he'd tried to capitalize on her ignorance to scare her away. If Billie could see at a glance that the pump was practically new, then so could he.

It was a minor irritation, but it caused her to scoop out the morning allotment of oats and cracked corn with more vigor than she might otherwise have expended. She would like for Clark Strong to know that he'd probably done her a favor, causing her to be more prepared for trouble with a malfunctioning pump than she would otherwise have been. Avery had searched for and studied the manual on the pump.

Unfastening the gate had its similar unpleasant associations. Avery's spine invariably stiffened and her mouth compressed slightly as she operated the latch with more force than was necessary. For the latch worked perfectly well now that it was kept lubricated, and she lubricated it to excess, if anything.

Clark Strong had given her straight information about the latch. Avery had to credit him with that. A chain and padlock weren't necessary.

To her dying day, she doubted that she would ever erase the vivid image of him standing at the gate on that fateful occasion she dubbed in her mind as the "Empty Pen Episode." The memory always caused a little shudder. But never any revulsion.

None of Avery's images of Clark Strong were revolting, which made her banish them all the more quickly.

During the past three weeks, she hadn't encountered him or talked to him. She'd returned the crutches and the screwdriver to him by Billie and also payment for the prescription of pain medicine.

Approaching the gate of the pen this morning, she could see him as clearly as if he were in the flesh, scowling and rattling the gate. Despite his unfriendly expression, it wasn't an unattractive vision.

Out of my way, Clark. Go back to your house. Stay there.

"I need to get out and be around people more," Avery confided to the goat and the flock of poultry as she entered the pen. They were used to her conversing with them by now, and she no longer felt any self-consciousness. "Apparently I'm so desperate for company that I keep conjuring up what's-his-name next door." The rooster clucked solemnly. "I know. I can't just recognize the problem," she agreed, addressing him. "I need to take constructive action. Today I'm going to church."

The goat raised his head from his pail, chewing reflectively. God help her, it looked like Billy nodded! Avery grinned, feeling more lighthearted than she'd felt in many months.

"It's going to feel strange wearing a nice dress, for a change," she mused. "And I'm actually going to fix my hair and make up my face. Your point is well-taken." These words were in response to a chorus of clucking by several hens. "The church I'm attending is a small chapel in the country. I shouldn't overdo the jewelry. The congregation won't be putting on a fashion show. Neither will I. I'll be there to commune with God."

Getting dressed for church wasn't the boost to her morale that Avery had planned. It felt so *wrong* that she had only herself to make presentable. For the past eleven years, when she'd gotten ready for almost any outing, she'd divided her attention between dressing herself and seeing that her twin boys were appropriately attired.

It felt just as wrong and terribly lonely climbing into the small pickup truck by herself and driving to the church without two towheaded eleven-year-olds, resplendent in their matching suits. Her heart was heavy during the drive through hilly countryside, past Thoroughbred farms, llama ranches and an occasional ostrich and emu farm. The unfolding scenery would have held such enchantment for the twins, with glimpses of frolicking foals and herds of grazing llamas and flocks of giant exotic poultry.

The church was a Roman Catholic chapel. Avery wasn't Catholic, but that didn't matter to her. Her attitude, she realized, was unusual. She didn't consider herself limited to worshiping God according to the teachings of a single denomination. She could commune with God in any church as long as the atmosphere was reverent and conducive.

St. Peter's wasn't located in the village of Felton, the name by which the whole area was known, but on a country side road in a beautiful, isolated spot with large oak trees. Avery had followed signs one day and found the chapel. It had clapboard siding painted a dove gray and a picture-book steeple with a bell. She'd pulled into the empty unpaved parking lot, turned off the engine and sat there a long moment, sensing the sacredness of the spot.

Today the parking lot was more than half-filled with automobiles when she arrived. Avery nodded and responded to friendly, but reticent, greetings on her way inside. She approved that people weren't doing a lot of chatting and socializing prior to the service. That was best left for afterward, she reflected, taking her place on a pew about midway to the altar.

The chapel filled up, and the priest appeared to say Mass. Avery listened to his words, spoken in English. Along with the sounds, beautiful in themselves, and the meaning, she absorbed the effects of the lovely light filtering through the high, narrow stained-glass windows. She was conscious of being one person among the congregation and yet of being a part of an assembly of human beings gathered together in private and communal worship.

Serenity eased into her soul, and she attained the quietly joyful state of prayer without words.

When the service ended, Avery rose, spiritually renewed. She was walking up the aisle when she saw Clark Strong, who looked her way and saw her, obviously for the first time.

They stared at each other, both unprepared, both unguarded. He recovered first and nodded. Avery nodded back. He glanced away and then back at her, catching her still gazing at him. Blushing, she turned her head.

It was so unexpected for her to encounter him here, in church. And to read on his face that attending the Mass had given him some inner peace, as it had her. Avery hadn't seen him before without a frown. Sober and calm and not seething with anger and impatience, he was a totally different man. He was a man to whom she was powerfully drawn.

Avery also hadn't seen him before in a sports jacket, dress shirt and tie, looking not only handsome, but distinguished. Her reaction to his appearance—deep, instinctive womanly approval—was another factor to reckon with.

Clark reached the open doors of the chapel ahead of Avery. Taller than anyone near him, he was briefly silhouetted, head and shoulders, against the outside brightness. Another larger-than-life image of him was stamped on Avery's memory.

A blurry recollection, completely lost before now, surfaced. She remembered that she'd made a silly comparison between him and a Superhero when he'd picked her up to carry her out to his van and take her to a hospital. More vividly, she recalled the sensations of being carried in his arms, and her utter confidence that he wouldn't drop her.

Avery breathed deeply, flushing out memory as she filled her lungs with oxygen. Today was a new day. This was a new meeting between her and Clark.

Outside, he stood a little distance from the steps, waiting for her. Avery noted with her first glance at his face that he'd put up his guard. His expression was still calm, but unreadable.

"Hello, Clark," she greeted him simply.

"Hello, Avery. I didn't notice your truck before," he said, glancing toward Larry's pickup.

"It didn't once occur to me that I would see you here."

"I don't attend regularly. I'm not Catholic," he added.

"Neither am I. Religious denomination has never been important to me in choosing a church to attend."

"Same here."

As though by common consent, they moved farther away from the steps, separating themselves more from the crowd of churchgoers who were lingering to visit with acquaintances.

Avery caught a whiff of his after-shave. "I hardly recognized you at first," she remarked. "Somehow I would have expected you to look more uncomfortable in a tie."

He shrugged shoulders that seemed even broader in his tailored sports jacket. "I got dressed like this to go to work every morning for a lot of years." He hesitated. "You look well."

Avery was expecting a comment on her appearance, something slightly more complimentary than "You look well."

"I am well," she said. "I've recovered almost a hundred percent from my accident."

After another hesitation, he asked, "Are you doing okay?"

"I'm doing fine. As well as can be expected under my particular circumstances."

He nodded in silent comprehension. It wasn't necessary to elaborate.

"How are you?" Avery asked.

"Like you, I'm getting along as well as can be expected under my particular circumstances. I work hard to keep my sanity."

It was her turn to nod in understanding. She mustered her nerve. "Well, if you ever feel the need for conversation, I'm next door, chattering to a goat and a rooster and a bunch of chickens."

He smiled mirthlessly, but it was still a smile. "I'm sure you have better conversations with them than you would have with me."

"I doubt that."

"You shouldn't have any trouble making friends if you get out and meet people," he said. "You're very personable."

"Thanks," Avery said lightly, hoping that she didn't show how rebuffed she felt by his response to her overture. Or lack of response. "Today you're showing a personable side yourself."

He glanced down at his shoes as though inspecting the polished cordovan leather. His gaze traveled the short distance across the ground to her white pumps and then slowly upward, finally coming to her face. He wasn't undressing her with his eyes, but looking at her with a man's appreciation of a woman whose appearance pleased him.

"Things aren't that simple that I can drop over at your place for a visit when the urge strikes me," he said.

Avery let her gaze travel over him appreciatively. "No, I guess that's unrealistic," she agreed. "At least after today we don't have to feel hostile toward each other. I'll find another church to attend."

"No, I don't attend regularly anyway, as I said. I'll go elsewhere."

"You've lived in Felton longer, and you're the permanent resident." Avery touched his arm. "I insist. Out of the two of us, you need a church here more than I do."

Clark nodded. "You take care."

With his hands thrust into his slacks pockets, he walked away from her hurriedly.

Struggling to contain her regret, Avery stood watching him until he'd reached his van, parked out on the shoulder of the two-lane highway. Evidently he'd been among the last arrivals.

She walked to Larry's pickup, thinking about how Clark had been among the congregation today. It put a different light on her sense of spiritual kinship with the collective body of worshipers.

Encountering him, despite the surprise element and the high degree of intensity of their exchange outside the church, hadn't destroyed her serenity. She felt just as lonely, but not as *alone* as she had prior to the service.

Avery was glad that she'd gone to church. Glad that Clark had been there. What had transpired between them caused her no shame. They'd acknowledged to one another honestly that sexual attraction stood in the way of neighborly friendship.

She had still another reason to be grateful to him. He'd made it easier for her to stick to her moral principles, which ruled out sex without commitment. It wouldn't surprise her to learn that his values, like his attitude toward religious denomination, were similar to hers.

He was well named, she reflected, just as she had on the first day she met him. Clark Strong was a man of strong character.

The highest compliment that Avery could pay him was that she wished her sons could know him. Or know the man he really was, as gentle and thoughtful as he was masculine. He could be the best possible male influence a mother could want for two eleven-year-old boys.

Avery didn't pursue that line of thinking any further.

I wouldn't be good for her.
I would be bad for her.
Only his conviction kept Clark walking toward his van, away from Avery Payton before he could make a wrong overture.

It had been on the tip of his tongue to invite her to have lunch with him. They could drive to Covington or Mandeville or Madisonville. Or across the Lake Pontchartrain

Causeway to New Orleans, for that matter. The options were there. The opportunity.

Clark shook his head hard. He couldn't *date* her. What the hell kind of craziness was that? Dating was something normal people did. He wasn't normal, and neither was she.

His demons would wake up. His anger would come back and eat at him. It would be foolish to think otherwise. Her sadness was lying in wait for her, like an insidious ailment that would dull her lovely blue eyes and crush her spirit.

He couldn't bear seeing her sad. He hadn't been able to bear it when he was walled in with his hostility. Clark had to think of self-preservation for Elizabeth's sake. He *was* a father even though he wasn't allowed to be.

Developing any more feelings for Avery Payton than he'd already developed presented a grave risk. If Clark began to feel helpless and angry on her behalf, too, it well might be more than he could handle.

Driving home, Clark was certain that he was doing the right thing not allowing himself to slow down and give Avery a chance to catch up with him. He glanced frequently at the side mirrors of the van. There was no sign of her pickup truck when he crested a hill and could see miles behind him.

At his house, Shep came to greet him, tail wagging. While Clark petted the dog and carried on a typical dog-master conversation, he found himself glancing at the woods that screened Wade's house from view.

Before now the woods had represented much-desired privacy, a buffer zone. That had changed, he realized. He wouldn't mind being able to glance over and see someone moving about outside—not if the person was Avery. He wouldn't mind being able to see her lights burning at night.

A poem that he'd studied in an English class years ago came back to Clark. He remembered the name of the poet—

Robert Frost. The subject matter of the poem, maintaining a wall between neighboring properties, hadn't seemed relevant at the time. Now it was.

Avery was only temporarily his neighbor. Wade was to return in a year, and she would be gone.

On that sober reminder, Clark went inside, aware that his inner calm was lasting longer than he'd dared hope. In his bedroom he was unknotting his tie when the phone rang, piercing the quietness of his house.

Was Avery calling him? She was the only local who knew his unlisted home number.

Clark moved quickly to the phone, letting the tie dangle. If it was Avery, taking the initiative, he wouldn't be shedding his clothes. He was going to act on his earlier impulse and invite her out to Sunday lunch.

"Hello," he said with a note of expectation.

"Hello, Clark, this is Betty Laird."

His former mother-in-law's voice raised immediate alarm. *Something had happened to Elizabeth.*

"Betty, what's wrong?" he asked harshly, gripping the phone hard. "Has Elizabeth had an accident?"

"Elizabeth is safe, Clark. She's very upset, but no harm has come to her. It's Marilyn who's in critical condition."

"Was it a car accident? Was Marilyn driving all doped up on tranquilizers?" Clark's enormous relief that Elizabeth was all right had left him weak, an easy prey for the savage anger and powerlessness that welled up. It was intolerable being in his position, that of a father who could do nothing to protect his child. Before his mother-in-law could answer his questions, he went on harshly, "If Elizabeth had been injured, Betty, you and Charles would have to take your share of the blame. As Marilyn's parents, you're more concerned about what's best for your daughter than what's best for your grandchild. I should have custody of Elizabeth, not Marilyn.''

"Charles and I believe that you should have custody, Clark. That's one of the reasons I'm calling, to tell you that and to make arrangements for you to come and get Elizabeth and take her home with you.''

Clark couldn't believe the words he was hearing. Numbly he sat down on the edge of his bed. "Are you expecting Marilyn to die?'' he asked bluntly.

"We're just hoping for the best at this point,'' Betty Laird replied, her voice choking up.

As much as he condemned her, Clark couldn't help feeling compassion for his ex-mother-in-law.

"Tell me what happened. Did Marilyn make another suicide attempt?'' he questioned soberly.

"She swallowed an entire bottle of tranquilizers. Elizabeth was staying with us overnight.''

"So she didn't wake up and find her mother. Thank God for that,'' Clark said fervently.

"Marilyn's been depressed.''

"I gathered that from Elizabeth's letters this summer. What have you told her about Marilyn's condition? Did you explain the truth to her?''

"No, of course not!'' The shocked denial was what Clark was expecting. "We just told her that her mother had accidentally taken too much aspirin for a bad headache. Clark, you have to promise not to tell Elizabeth bad things about her mother,'' Betty Laird pleaded. "For Elizabeth's sake.''

She and her husband had tried to sugarcoat reality for Marilyn all her life and now she was urging him to do the same with her grandchild.

"I would never lie to Elizabeth,'' Clark stated firmly. "If in my judgment a truth is too ugly for her to hear, I'll tell her the mildest version or simply say that she needs to be older before we discuss the matter. Now I'd better hang up and pack a few things for the trip to Shreveport."

"You're driving here today?"

"I'll be leaving within the hour. I'll plan to sleep in a motel in Shreveport tonight and bring Elizabeth back with me tomorrow."

He wasn't wasting any time and allowing the Lairds to change their minds.

"I'll have her things ready. Clark, you won't turn Elizabeth against us? You'll let her visit us? She's our grandbaby, and we love her very much—" Betty's voice broke.

"Elizabeth loves you," Clark replied sincerely. "I wouldn't think of turning her against you and Charles or of preventing you from being an important part of her life."

"You naturally have hard feelings toward us, though."

"Yes, I do."

"We had to side with Marilyn in the custody fight, Clark. She's our daughter. We never had anything against you. We appreciated how good you were to Marilyn and how hard you tried to make your marriage to her work. We never held you responsible for the divorce. We have a high regard for you and don't doubt that you'll be a wonderful father to Elizabeth."

"I intend to make being a good father to Elizabeth the number-one priority in life, Betty."

Maybe in future years he might be able to speak words of forgiveness to Betty Laird and exonerate her of her guilt toward him, but not now. For one thing, Clark knew that he couldn't depend on the Lairds to side with him in a new custody suit if Marilyn recovered and insisted on Elizabeth's living with her again.

Over his dead body, Clark resolved. He would do anything, *anything,* to keep his daughter with him.

Chapter Six

"Daddy, is Mommy going to get well, like Grandma Laird said?"

"I don't know, honey," Clark replied gently, reaching over for Elizabeth's small hand and holding it in his large one. "As soon as we get home, we'll call the hospital and get a report. Try not to worry, if you can help it."

They'd been traveling a couple of hours, and she was just now asking the question he'd been expecting her to ask much sooner. It was obvious that troubling thoughts weighed on her mind. She had been very quiet and listless.

"Mommy had lots of headaches. What causes headaches, Daddy?"

"There are various causes. A bump on the head, loud noise, a cold, even a bad case of hunger. Are you getting hungry, too?" Clark asked, hoping to sidetrack her. "We'll be stopping for gas soon. We could buy some snack food to munch on and hold us until lunchtime."

Under normal circumstances, he wouldn't have encouraged eating junk food, but he was willing to try anything to cheer her up.

"Okay," she agreed solemnly. Still pursuing the subject of her mother's health, she said hesitantly, "Mommy didn't ever buy aspirin for grownups. She only bought children's aspirin for me when I was little."

Elizabeth didn't believe her grandmother's phony explanation that Marilyn had accidentally overdosed on aspirin. She wanted to know the truth, but dreaded what she'd find out, Clark realized. What was he to say? *Let me handle this wisely.*

"You're wondering how your mother could have taken too many aspirin when she never took aspirin for her headaches, as far as you knew," he stated.

She nodded. "Mommy took pills from the doctor."

"Those pills are for a sickness called depression. Your mother has suffered from it for many years, since before she and I got married to each other." A medical history she hadn't shared during their courtship and her parents hadn't divulged, either.

"Since before I was born?"

"Long before you were born."

Elizabeth mulled over the information, seeming to gain some comfort from it. "She had headaches before she had me?"

"Yes, and she would go to bed and stay there sometimes for days. She would have spells of crying. Your mother's illness makes her very unhappy at times and no one can cheer her up, not even the people she loves."

The sadly comprehending expression on his daughter's young face hurt. It was clear that he was describing a pattern of behavior that was a common state of things for her. Clark had to quell a surge of anger. *Damn the courts, damn*

the Lairds for subjecting Elizabeth to the kind of home life
she'd had the past three years since her parents had di-
vorced.

"I try to make Mommy feel happy," she said with a sigh.
"I try to make her laugh."

"And when you can't, you feel very bad, like you're responsible?" Another nod of affirmation. "Well, you're not
responsible, honey. Do you believe me?"

"I know I can believe you, Daddy."

Clark's love and fierce protectiveness swelled his heart
almost to the bursting point. There was no way he would
ever return her to the unhealthy home environment from
which he was rescuing her. She deserved to grow up secure
and happy, not burdened with anxiety and vague guilt.

"Mommy's sickness got worse, and she swallowed too
many of the pills?"

"That's exactly what happened, honey."

"Not on purpose," she said after a moment.

"Your mother was alone. No one except her can really say
for certain," Clark pointed out.

"Grandma Laird made a mistake about the aspirin," she
suggested.

"Grandma Laird was mistaken." Clark spoke without
any censure.

Elizabeth sat up straighter, glancing at a sign that indicated an exit was coming up. "I didn't eat my breakfast this
morning. I am getting a little hungry now," she confided.

"We'll take this next exit."

Thirty minutes later they were back on the interstate, riding along companionably, sharing a bag of chips and sip-
ping from cans of soda.

"This is a nice van, Daddy," she complimented, smiling
at him.

Clark smiled back at her. "I'm glad you like it."

"It's going to be fun staying with you at your house. I wanted to visit you before, but I couldn't leave Mommy."

"I always understood," he assured her. "You didn't hurt my feelings."

Elizabeth had refused to spend any holidays apart from her mother. She'd even turned down chances to go with him on vacations that he'd proposed, like a trip to Walt Disney World. Clark hadn't insisted on his restricted rights the courts had granted him. He'd guessed that she was under psychological pressure to show loyalty to Marilyn. Given his own state of mind, too, he'd questioned whether being with him would be beneficial for Elizabeth. She had enough to handle living with a mentally unstable mother without being forced into the company of a bitter, angry father.

"Who's going to take care of me?" she inquired with no hint of concern.

"Mainly I intend to take care of you myself. During the day while I'm working, I'll hire a sitter. But I'll cook our supper at night and fix our breakfast in the morning."

She crunched on a chip. "The sitter will give me lunch?"

"Not necessarily. I may do that, too. I usually come home for lunch, since my work is so near," he explained. "The lady I'm hoping to hire lives next door. She may want to take a break in the middle of the day and go to her house. We'll just have to see."

"You can cook, Daddy?" The idea seemed to intrigue her.

"Yes, I can cook," Clark declared.

"Can you bake cookies?"

She apparently wasn't particularly interested in who her sitter was. He'd tried to sound casual, when he felt anything but casual about the subject. Avery Payton was the ideal person to put in charge of caring for Elizabeth. He could leave his daughter with her and never have to worry.

Avery *had* to take the job. Clark wouldn't take no for an answer.

"Now who can that be?" Avery wondered aloud, wiping her hands on a dishcloth as she went to answer the phone.

She'd just finished her lunch and was washing up the few dishes she'd used. Larry's kitchen was equipped with a dishwasher, but Avery seldom used it. Her problem wasn't saving time and labor, but keeping herself fully occupied. The several hours just past the middle of the day were the worst, when it was too hot to work out in the garden under the broiling June sun.

Instead of collecting her unemployment compensation, Avery would take any poor-paying job that she could get if it weren't for wanting to be free when the twins visited. A solution was finding some worthwhile volunteer work. Surely there was such a thing here in the country. This afternoon when she paid a visit to the tiny library branch to return some books, she thought she might talk to the librarian about helping out as an aide.

"Hello." She spoke cheerfully into the phone, thinking that the last time she'd spoken to another human being was Sunday, when she'd talked to Clark Strong outside the church. Today was Tuesday.

"Hello, Avery. This is Clark. How are you?"

"I'm fine, Clark," she replied once she'd recovered from her surprise.

"The reason I'm calling is that I need your help," he said, coming directly to the point.

"My help?"

"I want to offer you a job."

"A job? Doing what?"

"Could we discuss it in person? I think that would be better. Would it be convenient for you to come here to my house this afternoon?'' he asked, taking her by surprise once again.

He wanted to interview her at his *house,* not at his nursery.

''Yes, it's convenient,'' she said. ''I can be there in thirty minutes.''

''I would greatly appreciate it.''

He hung up, leaving Avery not only mystified but oddly uneasy. Why hadn't he just told her what the job was over the phone? Why was he home on a Tuesday afternoon and not at the nursery?

At least Clark had sounded calm. Though brief and businesslike, he hadn't been terse. *I need your help,* he'd said. Avery would welcome doing him a favor and repaying him for all he'd done for her.

She quickly finished her cleanup and changed into a cotton skirt and blouse and sandals, an outfit appropriate for her planned trip to the library. The waistband of the skirt fit, thanks to the five pounds she'd gained eating a healthy diet. Working in the garden and in the yard gave her a hearty appetite.

She'd also gotten the best tan she'd had in years. Her hair had developed highlights and turned a more golden blond. Without being vain, Avery saw evidence in the mirror that country life had enhanced her natural attributes and made her prettier than she'd been a month ago when she'd barged into Clark's backyard.

C. Strong's backyard. Avery recalled that day as she drove to her appointment with him. She grimaced at the thought of what she must have looked like—gaunt and pale and scared out of her wits.

Today she wasn't at all scared, but she *was* nervous. What sort of job did he intend to offer her at his nursery? An office job? A laborer's job? Was he in need of a salesperson?

Soon enough she would know.

Clark emerged from his screened porch when she pulled up. He was there in time to open the door of the pickup for her. Avery blinked in exaggerated surprise when he held out his hand to help her down. Her reaction was partly an attempt to check her rush of feminine pleasure in seeing him again.

He was wearing jeans and a dark red knit shirt. Some element of urgency seemed to heighten the impact of his rugged masculinity.

"You're certainly giving me the red-carpet treatment," she observed as she took his hand.

"Come inside," he invited. "There's someone I want you to meet."

About to step down, Avery stopped and looked at him blankly. "Someone you want me to meet? Who?"

"My daughter, Elizabeth." Her hand had gone limp in his. He gave it a firm squeeze.

His *daughter?* Avery made an ungraceful descent to the ground, her coordination seeming to be affected by her utter surprise and confusion. Why hadn't he mentioned on the phone that his daughter was visiting him? Clark ushered her gently out of the way so that he could shut the door of the pickup. For all her robotlike movement, Avery was aware of how much she enjoyed having him touch her body.

"I got a call on Sunday from my former mother-in-law in Shreveport informing me that my ex-wife was hospitalized and in critical condition," he explained. Clasping Avery's arm, he started them toward the house. "I drove to Shreveport on Sunday and brought Elizabeth back with me yesterday."

"She's going to stay with you until her mother's recovered?"

His fingers tightened. "She's going to live with me permanently," he stated grimly.

"You intend to try to get custody of her?"

"I intend to get custody of her, but I haven't discussed my intention with her. It's too soon."

Avery sighed. "Clark, without knowing any of the circumstances, I just hope you're not building up false hopes." She was afraid for him.

Her job interview had paled in importance. The mystery had been solved about why he wasn't at the nursery today. He was handling business here at home. Probably he foresaw having to be away from the nursery a great deal in the coming weeks and that was where she came in.

They'd reached the house. Avery held back, not entering through the screened door onto the back porch. "Before we go inside," she said, "whatever job you have for me at the nursery, I'll be more than glad to do it."

He squeezed her arm, but didn't show any marked relief nor make any reply. Nonplussed by his reaction, she let him guide her across the porch and into the air-conditioned coolness of the house.

They entered a large, pleasant country kitchen, furnished with an oak dining table that seated six. Avery glanced around curiously, noting a general state of neatness and cleanliness. Her attention to decorating details was short-lived because peals of childish laughter came from the next room, the sound automatically bringing a smile to her lips.

"Daddy! I think Shep remembers me! He's *licking* my face!"

Avery gasped, suddenly remembering the vicious German shepherd. Before she could voice her horror at the thought of the child playing with that dog, Clark called to his daughter, "I'm sure he does remember you, baby."

The deep, loving timbre of his voice did strange things to Avery. She wished she could leave and come back a little more prepared, less vulnerable.

Clark caught up her hand and led her into the adjoining room, an informal living room with a massive brick fireplace. On the carpeted floor, a little girl with dark brown braids lay on her back, wriggling with delight as the gray-and-black German shepherd lapped her pink cheeks.

"We've got company," Clark announced indulgently. "Sit up and meet Ms. Payton, our next-door neighbor. Shep." He spoke the dog's name in a stern tone, and the animal reluctantly sat on his haunches, tongue wagging.

Elizabeth was an adorable replica of her father with his hair color and dark brown eyes. She was a petite child, though, apparently having inherited her delicate build from her mother.

"Hello, Elizabeth." Avery smiled at the little girl as she scrambled to her feet, smoothing back tendrils of hair from her forehead. She was wearing pink jeans, a pink pullover and pink sneakers.

"Hi." Elizabeth shyly smiled back, winning Avery's heart. "I'm pleased to meet you."

"Sit down, Avery," Clark urged. Before she could respond on her own, he was walking her to the long sofa, upholstered in a beige tweedy fabric. "I'll let Elizabeth entertain you while I go out and put on some coffee."

Avery sat down, having little other choice. She arranged her skirt and then patted the seat beside her. "I don't need to be entertained, but I would love to have Elizabeth talk to me."

Clark retreated to one side, watching, as his daughter came over to perch on the sofa, daintily crossing one leg over the other.

"Are you going to be my sitter?" Elizabeth inquired.

"Your sitter?" Avery repeated, staring at the little girl. Clark had tensed and was as still as a statue. The only sound was Shep's panting.

Elizabeth's expression grew uncertain. "My daddy said that he was hoping to hire the lady who lived next door to be my sitter." Her gaze went to her father. "Is there another lady, Daddy?"

Avery glared at Clark, waiting for his answer.

"No, baby," he said quietly. "Ms. Payton is the person I want to hire. I haven't had the chance yet to offer her the job."

"I believe your father wanted me to meet you first, Elizabeth." Avery looked daggers at him as she spoke calmly. "Maybe he wanted to make sure you and I liked one another before he asked me."

"I like you, Ms. Payton," Elizabeth ventured bravely. "I think you're pretty."

Avery patted her small knee. "I think you're cute as a button and very sweet." *My opinion of your father isn't so positive.* Clark's manipulativeness was not only offensive, but disappointing. She wouldn't have thought him capable of such tactics. "I would enjoy looking after you, Elizabeth," Avery went on. "It wouldn't be like a job at all." She addressed him crisply. "The only condition is that I can bring Elizabeth to my house and take her places with me. Also, when my sons visit near the end of summer, you would have to make other arrangements."

Clark inclined his head humbly, agreeing without hesitation at her stipulations. Open relief was written on his face. "All I ask is that you let me know when you're taking her somewhere."

"Of course."

"We'll have fun, Elizabeth. Goodbye now." Avery smiled at the little girl in parting and then stood up.

"Won't you stay awhile?" Clark asked.

"No, thank you. I'm on my way to the library. But I would like a word with you."

He accompanied her outside. On the porch, Avery turned to face him. Her voice resonated with her indignation as she chastised him. "I just want you to know what a low opinion I have of the way you handled this. It wasn't necessary for you to *use* Elizabeth and sell me on being her sitter. You could have been direct. You could have explained your situation over the phone, and I would have been happy to help you out."

"I'm sorry that you're upset. My motives were the best. It was just of the utmost importance to me to have you as Elizabeth's sitter." He made a movement as though to touch her and then dropped his hand when Avery flinched. "I was functioning as a father."

"Well, you accomplished your objective. I'm available whenever you need me."

"I really should get back to the nursery tomorrow. Don't you see that I couldn't bring Elizabeth home with me and leave her with just anyone? You're a very maternal woman, Avery. That was my dominant impression of you the first day I saw you."

While she was noticing that he was a virile man in his prime, while she was being attracted to him against her will and subconsciously fueling fantasy, he was noticing that she would make a good baby-sitter. Avery's pride smarted at the memory of her dream about being ravished in the woods by him.

"I give you credit, Clark, for being a concerned father. Let's just leave it at that," she said crisply. "What time do you go to work in the morning?"

He sighed. "I'd like to leave about eight o'clock. I'll wake Elizabeth and give her breakfast."

"I'll come over at eight. And I don't mind giving her breakfast, if she's sleepy and doesn't want to get up early."

"Shall we play it by ear?" he suggested.

"Will you want to come back here at noon and have lunch with Elizabeth?" Avery briskly continued with arranging the next day's schedule.

"I'd like to."

"That's fine."

"I'll knock off by five or five-thirty now that she's with me. Before, I might have worked until dark or after dark."

"If you're running late, it's no problem," Avery stated. "It's not as though I have any other pressing obligations."

"We need to discuss salary," he said.

The gentle apology in his tone and manner threatened to erode her defenses. She glanced at her watch, noting that only fifteen minutes had elapsed. It seemed a much longer time.

"I really don't care if you pay me or not. This afternoon I was going to talk to the librarian about doing volunteer work. I'd much rather be Elizabeth's sitter."

"I insist on paying you. I couldn't take advantage of you for the length of time we're talking about. You said you'd be living in Wade's house a year," he reminded.

Avery nodded. "Whatever you can afford is agreeable."

"Are you sure you won't change your mind and stay awhile?" Clark asked hopefully.

"I'm sure." She decided to be blunt. "It would be too much of a strain being friendly to you in front of Elizabeth. I'm not very good at hiding my true feelings."

Her reservations were more complicated than that, but a portion of the truth would suffice. Avery realized that she was holding on to her grudge for dear life. Without it, she was far too vulnerable where he was concerned.

Clark didn't persist. "I admire your honesty," he said with a ring of sincerity.

In his overzealousness, he'd bungled badly, Clark reflected, going inside after Avery had left. *Thank goodness that he was dealing with a woman who was one of a kind.* A lesser woman might have gotten upset and walked out in a huff.

Not Avery. She was too fine a person to behave in a petty fashion. Too mature and fair-minded not to keep matters in perspective.

Clark deeply regretted that he'd earned her disapproval. He definitely wanted to reinstate himself.

Elizabeth had rejoined Shep on the carpet and was petting him. She jumped up as her father entered the living room.

"Can we play one of my games that I brought with me, Daddy?"

"Sure thing. If you think I'm smart enough that you can teach me the rules," he teased.

She giggled, heading at once for her room. "You're real smart!"

I'm not feeling very smart at the moment, Clark thought, dropping down onto the sofa and stretching out his long legs.

As a man, he could make mistakes. As a father, he couldn't. Clark had to show good judgment one hundred percent of the time when Elizabeth's well-being was involved.

There was no margin for error. Now that he'd succeeded, after a fashion, in getting Avery as a sitter, he could proceed to the next important order of business: retaining an excellent attorney to start custody proceedings.

This time Clark had a case for proving that he was the stable parent. Before, there hadn't been any way to substantiate Marilyn's mental problems. There'd primarily been his testimony. She'd denied the seriousness of her bouts with depression and so had her parents. Her treatment had been in private clinics. Clark's attorney hadn't been able to come up with any documentation of her suicide attempts.

Not so with this latest near-successful effort to take her own life. Paramedics had been called to the scene. She'd been rushed to a hospital. There was concrete evidence that she'd swallowed a whole bottle of tranquilizers.

Clark wasn't going to waste any time. He meant to file suit right away.

This time he had more than a fighting chance to win custody of Elizabeth, especially with Marilyn incapacitated. But what worried him was that he might have another fight on his hands in a year or two if Marilyn recovered, and her prognosis had improved he'd learned last night when he called for a report.

In a custody battle between single parents, a father was automatically at a disadvantage, as unjust as that was.

Clark could remarry and reduce that disadvantage.

With a wife standing beside him in court, a stepmother for Elizabeth, suddenly he was in a much better position.

It wasn't a new idea, but before now it hadn't been a feasible idea. Clark was amazed at how entirely feasible it did seem.

Avery was a natural as a stepmother.

She also had a lot to recommend her as a wife, based on short acquaintance.

"I brought two games, Daddy. You can choose."

Elizabeth was back. Clark gave her his full attention.

"Let's play your favorite first," he suggested. "Then we'll play the other one."

"All right." She smiled at him happily, climbing up on the sofa and busying herself with setting up a game board. "This is fun, huh?"

Clark smiled back. "This is the most fun your daddy has had in ages."

Chapter Seven

"Why don't we make up my daddy's bed after we make up mine?" Elizabeth asked innocently.

Avery continued smoothing out the pink candy-striped sheet, annoyed with herself that her pulse had speeded up at the thought of entering Clark's room and making his bed.

"Your daddy didn't hire me to do housework," she explained. "My job is to take care of you. One reason I help you make up your bed every morning and straighten your room is to teach you how to be neat."

"Oh," the little girl said. She never argued and tried to get her way, like a normal child invariably did at least occasionally. In a week's time, Avery had found her much too obedient and eager for approval. Grasping her side of the bedspread, Elizabeth inquired anxiously, "Am I doing it right?"

"You're doing it very well," Avery assured her.

"When I helped Grandma Laird make my bed at her house, she did my side over. But you don't have to, huh?"

"No, I don't have to."

Elizabeth probably hadn't been spanked or treated harshly by her mother or her grandparents. Avery hadn't gotten any inkling of that, but Clark's little daughter showed signs of being very insecure. Until he showed up. Then she blossomed.

"You could make up your daddy's bed by yourself, if you wanted to do something nice for him," Avery remarked, careful not to turn her words into a suggestion, but rather open up an option.

"But I might not do it good enough."

"I'm sure you'd do a very good job for your age. That's all any of us can do. Our best." *Which sometimes wasn't good enough.* Avery plumped a pillow. Doing her best as Elizabeth's sitter required fighting off self-pity when it sneaked up on her.

"Will you come and look when I'm finished?"

"I'll take a peek from the doorway."

Avery heard her own faintly guilty note and reminded herself virtuously that she hadn't given into temptation and peeked into his bedroom before today, despite having every opportunity. Elizabeth had volunteered that her daddy's room was located around a bend in the hallway, adding that he had his own bathroom. Avery assumed that he occupied the so-called master suite in the house.

It was a spacious house with four bedrooms, three full bathrooms and a half bath. The former owners of Pleasant Hollow Nursery, who'd built the house, had had five children. They'd put both home and business on the market together, wanting a single buyer. Clark had been that buyer, as Avery had learned in the village on that same fateful day she'd met him.

Evidently he'd wanted to buy the nursery and undoubtedly he'd liked the seclusion of the house and the convenience of living near his work. It hadn't deterred him that the house was actually too large for his needs. The whole setup must have been made to order for him at the time, Avery recognized, allowing him to be a recluse.

It touched her that he'd had a delightful little girl's room all ready for Elizabeth to move into. There hadn't been time for him to rush out and buy the pretty white-painted furniture, the pictures on the wall depicting scenes from fairy tales, the giant-size stuffed animals.

Avery doubted a mother could have done any better as a decorator, a compliment that she would pay him eventually. When she allowed herself to thaw and be slightly more friendly.

"I'll be in the laundry room," she called after Elizabeth as the latter disappeared down the hall. "I'm going to wash a load of your clothes."

Doing laundry wasn't technically one of her duties, any more than housework, but it was hardly a chore. Avery could help Clark out that much.

It didn't occur to her until she entered the laundry room and surveyed a wicker basket overflowing with soiled clothing that she was going to have to sort through his dirty clothes if she planned to follow through with her good intentions. Elizabeth's small garments were mixed in with his jeans and shirts and underwear and socks.

He came home at noon each day usually sweaty and sometimes dirty. If either was the case, he changed into clean clothes, which he wore to work that afternoon. Avery wouldn't have been very observant if she hadn't noticed that he was wearing a different shirt morning and afternoon. It didn't surprise her that his laundry piled up on him, she reflected, gingerly lifting a pair of his jeans by the waistband.

Elizabeth entered, announcing in a disappointed voice, "My daddy had already made up his bed."

Avery shared in the little girl's disappointment. No inspection was going to be necessary.

"Maybe another day he'll forget," she consoled.

"Can I help you wash my clothes?" Elizabeth asked.

"You can, if you like," Avery agreed and ended up standing patiently to one side, supervising while Clark's daughter rummaged through the basket, making it unnecessary for her to handle his underwear. She couldn't help noticing that he apparently preferred dark-colored cotton briefs. There wasn't a single white pair.

As luck would have it, a pair of maroon briefs ended up on top when Elizabeth had finished. To Avery's private discomfort, Clark's discarded underwear retained the shape of his body, the crotch of the garment forming a cup. Unobtrusively she pulled out a pair of jeans and draped them on top.

"Now what would you like to do?" she inquired when the washer was loaded, the soap powder measured and poured and the proper settings all selected. With Elizabeth's "help," it had been a lengthy process.

Typically the little girl looked to Avery, the adult in charge, to set up the parameters and give her her choices. "What can we do?"

"Any number of things. I'm feeling lazy. Why don't you think of an activity?"

"Could we cook something?"

"I don't know why not. What did you have in mind?"

Elizabeth thought hard, her small brow furrowed. "Tuna salad?"

"Tuna salad?" Avery repeated in mild surprise.

"For me and my daddy's lunch. I could surprise him."

"What a nice idea. We'll make sure he knows it was *your* idea," Avery said. *So much for fostering initiative,* she thought. She was going to end up preparing Clark's lunch.

"I could set the table and have everything ready when he comes home!" Elizabeth was figuratively off and running with her idea.

"Let's check and see if we have all the necessary ingredients."

A search of the pantry shelves in the laundry room didn't turn up a can of tuna.

"Are you sure your daddy likes tuna salad?" Avery inquired, the thought occurring to her that Clark might not simply be out of canned tuna.

"He likes lots of different food" was Elizabeth's answer. "Can we go to the store and buy some tuna?"

"It's not necessary to go to the store. I have several cans at my house. We'll walk through the woods." There was a well-marked path by now. Avery had decided that it was silly to drive back and forth to the Clark's house.

She and Elizabeth spent the morning busily employed in his kitchen. Regardless of the mess, Avery let the little girl do every step that didn't pose any danger. Tuna salad was apparently popular lunch fare with Elizabeth's grandparents, the Lairds. Elizabeth had her Grandma Laird's recipe memorized.

"By the time this is chilled, it'll be delicious," Avery stated in all sincerity when she and Elizabeth tasted the finished product.

Elizabeth beamed and then looked anxious. "I just hope I made enough. My daddy gets real hungry."

"There's plenty for the two of you. And we'll put out sliced bread and cheese and pickles, like your Grandma Laird does."

"I wish you could eat with us."

"That's sweet, but I'm going to my house for lunch," Avery refused firmly.

"Daddy always asks you if you'll stay."

"He's being polite." Avery gave the little girl a hug, pleased that she was being somewhat argumentative.

Clark arrived home at twelve-thirty. Elizabeth had the table set, complete with a vase bearing a cluster of glorious peach-colored daylilies blooming on a single stalk. The bed of hybrid daylilies that Larry's goat had munched on was in bloom, a marvel of exquisite varieties that he'd hybridized himself, Avery had learned.

Hearing his deep voice as he greeted Shep outside, she jumped up to leave.

"Wait and see my daddy's face when he walks in!" Elizabeth implored.

Avery wished that the suggestion didn't appeal to her quite so much. It not only warmed her heart to watch Clark's face light up with paternal love when he spotted Elizabeth, she couldn't for the life of her not take a woman's pleasure in looking at him. And not just looking at his face, but at the rest of him, dirty or clean.

"What have we here?" he demanded, entering the kitchen and taking in with a glance his daughter, Avery and the table, in that order. Today he wasn't sweaty. His shirt didn't cling damply, molding his shoulders and chest.

"I made us lunch, Daddy," Elizabeth explained as she ran to him.

Clark picked his daughter up and hugged her tightly, his strong arms enfolding her small form. Avery felt something tighten inside her, then spring loose, leaving an empty sensation, when he set Elizabeth back down.

"This is a treat," he said, walking toward the table and nearer Avery.

"It was all my idea, and I did almost every single thing," his daughter claimed proudly.

"She did," Avery confirmed. "We spent the entire morning laboring here in the kitchen."

"We're having tuna salad, whole-wheat bread, Swiss cheese and cheddar cheese and bread-and-butter pickles." Like some diminutive Julia Child opening a cooking segment, Elizabeth pointed to each item of the lunch feast she was serving.

Clark was eyeing the shallow bowl of tuna salad nestled in lettuce leaves. "Tuna salad," he said. His gaze met Avery's.

Suddenly she *knew* he wasn't fond of tuna.

"You probably don't often make tuna salad for yourself," she suggested with a note of apology that said, *I had no idea.*

"You might say I never make it for myself," he replied. "Charlie the Tuna isn't in any danger from me."

He *hated* tuna salad.

"I hope I made enough, Daddy," Elizabeth put in. "Ms. Payton said it's delicious."

"You made an ample amount, baby. We'll set another place. Since Ms. Payton likes your tuna salad, she should enjoy her share of it."

Avery could hardly refuse.

Nor did she really want to refuse.

"You run to the bathroom and wash your hands, Elizabeth," she instructed. "I'll take care of setting a place for me." The little girl obediently left. "I feel terrible about this," Avery told Clark in an undertone. "You're being a good sport."

He'd gone to the sink and was washing his hands, using dish detergent. "I can't hurt her feelings. Besides, if it will help to get me out of the doghouse with you, I'll gladly choke down a helping of tuna salad," he added.

Glancing over his shoulder, he smiled at her. Avery's heart skipped a beat. "That kind of language hardly applies," she said stiffly, turning away. "I'm Elizabeth's sitter."

"I'm sorry," he apologized quickly. "I didn't mean to trivialize your grievance. I would just like to get in your good graces somehow."

Fortunately—and regrettably—Elizabeth returned, saving Avery from having to answer.

Sitting down to lunch, Avery knew her so-called "grievance" against him was doomed. It couldn't withstand the interest in his eyes, the warmth of his smile, the sheer stimulation of his masculine company. His anger and bitterness had disappeared, leaving him much more relaxed, but not low-key. He emanated vitality. Even his quiet emotion was intense.

Clark was a likable man. So why not let herself like him? Why not be friends? He obviously had decided he wanted to be friends with her now that he had Elizabeth living with him.

Sympathizing with his predicament that she'd unknowingly helped to create by letting Elizabeth prepare lunch, made it easier for Avery to unbend. He forked the tuna salad into his mouth and washed it down with water, getting up several times to refill his glass.

"That was the best tuna salad that I've ever had, by far," he complimented his daughter, having finally disposed of his helping, along with four slices of bread and at least that many slices of cheese and half a jar of pickles.

"There's a little more left, Daddy."

Clark held up his hand. "I really couldn't eat another bite."

Avery spoke up. "Then I'll finish up the rest. It's really excellent tuna salad."

"Please," he said fervently, handing her the bowl.

She smiled at him. He smiled back, thanking her, but his gaze had a disturbing intentness.

"So you two cooked all morning?" Clark pushed aside his plate, addressing his question to both of them. Avery let Elizabeth answer.

"First we made up my bed and straightened up my room. I was going to make up your bed by myself, Daddy. Ms. Payton wasn't going to help me. She was just going to come to the door when I'd finished. But you'd already made up your bed."

"After a fashion," he said.

Avery kept her eyes on her plate. She knew he was probably translating for himself, *Ms. Payton didn't want to help me but was agreeable to looking inside your bedroom.*

Elizabeth continued with her report of the morning's activities. "We washed a load of my clothes. I picked them out of the basket and put them in the washing machine and poured the soap powder and pulled out the knob that started the water. Didn't I, Ms. Payton?"

"You certainly did all that," Avery confirmed. "I just selected the setting."

There was nothing especially intimate about the conversation. She didn't know why she should be embarrassed. He couldn't read her mind or know that she was remembering his maroon briefs.

"We didn't wash your dirty clothes, Daddy."

"It was a big help that you and Ms. Payton did your laundry. I certainly don't expect you to do mine," he said.

Avery and Elizabeth overruled his offer to clear the table by himself. He gave in without argument, and the three of them worked together, actually making a longer job out of it than if either Avery or Clark had worked alone, without Elizabeth's help. Clark gave every indication that he was enjoying the homey scene thoroughly, while Avery was aware that she found being a part of it too enjoyable for comfort.

She was seeing a lighthearted side of him that she hadn't seen before as he teased Elizabeth, much to her delight, and carried on tongue-in-cheek adult exchanges with Avery. He touched his daughter often, tweaking her braid, patting her on the head, lightly trailing a finger across her cheek. Observing those gestures of paternal affection, Avery felt a yearning sensation. When once or twice he casually touched her, she had to bear down on the yearning.

She shared some of Elizabeth's regret at his announcement that he had to return to work, but also welcomed his departure. He bent and kissed the little girl on the cheek. She wrapped her arms around his neck and hugged him tightly.

"Goodbye, Daddy."

"Thank you again for lunch, baby," he said tenderly. Straightening, he hesitated a fraction of a second and then, taking Avery totally by surprise, he bent and kissed her on the cheek. The longing welled up in her to follow his daughter's example and put her arms around his neck. Grabbing on to something was nearly a necessity with her whole body seeming to lose all strength. "Thank you for everything," he said softly.

"You're welcome," Avery managed to reply.

After he'd gone out, closing the door after him, she put her hand up to her cheek and surreptitiously rubbed the spot where his lips, warm and firm, had pressed and lingered a second. His kiss hadn't been a playful peck. Avery breathed in deeply, sucking in oxygen and willing away the awareness of how close to her lips his mouth had rested.

Elizabeth apparently found nothing amiss with her father's having kissed her sitter.

"Let's go to my house this afternoon," Avery proposed, and the little girl readily went along with the suggestion, having no inkling, of course, that Avery was fleeing Clark's house where his presence was strong.

She'd regained her perspective within a matter of minutes and was back on emotional track. All it took was thinking about the twins. They were her children. She was their mother. Her mother-child relationship with them was the all-important relationship in her existence, coming before any other relationship. It determined her plans, her future, whether or not she had custody of them.

Being Elizabeth's sitter was temporary, like living here in the country was temporary. Avery shouldn't grow too fond of the little girl. Or her father.

"I'll drop you off at your house. Your daddy's probably home by now."

"Before supper I want to address my card to Mommy and write her a note."

"I'm sure he'll help you."

Elizabeth sat holding a small bag containing a get-well card that she'd selected at the village pharmacy. The little girl had had an attack of missing her mother that afternoon, after the morning's excitement. Avery had thought it might cheer her up to go shopping for a card, and it had. They'd prolonged the trip, browsing in the few stores, which included a feed and seed store and a surplus merchandise store that sold everything from canned goods to rubber boots.

Avery turned into Clark's driveway past his black mailbox with C. STRONG lettered in white paint. Her intention was to drop Elizabeth off, if his van was there.

To her surprise, his parking spot was vacant. "Your daddy's running late," she commented to Elizabeth with mixed feelings. This meant she'd have to go inside and be there when he arrived home. After that kiss on the cheek, she felt awkward, some barrier having been lowered.

The wall phone in the kitchen began to ring just as Avery opened the door. Clark was calling, apologizing because he was delayed at the nursery, loading a truck of hibiscus plants.

"The driver had a breakdown and only got here a few minutes ago," he explained. "I should be home in a half hour, at most."

"There's no big rush," Avery assured him. "Take as long as you need."

After she'd hung up, it occurred to her that she could have offered to start supper for him and Elizabeth.

"Would you help me with my note to Mommy?" the single-minded little girl requested.

"I'd be happy to," Avery replied, deciding that it was better that she hadn't offered to help with supper preparations. She needed to preserve certain boundaries. "Let's sit at the kitchen table, shall we?"

"I'll be right back. I want to get my pen that writes pink."

The search took her five minutes. Avery was about to go and check on her when she returned and climbed up on a chair, ready to begin. "I'm going to make my letters small so I can write a lot of words. I'm going to take my time and write real neat," Elizabeth confided, giving Avery her first clue that composing the note might be a more laborious process than she'd anticipated.

Sure enough, when Clark's van drove up outside, his daughter was still at her task. "I hear Daddy," she said absently, her small brow furrowed with concentration. "How do you spell *pharmacy?*"

Avery was patiently answering, letter by letter, when Clark opened the kitchen door. She looked up, seeing that he was wringing wet with sweat; even his jeans soaked with perspiration. He apparently had helped to load the hibiscus plants himself, not just supervised. "Elizabeth is writing a note to her mother. She bought her a get-well card today," Avery explained, lowering her gaze.

"Hi, Daddy," Elizabeth put in. "I need to finish before we have supper."

"Don't let me interrupt," he said. "I'm headed straight for the shower."

He was taking an indirect route, heading first for the laundry room, peeling off his sodden shirt as he went. Avery raised her eyes and watched the ripple of muscles in his back as he stripped the shirt over his head, disappearing through the doorway, naked from the waist up. She breathed in and intoned the last letter of pharmacy. *"Y."*

From the laundry room came the dull plop of Clark's shoes hitting the floor. Shortly he emerged, barefoot, wearing only the sweat-soaked jeans, his front upper torso magnificently exposed to her view. The growth of dark body hair on his muscular chest tapered to a narrow trail down his taut stomach to the waistband of his jeans. After one close look that she hoped didn't convey her feminine appreciation, Avery trained her gaze on Elizabeth's hand grasping the pen and said, "That's very good."

Under the table she pressed her hand to her stomach, which was aquiver. It didn't help at all to realize that his keeping his jeans on was a concession to modesty. If she and Elizabeth hadn't been there, he undoubtedly would have shed them and his underwear, too, and passed buck naked through the house to his bathroom. Probably that had been his usual practice when he lived alone.

Avery was upset with herself that she found the sight of Clark without his shirt on downright arousing. But she had. That was the fact of the matter. And her reaction was hardly baffling. She was physically attracted to him. What woman wouldn't be?

Clark returned shortly, his dark brown hair wet but combed. He was wearing clothes that were a fresh version of those he'd taken off, jeans and knit shirt open at the throat. Pausing behind Elizabeth's chair, he silently scanned her note.

"About finished?" he inquired.

Elizabeth sighed. "I'm almost out of room, and I haven't told Mommy about Ms. Payton yet."

"Ms. Payton is too important to omit," he said.

Avery got up. "On that I'll leave and let you take over," she told him.

"I was hoping that you would go out for supper with us tonight. Have you tried the Barbecue Pit? It has pretty good barbecue ribs."

"Why, no, I haven't eaten there."

"The place has no atmosphere, of course."

"Maybe some other time," Avery said.

"Please—unless you really would rather not join us," he added. "We'd like your company."

And she would like their company—his and Elizabeth's. Her alternative was going home and eating a solitary supper. It seemed a lonely prospect compared to the informal meal out he was suggesting.

"Thank you. I will join you."

"Good," Clark replied. "If we can help Elizabeth finish up, we'll get in the van and go. I'm hungry enough to eat a side of beef." He leaned down, rubbing his clean-shaven cheek against his daughter's pink cheek. "How about this for a final sentence that will fit your space? 'My sitter, Ms. Payton, takes good care of me.'"

"Okay." Elizabeth painstakingly wrote the words and signed the card, agreeing to wait until the next morning to address the envelope.

On a weeknight the Barbecue Pit wasn't packed with diners, but there were a few tables with teenagers and several occupied by families. The Western decor might have been best described as shabby. But the place was reasonably clean, and the food tasted good.

Avery was glad she'd come along.

During the meal, Elizabeth unexpectedly brought up the twins, asking, "Do Bret and Bart like barbecue?"

"Who?" Clark inquired. He glanced from Elizabeth to her, comprehension dawning on his face.

"Bret and Bart are my twin boys," she explained, telling him with her tone that it wasn't painful to have them come up in conversation. Surprisingly, it wasn't. "Yes, they do like barbecue. When they visit me, I'll have to bring them here, won't I?" she said, replying to his daughter.

"Can I come, too?"

Clark spoke up indulgently, "It's always best to wait and get invited, not invite yourself. When are the boys coming?" he asked.

"The first week in August."

"This area offers a lot to do that boys of that age should enjoy. I'm acquainted with most of the ranch owners. I can probably arrange for you to take Bret and Bart on some tours of the stables and racetrack training facilities. They might be interested in visiting an ostrich farm and an emu farm. I can set that up, too."

"I would love to do all that with them!" Avery exclaimed. "I would enjoy everything you've mentioned myself."

"Then I'll see what I can do."

"What about me, Daddy?" Elizabeth piped up.

Clark wiped away a smear of barbecue sauce from the corner of her mouth, using his napkin. "What about you?" he mocked gently. "Don't worry. You'll get to visit some of the same places where Ms. Avery takes her boys."

"You'll take me?"

"I sure will."

Avery noted the changed reference to her as *Ms. Avery* instead of *Ms. Payton*.

It was still daylight when they were leaving the restaurant. The short drive to Clark's house took only fifteen minutes, and dusk was just beginning to fall. The purple martins hadn't come out yet to swoop across the sky and patrol for insects. He drove past his driveway to hers.

"My truck is at your house," Avery reminded him.

"I know. I thought you might need to let Wade's old dog out. And I also thought you might like to turn on some lights so that you don't come home to a dark house."

"It won't be dark for another half hour."

"I was hoping that you would keep me company awhile tonight," Clark replied. "Elizabeth will be going to bed."

"You won't find me very good company, I'm afraid," Avery warned. "I may start yawning at nine-thirty. I've fallen into the 'early-to-bed-early-to-rise' habit."

"I don't promise to be good company myself" was his answer. "You don't have to be sociable."

At Avery's house, Clark and Elizabeth waited in the van while she went inside, taking his advice and turning on lights while Sam obligingly made a brief trip into the yard. The old dog didn't like to leave his rug for long.

"Keep the burglars out, Sam," she admonished him, as he flopped back down with a great sigh after he'd returned. "I'm visiting next door for a little while. No reflection on you, but you're not the greatest conversationalist in the world."

Last night she'd written the twins a newsy letter and mailed it today. She wouldn't have written them again tonight anyway. Receiving a daily letter from her wasn't a good thing for them.

It was okay for her to spend an hour or so with Clark, enjoying some adult companionship. She didn't have to feel guilty over not choosing to be by herself with just the twins' pictures and Sam for company.

Clark had no thoughts of seducing her, not with Elizabeth in another room in the house. Avery wasn't in the least worried about having to fend him off. The butterflies in her stomach were just nervousness at the prospect of being alone with him.

Chapter Eight

"You haven't had any more trouble with that latch on the gate?" Clark inquired when she got back into the van.

"No. It works fine. I oil it regularly."

"That goat looks like he's put on a few pounds. Are the chickens laying eggs?" Clark was backing up to turn around.

"Every single one of them is laying. I keep Billie supplied. Would you like some fresh yard eggs?"

"Love some," he replied and grinned. "Although I wasn't hinting."

"You would be more than welcome."

Elizabeth, who had been quiet, joined the conversation. "Are fresh yard eggs good for making tuna salad?"

Clark and Avery looked at each other in silent communication. *Please, no more tuna salad,* he implored. She assured him with her sympathetic expression that she wouldn't subject him to eating any more tuna salad in the future.

"Actually hard-boiled fresh eggs don't peel as easily as eggs from the supermarket that aren't quite as fresh," Avery remarked to the little girl. "But the fresh eggs are delicious when they're fried or scrambled. There's really a difference."

"My daddy and I like scrambled eggs for breakfast," Elizabeth volunteered. "But he likes his gummy, and I like mine dry."

"My boys like theirs dry," Avery commented.

"And you?" Clark asked.

"'Gummy,'" she admitted, using Elizabeth's term for *moist*.

"What's their favorite breakfast in all the world?" Elizabeth wanted to know.

"French toast." Counteracting a tinge of sadness, Avery had spoken lightly, but Clark glanced over at her.

"Mine, too!" his small daughter exclaimed. "But Daddy doesn't know how to make French toast."

"Ms. Avery will have to write down her recipe for me," he said.

They reached his house and trooped inside, as though the three of them going out to supper was a common occurrence. Shep had licked Avery's hand in welcome out on the porch, apparently accepting her as a member of the family. The German shepherd was primarily an outside dog, and slept on the porch at night, Avery had learned in the course of the past week, as she'd learned various and sundry other bits of information about Clark's household.

"If you don't mind, I'm going to throw a load of clothes into the washing machine," Clark said over his shoulder as he headed into the laundry room. "Make yourself comfortable and watch TV, if you like."

"Why don't I draw Elizabeth's bath?" Avery offered.

"Don't feel that you have to," he replied. "This won't take me but a minute, and I can do it."

Given the option, Avery followed Elizabeth. Helping the little girl get ready for bed held far more appeal than going into the living room and turning on the TV.

When Clark stuck his head in the bathroom door a few minutes later, Avery was crouched beside the tub, washing Elizabeth's back at her request.

He smiled at them both. "If I'm not needed in here, I have a phone call to make."

The bath ritual was different enough that Avery wasn't engulfed with painful deéjà vu. Bathing one little seven-year-old girl wasn't similar to putting a pair of seven-year-old boys in the same tub together.

Elizabeth hugged Avery after Avery had dried her off and slipped her nightgown over her head. "Thank you, Ms. Avery," she said sweetly.

"You're very welcome, dear," Avery replied, tenderness welling up inside her as she hugged the little girl back.

"Is it all right to call you 'Ms. Avery'?"

"It's perfectly all right with me."

Clark came into his daughter's bedroom as she was climbing into her bed. Avery said good-night to Elizabeth and left him to tuck her in.

In the living room, Avery stood a moment in indecision. Then she sat on the sofa rather than in an armchair. The TV remote control was in easy reach on the coffee table, but instead, she picked up a copy of *National Geographic* and thumbed through it, wondering which articles he'd read.

Clark joined her after about five minutes and sat down on the sofa a comfortable distance away. "She fell asleep in the middle of the story I was reading her," he said.

"She's a sweet child. She gives me no trouble at all."

He stretched his arm along the back of the sofa, shifting his big body slightly so that his knees angled toward hers.

"When Marilyn got pregnant, I was really hoping the child would be a boy," he reflected.

"That's natural, I suppose, for a father to want a son."

"Did you want a daughter?"

"Oh, yes," Avery admitted. "When I learned I was pregnant, I secretly hoped it was a girl. Instead, of course, I had twin boys, and I wouldn't have traded them. If I'd stayed married to their father, I'm sure I would have tried to give them a little sister. But that wasn't in the cards."

"What did go wrong with your marriage, if you don't mind my asking?"

"In a nutshell, my ex-husband, John, fell out of love with me and in love with the woman he's married to now, Cindy. He was genuinely apologetic about hurting me and breaking up our family. Apparently theirs was a kind of soul mating, not just a wild physical attraction. He didn't have an affair with her behind my back. A week after he'd met her, he asked me for a divorce so he could marry her. I was quite devastated," Avery concluded matter-of-factly.

"That bastard," Clark said grimly, his jaw set.

"If he'd been a real bastard, it might have been easier. But he wasn't."

"You don't seem bitter."

"I'm permanently disillusioned about the whole business of falling in love. Marriage vows lost a lot of their credibility for me, sad to say." She could never be so gullible again as to believe a man could love her forever.

He nodded. "Same here. I'm a real cynic about romantic love, having gone the whole route once. Give me respect and admiration for a woman over being swept off my feet by her beauty and all that other claptrap that has no substance. The kind of love that makes a marriage hang together is mutual devotion, or at least that's my opinion."

"You may be right. I guess both of us can only speculate about successful marriages," Avery pointed out. It disturbed her that she didn't want to agree with him. She wouldn't have suspected that she was still a foolish romantic at heart, however disillusioned. Picking up the *National Geographic* on her lap, she laid it on the coffee table and asked, "What caused your marriage problems? Did your exwife have postpartum depression after giving birth to Elizabeth? Was that the beginning of her mental instability?"

Clark didn't answer at once, almost as though he didn't want to shift conversational gears. "No, it wasn't the beginning," he denied. "Marilyn started having psychiatric therapy in her early teens. Her parents are well-to-do. They've spent a small fortune on psychiatrists and treatment in private clinics. On our honeymoon I discovered that she took tranquilizers. She hadn't told me any of her history of suffering from depression. We were married six months when she slit her wrists after we'd had an argument. Then the story came out. She was pregnant at the time," he added. "The argument was over her taking overthe-counter medication without her doctor's permission and possibly doing harm to the baby."

"My God!" Avery murmured, horrified. "She was pregnant and tried to kill herself? Did you find her?"

"No. I later wished that I had. Then I would have had medical proof that it had happened. She packed a bag after I left for work and drove most of the way to Shreveport, apparently with some intention of leaving me and going to her parents' house. She checked into a motel, made her suicide attempt and then called them. They rushed to the motel. That night they notified me."

"Weren't the scars on her wrists proof of what she'd done?"

"She was in an automobile accident a couple of years later. Lacerations from the broken glass left her with similar scars."

"You were still married to her?"

"Yes. I suppose I would still be married to Marilyn now, if she hadn't divorced me, after leaving me numerous times. We've been divorced three years."

"You still...love her?" Avery asked hesitantly.

He shook his head impatiently. "I feel pity for her when I can allow myself to feel anything for her. How about you? Do you still care for your ex-husband?"

"Not after this amount of time. We've been divorced for eight years. He left me when the twins were three."

"He paid child support?"

"Yes, he made his payments faithfully from California, where he and Cindy moved. I had to get a job, of course. Fortunately, I was lucky enough to get a good one, considering my education and qualifications. I managed okay financially until this past December, when I was laid off." Avery picked up the TV remote control. "Are you sure you wouldn't rather watch television?"

"I'm interested in what you're telling me," he answered simply. "So it was financial hardship that made you send your two eleven-year-olds to live with their father?"

"No, financial hardship just made it that much more difficult for me to refuse to let John try to turn them into happier children, as he insisted he could do. With a smaller income, I faced having to move them to a cheaper apartment in a worse neighborhood and increase the chances that they would experience more city violence." Avery described the incidents that had terrorized her sons, affecting their personalities and their performance in school. "If their father could give them a better home in every sense of the word, then for me to keep them with me, to their detriment, was unforgivably selfish. That was the conclusion I inevitably came to. My sending the boys to John was conditional. I made that clear. I was giving him a chance to prove he could meet their needs better than I could. I wasn't giving up custody."

Clark moved closer to her on the sofa and put his arm around her shoulders. "What you did was remarkably unselfish," he said gently. "How is it working out for Bret and Bart?"

Avery spoke with difficulty, struggling to control her emotion. "It seems that I did the right thing for them. They've sounded happy and excited when I've talked to them on the phone."

"Are there any half brothers and half sisters?"

"No, John and Cindy haven't been able to have children."

"Is she the type to be a good stepmother?"

"Yes."

"So your boys will have a home with two parents, not one." He hugged her shoulders. "I think you're a very admirable woman, Avery. Your sons are fortunate all the way around to have you for a mother. Someday they'll realize just how fortunate." With his free hand he took the TV remote control from her. "Do you like old movies?"

Avery nodded, not really trusting herself to say another word for fear of breaking down and crying. His complete and sincere approval was comforting and yet it failed to ease her despair. However right she'd been, the personal sacrifice was overwhelming. *I can't bear not having my children with me.*

In just a few minutes, she would leave, after she'd gotten a grip on her emotions.

Clark had turned on the television set and was flipping through channels. "While you were bathing Elizabeth, I called and got a report on her mother," he said, his tone grim. He'd switched his thoughts from Avery's situation to his own.

"How is she doing?"

"She's well enough to be moved to a sanatorium." His voice, still grim, held a note of satisfaction. "The Lairds told me the name of the place. I won't need to pay a private investigator to dig out the information."

"Will you start custody proceedings while she's there?"

"I'll start custody proceedings as soon as I hire an attorney. I've contacted several this week. It may involve an overnight trip since I'll want to meet him or her personally."

He looked at her inquiringly.

"Elizabeth can always spend the night with me."

"I'm sure she'd like that anyway." He gave her shoulder a squeeze and left his hand there, moving away a few inches to make the position comfortable for him as he transferred his attention to the television screen. "What do we have? An old Clark Gable movie?"

Avery's emotional turmoil subsided as she watched the movie with him. Her earlier resolve to leave right away deserted her, although she still thought that it would be wise for her to go home. She just couldn't summon the willpower. It was so companionable sitting next to him. *Too* companionable, if anything.

The casual, friendly contact of his hand resting on her shoulder sent relaxing warmth all through her body. She knew she shouldn't be quite so at ease—this wasn't a safe, dull relaxation.

Clark inquired during a commercial break, "Can I get you anything?"

"What are you offering?" Maybe it was a good idea to send him out to the kitchen and interrupt this harmony, Avery was thinking.

He smiled wryly. "Wrong answer. You were supposed to say, 'Nothing, thank you.'"

"Oh, I didn't realize that you were just paying lip service to hospitality."

His smile slowly faded, and his expression grew intent. "Maybe I should make us some microwave popcorn. Munching on something might help me resist the urge to kiss you."

It was too late for microwave popcorn. He was going to kiss her. His intention hung in the air between them. Avery was helpless to stop him, her relaxation having turned to languorous expectation.

Clark framed her face and tilted up her chin. Then he brought his lips to hers. His kiss was similar to his kiss on the cheek earlier in the day. Or it was similar for about the same length of time. Then it changed, growing in intensity as he moved his head, not exerting any pressure, but asking her with his mouth to respond.

Clark, we shouldn't....

Avery's plea was silent and not effectual, because her arms were closing around his neck and her head moved in conjunction with his, helping him to discover all the angles for kissing her.

His clean male scent filled her lungs. His warm breath fanned her face. Avery's senses demanded more involvement in kissing him back. She wanted to absorb his masculinity into her very pores, sate herself on his potent physical appeal.

There was no intention to incite him to passion in her actions as she stroked with one hand down the back of his head, feeling the strands of his neatly barbered, dark brown hair. It was medium-textured, not coarse, not fine, smooth and surprisingly soft. At the nape of his neck she ran her fingers along the blunt edge where the barber had trimmed with scissors. She rubbed her fingertips on the stubble of shaved hair just below the line.

Using both hands, she caressed the curve of his neck and shoulders, feeling beneath his shirt the powerful symmetry that she'd observed with such feminine pleasure. Kneading with her fingers, she felt resilient skin and hard muscle. Smoothing outward with her palms, she measured the broad span of his shoulders. The glutting of the senses that was supposed to work some sort of cure for her was suddenly brought to a halt.

Clark flexed his shoulders and made a sound in his throat. Then he was kissing her harder, asking her with bruising pressure to open her lips and mate with his tongue. Avery hung on for dear life, her arms wrapped around his neck, resisting the intimacy, saying in her mind, *No, Clark, no...*

The hot passion in him made him deaf to her plea for sanity. His hands moved down to her breasts, captured them and squeezed. Avery moaned with the ecstasy and *no* turned to *yes.*

All resistance burned away by his heat, she deepened the kiss with him, arching her back to surrender her breasts more fully to his wonderful, strong hands. *I want you* was his primal, urgent communication. Her mindless, shameless answer was *Take me.*

It was Clark who stopped what was happening.

Avery uttered an incoherent protest when his hands loosened and released her. He turned his head aside, gathering her into his arms. A hard shudder ran through his body as he hugged her tight.

For all too short a time, Avery was totally encompassed in his strength. Then his embrace slackened. Along with her unsatisfied physical desire, she was left with a deep emotional yearning.

"I honestly didn't have anything in mind other than kissing you," Clark apologized. "On top of everything else, you're more sensuous and passionate than I had figured you to be."

"Don't you mean 'more sex starved'?" Avery countered. She would have pushed away if she hadn't welcomed keeping her face hidden from him.

"My remark was intended as a compliment. Don't look for hidden meanings in what I say," he told her earnestly. "Like you, I say what I mean."

"Well, believe me when I say that I'm appalled over getting that turned on. I certainly enjoyed sex when I was married, but I've had no trouble getting along without a sex life."

"I'll take it as a compliment that you got turned on." He tightened his arms briefly, giving her a little warm squeeze. "You woke up my sex drive that first day I met you."

The conversation wasn't easing any of her dissatisfactions and a feminine resentment was growing. Since he admired her openness so much, Avery decided to be outspoken.

"Your sex drive must not be awakened to full capacity or you wouldn't have been able to stop so easily just now."

"It wasn't *easy* to stop," he denied, pulling back to look at her. "I was completely aroused. I still *am* aroused, for that matter. Avery, you aren't insulted because I didn't make love to you here on the sofa when we haven't even discussed getting involved in an intimate relationship?"

"I don't feel flattered, considering that I completely lost my morals in the heat of passion," she admitted honestly. "I guess a part of me wishes that you'd lost your self-control, too. Because it won't happen again. There's nothing to discuss. I won't have an affair with you. Aside from it being wrong in my own eyes, it would be setting a bad example for Elizabeth.''

He let her sit apart from him, his actions a kind of acquiescence.

"I agree with you completely that carrying on an affair wouldn't be good for any of us," he said reasonably. "Aside from issues of right and wrong, I can't be too careful. Getting custody of Elizabeth is too important to me to risk charges of immoral behavior.''

"Of course, it is." Avery put her hands to her cheeks, shaking her head in disbelief. "To think that I forgot all about her! She could have woke up and walked in on us! We'd better avoid any more evenings of my keeping you company.''

Clark reached and took her hand and held it in a firm grip between them on the sofa cushion. "That's exactly what I *don't* want," he declared. "What I *won't* agree to. I'm forty years old. I can control my hormones. I'm *not* giving up your company, Avery.''

"You'll have to make a conscious effort to help me control *my* hormones." She made a little face in self-deprecation. "For example, from now you need to keep your shirt on and not sport your manly physique.''

"Keep my shirt on?" he repeated. His puzzlement soon cleared. He smiled with a hint of sheepishness that Avery found enormously appealing. "You don't mean that you're that easy?" he teased. "All I have to do to seduce you is take off my shirt?''

"Imagine how you would react if I breezed past you half-dressed.''

"No, I had better not imagine that." He squeezed her hand. "Are you okay?" he inquired gently.

"I'm feeling less frustrated." The deeper aching dissatisfaction had eased somewhat, too, but was still there.

"Is there anything I can do?"

Avery started to say *no.* Instead she said slowly, "There *is* something. Could you hug me in a completely nonsexual way? And hold me very tight?"

Without a word, he put his arms around her and gathered her close. She closed her eyes and absorbed his strength, his caring.

"Thank you," she murmured after he'd held her for a minute or two. "I've needed that for such a long time."

"Would you do something for me?" Clark asked.

"Yes, what?"

"Hug me tight."

Avery's arms loosely circled his waist. She tightened them and hugged him with all her strength.

"That's good," he murmured. "Thank you."

They continued to hold each other in a warm, comforting embrace.

"I never realized that a man could need to be hugged," Avery mused. Raising her head, she smiled at him and asked the question he'd asked her earlier. "Are you okay?"

He kissed her gently on the lips before answering, "I'm fine."

"Then I'll tell you good-night and go home."

Clark walked with her to her truck. He hugged her again and gave her another tender kiss in parting. It occurred to Avery that he could hardly have been more solicitous if he had become her lover tonight.

Clark stood and gazed down his driveway until the red taillights on Avery's truck had disappeared.

Are you okay? she'd asked, her pretty blue eyes mirroring concern. He'd answered truthfully that he was fine, not meaning that he wasn't suffering from any sexual frustration.

His jeans were uncomfortably tight in the crotch. He was still partially aroused, but his state of dissatisfaction was purely physical. Clark was so damned grateful that Avery had come into his life.

What a special woman she was.

The better he got to know her, the more he liked and respected and admired her. Tonight had removed any vestige of doubt he might have had about the advisability of marrying her. She would make a wonderful stepmother for Elizabeth and a wonderful marriage partner for him. The three of them would click as a family unit with relatively little adjustment. For him now, it was simply a matter of being patient and giving her enough time to reach the same conclusions.

Clark hoped she didn't take too long. He was ready to propose. A better description might be *hot to propose,* he reflected with a dry humor, tugging at the fly of his jeans and walking stiff-legged toward his house.

The sexual chemistry between them was icing on the cake. Whether or not his second wife was a good bed partner for him hadn't even been a consideration for Clark. What was important was that Elizabeth had a terrific stepmother. He could content himself with affectionate marital sex.

Judging from tonight, there was a lot of pleasure in store for him as Avery's husband. It didn't bear thinking about. For his own comfort, he would do well not to indulge in fantasy.

Clark had never expected to feel ardent as a lover again. Not after Marilyn and the nightmare of his marriage to her. He'd never expected to feel so damned *eager* about remarrying.

Being patient wasn't going to be easy. He'd come within a hair of jumping the gun tonight and telling her how she figured into his plans for the future.

It scared Clark a little that that future seemed so promising all of a sudden. His future had looked completely bleak to him for so long.

Being optimistic took some getting used to.

"You like Avery, too, don't you, Shep?" Clark stopped to pet the German shepherd on the porch. "She's going to be a permanent fixture around here, if my luck holds up."

Remembering the load of clothes that he'd washed earlier, he went inside and transferred it to the dryer. Then he went and checked on his daughter, easing her bedroom door open and tiptoeing over to her bed. She was curled up on her side and was smiling in her sleep.

"Sweet dreams," Clark whispered tenderly and bent to kiss her cheek.

Raising up, he knew that for Elizabeth's sake he *could* be as patient as he needed to be and let matters take a natural course with Avery.

Chapter Nine

"Good night, Ms. Avery," Elizabeth mumbled sleepily, closing her eyes. Her dark eyelashes formed curly crescents against her pink cheeks.

"Sweet dreams, Elizabeth." Avery bent and kissed the little girl's forehead.

"Would you rub my back?"

"I'll rub your back and sit right here until you're fast asleep," Avery assured. Elizabeth turned on her side, and Avery massaged her small back and shoulders. "Remember that my bedroom is just down the hallway. If you wake up during the night, just call out. I'll leave a night light on."

Elizabeth nodded, rubbing her cheek against the pillow. Her breathing became regular. Avery continued stroking her warm, inert little body, in no hurry to go downstairs.

I probably feel as insecure as Elizabeth tonight, not having Clark nearby, she thought. He'd gone to New Orleans to interview attorneys from two different firms and wouldn't be back until tomorrow. Avery visualized him as he'd looked that morning, dressed to leave, and felt an absurd pride.

She also felt a pang of jealousy. One of the attorneys—the one he was meeting with today—was female. What if the woman had turned out to be attractive and unattached? What if she and Clark had liked one another? There he was, handsome and unmarried and free to ask any woman to go out with him. Right this minute he might sitting in a New Orleans restaurant with her, having dinner. Then afterward they might go to her place or his hotel—

Avery couldn't *stand* to think about it and yet she couldn't keep herself from thinking about it. All afternoon she'd tortured herself with pointless speculation. She felt so threatened and that was ridiculous, given the circumstances. Clark didn't owe her fidelity.

Almost a week had passed now since they'd kissed in his living room, and, true to his word, he was keeping his hormones under control, apparently without any great difficulty. His kisses and hand-holding and hugs were affectionate and chaste, even if his gaze did stray to her breasts.

Off in New Orleans on his own, he could get relief for his pent-up sexual need. Elizabeth wouldn't pose a problem.

Avery couldn't bear the thought of him taking another woman to bed. And her extreme jealousy was mixed with resentment. What about *her?* How was *she* supposed to get relief from her repressed sexual needs that *he'd* aroused?

Elizabeth sighed in her sleep, drawing Avery's full attention again. She looked so sweet and vulnerable. Avery bent and kissed her on the cheek. The little girl smiled and turned over on her back.

''I love you,'' she murmured, her lips still curved trustingly in a smile.

Her words were probably part of a dream, but they prompted an answer straight from Avery's heart: *I love you, precious child.*

Despite her advice to herself at the outset, she'd grown deeply attached to Clark's little daughter. But that had been inevitable. Elizabeth was a lovable child, and Avery was maternal by nature.

Leaving the hall light on and the bedroom door open, she went downstairs. A glance at the telephone reminded her that Clark had said he would call tonight. She'd expected him to call before Elizabeth's bedtime, but he hadn't. Evidently he'd either forgotten or else he'd gotten involved—

Avery broke off midthought, hearing the sound of an automobile approaching her house. It wasn't quite full dark yet. She walked quickly to a window and peered out. Recognizing Clark's van, she exclaimed his name aloud, hearing the joy in her own voice. *"Clark!"*

He'd come back tonight!

Her impulse was to react exactly as Elizabeth might have done and rush out to greet him with open arms. Avery restrained that impulse and walked out sedately.

He climbed down from the driver's seat, wearing the tailored slacks and dress shirt with muted stripes that he'd donned that morning, but minus his tie and with several buttons of the shirt unbuttoned. Striding toward her, he looked like a professional man home from the office after a successful day.

"This is a nice surprise," Avery allowed herself to say. "If I'd known, I could have kept Elizabeth up."

"I considered calling and telling you that I was on my way. But I decided against it," he said. Reaching her, he bent down and kissed her on the cheek, not on the mouth. Then wrapping an arm around her shoulders, he gave her a hug and headed them back toward her back porch.

"You're going back to New Orleans tomorrow?" Commuters made the long drive daily, she knew, but she hadn't brought up that fact when he'd told her he'd booked a room in a downtown hotel.

"No, I finished up my business today. Faith Willis and I struck an instant rapport. She's a nice human being as well as a sharp, qualified attorney."

"You went ahead and hired her without meeting the other attorney?" A male attorney.

"Yes, I was leaning toward hiring her anyway if she seemed equally competent. I think having a woman attorney is a good tactic in a case like mine. Don't you agree?"

"I suppose. Did you have dinner in New Orleans?"

"Faith and I had dinner together and discussed our legal agenda."

Faith. They were on a first-name basis.

Clark went on. "She wanted to know everything about me, past, present and future." He tightened his arm around her shoulders, giving her a hug that felt brotherly. "I told her about you and about what a special person you are. She gave me some urgent advice."

"What was it?" Avery asked. How old was Faith Willis? What did she look like? Was she single? Those were some of the questions she wanted to ask him.

They'd reached the tiny back porch, which unlike his, wasn't a screened porch. Clark glanced toward the swing that would comfortably seat two people. He seemed to be weighing in his mind whether to steer her over to it. Apparently he decided not to.

"I'll explain later," he said. "First let me look in on Elizabeth."

Avery accompanied him inside the kitchen. "Why don't you go up by yourself?" she suggested. "It's the bedroom to the right when you reach the top of the stairs."

Clark took her hand. "Come up with me."

"I'm not afraid of you sneaking into my bedroom and stealing my valuables," she protested.

He drew her along with him to the stairs. In the upstairs hallway, he took her hand again. Together they entered the bedroom where his daughter slept and together they walked silently to the side of the bed. She lay in the same position.

Holding tight to Avery's hand, Clark bent and kissed Elizabeth on the forehead, then on either cheek. He straightened and gazed down at her soberly.

"She means the world to me," he said in a low voice.

"I know she does," Avery whispered.

Clark looked at her. "I can't be mother and father to her, Avery."

She stared at him, befuddled. What had led him to make that fervent statement? Sudden understanding made her gasp. *The urgent advice he'd been given today by the woman attorney was to remarry before his case came up.*

Was it his idea or Faith Willis's that Avery might suffice as a second wife and stepmother? she wondered numbly as she turned from him and led the way toward the door.

Her shock was fast changing to anger and indignation by the time she'd preceded him down the stairs. Now she understood his hesitation out on the porch. Before he put his cards on the table, he'd taken her up to see Elizabeth with him, setting the stage and making sure Avery was receptive.

It was the same manipulativeness he'd displayed when he'd invited her to his house to meet Elizabeth before he asked Avery to be her sitter.

"Let's go out on your back porch and talk." Clark made the suggestion in the living room, catching up with her.

"No, let's *don't* go out on the porch. Let's talk right here," she replied. "With the pictures of my sons looking on. I think they have a stake in this discussion. Although I don't think that's occurred to you. Or your attorney."

He frowned, studying her face uncertainly. "What do you mean?"

"Correct me if I'm jumping to a wrong conclusion. Didn't you come here tonight with a mission? To offer me a promotion from being Elizabeth's sitter to being her stepmother?"

"I came with the intention of trying to persuade you to marry me," Clark admitted. "Why does that make you angry?"

"The whole way you went about it makes me angry. I'm humiliated to think that you sat and discussed this with your attorney! Marrying me was an item on your so-called 'legal agenda' that you hashed over with her during dinner tonight, wasn't it?" Avery demanded.

He sighed, wiping a hand across his face. "I told her that I planned to marry you. I phrased the intention in a hopeful context. She recommended strongly that I not delay, her reasoning being that the longer length of time I've been married when the case comes up, the better. There shouldn't be any hint of my having gotten myself a wife at the last minute just to improve my chances of getting custody."

"That's the main purpose, though?"

"Not the main purpose, but certainly it figures in. As I said upstairs just now, I can't satisfy Elizabeth's need for maternal care and love. It's obvious to me that you're fond of her. With time, couldn't you love her like you would a child of your own?"

"Of course, I could. That's not the point. You took it upon yourself to map out my future, Clark, without even consulting me. Without considering my needs and wants and what was good for me."

"That isn't true!" he denied. "I am considering you and what would make you happy. I'm not a rich man, Avery, but I can give you financial security. You wouldn't have to work at a job outside our home. We can have a good life as a family, the three of us. There's nothing to say that the number can't be increased to four," he suggested tentatively.

No mention of love, because he didn't love her.

Avery turned away abruptly and walked over to a set of bookshelves against the wall. She picked up a framed photograph of her twin sons and clasped it to her breast.

"What about Bret and Bart? Am I supposed to just forget about them?"

"No, of course not. They can come for visits. We can make trips to California."

She closed her eyes, shaking her head.

"You said yourself that your sons are adapting to living with their father," Clark said gently. "Is there any reason you can't have a fulfilling life rather than just an existence? When Wade comes home after his year in the Persian Gulf, you'll have to move out. Where will you go? What will you do?"

"I plan to move out to California," Avery informed him with a quiet dignity. He'd made her sound like a poor homeless woman out on the streets, which apparently was his view of her. "By then, my living in a nearby town or community shouldn't be disruptive for Bret and Bart. I can see them often and be a part of their lives."

Clark took a step and gripped the back of the sofa, supporting himself. From his sick expression, she might have just kicked him in the groin. "You've never even hinted of having such a plan," he protested. "I had no idea."

"This is the first time the subject has ever come up," she pointed out. "I love my boys, Clark, just as much as you love Elizabeth."

"I've never questioned that, Avery." He closed his eyes, shaking his head. "I just can't *accept*—"

He didn't finish the sentence. A clamor of loud squawking had risen outside.

"The chickens are upset about something," she said dully.

He sighed heavily, straightening. "It may be a hawk. I'd better go out and scare him off. Wade has a shotgun. I've heard him firing it a few times."

"There are several guns with barrels on a rack in the utility room. And boxes of bullets on the pantry shelf. I'll show you."

"He probably kept his shotgun loaded."

The raucous commotion hadn't died down. In a kind of delayed reaction, Avery was suddenly alarmed.

"Will a hawk actually attack a full-grown chicken?" she inquired anxiously, following after Clark, who was on his way to the utility room.

"If the chicken is foolish enough to leave the safety of the hen house," he replied with a grim matter-of-factness.

"We'd better hurry. I'm so glad you're here! I wouldn't have known *what* to do!"

Avery hovered at his elbow as he took one of the guns down, handling it with familiarity. Expertly he checked to see if it was loaded and reported that it was. In a state of panic now, she hurried outside with him, having to take running steps to keep up with his long stride.

Two-thirds of the distance to the chicken pen, he raised the gun and shot it without sighting along the barrel. The loud booming report made Avery jump and utter a gasping sound.

"There he is. See him?" Clark pointed.

"Yes, I see him. He's *huge*." Avery gazed with a horrified admiration. The hawk was silhouetted against the paler black of the sky, his predator's wings outstretched.

"You're not to kill him!" she protested as Clark pointed the gun upward again.

"No, indeed." He pulled the trigger and fired.

By the time the boom had died away, the hawk had flown off into the pine forests.

"Hush now," Avery scolded the excited chickens. "Just settle down and go back to sleep. The big, bad hawk is gone." In an undertone, she asked Clark worriedly, "Is he gone?"

"He's gone, but he may come back." There was reluctant amusement in his voice as he observed, "You lowered your voice just now. Were you afraid these chickens would overhear our conversation?"

Avery smiled sheepishly, realizing that she had lowered her voice. "Tomorrow morning when I feed them, I'm going to tell them that you were the hero of the hour."

"I'll reload this shotgun and keep a watch out on the porch for a half hour or so," he said quietly, turning toward the house.

She walked beside him, realizing for the first time that she still clutched the twins' photograph. "One of us should go up and make sure Elizabeth wasn't disturbed by the gunfire."

"I can take her home with me tonight."

"Please don't."

He nodded, assenting to her wishes.

The hawk episode had dissolved the dissension, without raising any hope for a happy solution. Clark seemed resigned.

"Why don't I go upstairs and check on her?" she suggested as they went back inside.

"All right."

He went into the utility room. Stopping at the living room bookshelves, Avery replaced her sons' photograph among the small gallery.

Elizabeth was sleeping peacefully. Avery stood beside the bed, looking at the little girl with the new knowledge that she could be Elizabeth's stepmother.

And Clark's wife.

Did he even begin to grasp how difficult it was for her to refuse what he offered? No, she didn't think he did or he wouldn't have stressed the fact that he could give her financial support. It had helped that he pressed his suit with such honesty and pragmatism.

When Avery went back downstairs, Clark wasn't in the living room. She found him out on the porch in the swing. The shotgun wasn't in sight. Evidently he'd left it in the utility room.

"She slept through the excitement," Avery reported, going to sit beside him. He stopped the motion of the swing and then resumed it after she'd sat down.

"She's a sound little sleeper," he remarked. "I was prepared for having her wake up with nightmares, but fortunately that hasn't happened."

"Elizabeth feels very secure with you. It's a tribute to you as a father that she trusts in you to take care of her."

"I'll do everything in my power to give her what she needs," he said.

Did that *everything* include finding another stepmother besides Avery? She waited for him to say more, but he seemed buried in his own somber thoughts. They sat in silence except for the faint squeaking of the swing.

"Are we going to resume our interrupted conversation?" she finally asked.

"Frankly, I don't have the heart for it tonight," Clark replied in a defeated tone. "So much was riding on the hope that you might want a ready-made family. I have to regroup mentally. Let's talk about something else, shall we?"

"Okay." Avery sighed. "No sign of our hawk?"

"No, with any luck he's taken the hint and won't come back."

"You handle a gun with authority," she commented. "Are you a hunter?" If he were, he had his guns concealed because she hadn't seen them in his house.

"I did some hunting when I was a kid growing up in Texas, but I'm not a hunter and never had any desire to be one."

"It was expected of you?"

"It was expected of any boy. I was given my own rifle for a Christmas present when I was twelve."

"When you were twelve? You were only a year older than the twins!" Avery exclaimed. "I can't imagine putting that kind of responsibility on them, giving them a dangerous weapon and sending them out to kill animals. Of course, hunting isn't in my background."

"It was in my background, and I had to hide the fact that I hated killing wild animals. It made me sick to my stomach when I bagged my first deer with that brand-new rifle. One minute he was a live, beautiful creature and at the crack of my gun, he was dead. Just a carcass on the ground."

"Did your family eat wild game?"

"Yes. But I didn't relish eating it any more than I could relish eating one of Wade's hens after I'd wrung its neck and cleaned and gutted it. That's part of the whole hunting tradition, you see, that the hunter has to skin and clean his kill.

After I'd brought down that buck deer, I had to slit his throat and bleed him.''

"And you were only twelve years old!" she murmured sympathetically. "Why is it that society won't allow boys to be sensitive? I'm sure you were a tall, big boy, too, which meant you had to act tough. I guess you had to play contact sports, like football?"

Clark shrugged. "I liked sports. I didn't have any problems with tackling opponents in a football game." He paused, cocking his head. "Do I hear your telephone ringing?"

Avery could hear the phone now, too. She regretted the interruption as she excused herself and hurried inside, leaving the kitchen door open. If anyone except the twins were calling, she would make the phone conversation brief and rejoin him as soon as possible on the porch.

"Hi, Mom! It's us!" Bret's and Bart's boyish voices greeted her in chorus.

"Hi, darlings!" Avery exclaimed warmly. "What a nice surprise! A call from my two favorite guys in all the world!"

The kitchen phone had an extralong cord, allowing her to walk over to the dining table and pull out a chair and sit down. She could have closed the door, but she didn't. Avery didn't mind that Clark could overhear her talking to her sons in California. Quite the opposite, in fact.

It was a comforting thought that after she'd hung up, Clark would be there, rock-solid and strong. If Avery asked him to put his arms around her and hold her, he would, she knew.

Clark could not only hear Avery conversing with her sons, her voice resonant with her mother's love and interest, he could see her through a kitchen window. She smiled as she listened.

The picture she made was unbearably maternal and lovely. He felt privileged and touched to gaze at her and yet excluded and envious of her two towheaded sons, who, from their pictures, had her blue eyes and fair coloring. Yes, he was *envious*. *Jealous* of a couple of eleven-year-olds. Those weren't worthy emotions for a grown man. Even worse, Clark felt a helpless resentment.

He was going to *lose* her because her children came first with her, like his daughter came first with him. She meant to move all the way across the country. And she wouldn't be truly happy, truly fulfilled, being a part-time mother.

If any woman had ever deserved to be happy and fulfilled, that woman was Avery. Clark wanted her to be happy. He wanted to *make* her happy as much as he'd ever wanted anything.

She was so right for him.

Clark *couldn't* give her up and yet how on earth could he fit all the pieces of his life and her life together?

With this custody suit looming and Elizabeth's welfare to consider, he couldn't just sell out and relocate at the drop of a hat. California might be a fine place to live, but Clark had never had any desire to live there himself. He liked Felton. He wanted Elizabeth to grow up here in this wholesome country atmosphere. He liked owning and operating his own nursery. He didn't really want to go back to being a landscape architect.

Everything would be ideal for him with Avery as his wife. Without her—

No, there had to be a way.

It would be wise for him to leave while she was on the phone. He'd already made a big enough mess of things for one night. When she came out, God knows what he might blurt out. In his present state, he might get on his knees and beg Avery to marry him. That wouldn't be fair to her, and

Clark had to think about Elizabeth. It wouldn't be good for any of them to create tension.

Tomorrow was another day, a day when he'd have his daughter with him and he'd see Avery and have her as a part of his daily routine.

Clark rose from the swing and, with a lingering glance through the window, walked out to his van and drove away without saying good-night.

Avery heard the sound of the van engine starting up. *Clark was leaving?* Momentarily she lost track of the phone conversation with the twins, dismay washing through her as she listened to him driving out toward the highway.

"And guess what, Mom?"

"Yeah, guess what, Mom?"

She dragged her attention back, smothering a sigh of disappointment. "I give up. Why don't you just tell me?"

Muffled snickers.

"You're not gonna like it," Bart warned.

His brother seconded the warning, "You're gonna probably get all upset."

"Would one of you please explain?" Avery requested.

"We were wrestling around, and Bart took a swing at me and hit me in the nose."

"He bled all over his clothes."

"But I didn't bawl like a little crybaby. I hit him in the nose and gave him nosebleed, too. Dad thought it was great. He gave us five dollars apiece."

Avery couldn't believe her ears. "Your father thought it was 'great' that you bloodied each other's noses?"

"Dad wants us to be rough, Mom."

What would be Clark's reaction to John's encouraging violent behavior? She wished that he hadn't gone home. She would have liked to discuss with him her doubts about how

John was going about helping the boys to be less timid and more aggressive. First, karate lessons and now rewarding them for hurting one another.

Was Avery just looking for grounds to be critical of John? She would have liked to voice her question aloud to both Clark and herself.

He was the most masculine man she'd ever known and perhaps the gentlest and most sensitive. When the twins visited, Avery hoped that they got to spend a lot of time with him. She would like to develop his kind of manliness in her sons. His kind of strength of character.

After she'd hung up, Avery went back outside on the porch and curled up in the swing. Her heart was heavy. She felt the wrenching sense of separation that was worse after a phone call from the twins.

Gazing over at the dark woods on Clark's property, she also felt lonely for him and concerned about him. *Why had he gone home like that?*

Avery could only guess that he'd wanted to be by himself and recover from his disappointment. *I have to regroup mentally,* he'd said in that defeated tone of voice.

By tomorrow would he have come to terms with her refusing to marry him? The possibility filled her with aching regret. Yet she knew that it would be better for both of them if he had.

Because then Avery would have to come to terms with turning down the chance to be his wife. The chance to be Elizabeth's stepmother. The chance to be pregnant with his child.

Chapter Ten

Clark had slept restlessly. He'd dreamed crazy, disjointed dreams that switched from past to present to future. In some segments he'd been a boy on hunting trips. Then suddenly he was a grown man. There was no logical sequence and no realistic accuracy. Avery had been along on one of the hunting trips, he remembered, swinging his legs to the floor and sitting up on the side of his rumpled bed.

She'd been in most of the dreams, some of which had been erotic. Clark had woken up several times, hard and aroused. He didn't have to glance down to know that he was in an aroused state now.

Closing his eyes, he tortured himself for several moments, imagining that Avery came to sit beside him on his bed and caressed him intimately. The fantasy made him groan.

How he needed for her to touch him.

His physical desire went beyond just needing to have intercourse. He wanted to be naked with her, caress and fondle and kiss her entire body while she took every liberty with him.

That wasn't going to happen today, but it *was* going to happen. Clark couldn't accept the notion of permanent frustration any more than he could accept that Avery wouldn't be a permanent part of his and Elizabeth's lives.

As resolute as he was dissatisfied, Clark rose to shower, get dressed and have his breakfast.

Normally he gave Elizabeth her first wake-up call on his way to the kitchen, stopping at her door and saying something cheerful and trite like, "It's time to rise and shine, sleepyhead." After he'd started his coffee brewing and had breakfast nearly prepared, he made a trip back to her bedroom, picked her up in his arms and carried her to the table. After a few sips of orange juice, she smiled and started to perk up and become alert.

Today the damned house seemed as quiet as a tomb. Passing Elizabeth's room, Clark glanced at her neatly made bed and regretted that he hadn't brought her home with him last night. He missed the morning routine.

After breakfast, he would walk over to Avery's and see if they were up. If they were, he would visit a few minutes before he went to the nursery. That plan put a spring in Clark's step.

In the kitchen he took the glass carafe from the coffeemaker over to the sink to fill it with tap water. With his hand on the single-lever faucet, he stood there a moment, wondering if Avery had coffee already made.

She'd joked about adopting an early-to-bed-early-to-rise schedule here in the country. Maybe she was drinking her first cup of coffee while Elizabeth was still fast asleep upstairs.

Clark set the carafe down in the sink, made his exit through the kitchen door and struck out across his back yard. He took the route through the woods that was no longer just a well-defined path. He'd recently broadened it wide enough for two to walk abreast.

His next project, he reflected, was to clear out the underbrush and saplings so that he could see Wade's house from his house.

Avery was up. Emerging from the woods, Clark saw her disappearing into her kitchen from the back porch. Evidently she'd gone out to feed the goat and poultry, because the denizens of the pen were busy eating. He speeded up his already rapid pace.

Reaching the back door, Clark rapped his knuckles lightly on a glass pane to alert her to his presence, opened the door and stuck his head inside. "Is it too early for visit... for visitors?" he finished up in a different tone.

Avery was near the sink, her back to him, replacing a coffee canister on a shelf in an upper cabinet. With her arms upraised, the garment she was wearing—the same purple T-shirt sort of nightgown she'd had on when she'd fallen down the stairs—was hiked up, exposing the backs of her thighs and the rounded bottoms of her bare buttocks.

His glimpse of her entering the house hadn't prepared Clark for the fact that she hadn't gotten dressed yet. He stepped into the kitchen, fully appreciative of the unexpected, tantalizing view and instantly responsive.

"Clark!" she blurted out in surprise and embarrassment, glancing at him over her shoulder. "You caught me in my nightgown!" Quickly closing the cabinet door, she turned around, reaching back to tug down the purple garment. But then she raised her arms to smooth her hair, raising the hemline enough to tease him with what lay beneath. Simultaneously her motions with her hands made the nightshirt pull across her breasts, emphasizing that they were full and firm without the support of a bra. Gazing hungrily at the imprint of her nipples Clark could feel himself growing hard.

"I've seen you wearing that before," he reminded her. Powerful urges and forces of sheer inevitability drew him over to her, over to what was clearly a danger zone. Clark gave in to the urges and forces without a fight, moving toward her.

Blushing a deeper shade of pink, she crossed her arms over her breasts. With a breathlessness in her voice, she explained, "I was afraid Elizabeth would be disturbed by the morning ruckus. I got up out of bed and slipped downstairs. No one can see me from the highway so I went outside and fed the starving critters. As soon as I had put on some coffee, I was going back upstairs to make myself presentable, in case you came over." She sighed.

Clark had reached her. "You look more presentable than you did in some of my dreams last night," he said softly.

"You had dreams about me, too?"

Her guilty note did nothing to cool the warmth coursing through his body. "I spent most of the night with you, in some time frame or another," he said, taking her by the shoulders. One gentle tug was all it took. She stepped forward, unfolding her arms and sliding them up around his neck while in one exuberant motion he gathered her close, picked her up and held her tightly against him.

"I'm too heavy!" Avery protested unconvincingly. "You'll strain your back."

"You aren't a pound too heavy," Clark denied. "It's not my back that's feeling the strain. And if I put you down, I might take off that purple thing you're wearing."

"Oh, *Clark.*" She closed her eyes and, hugging him tighter, pressed her cheek to his. "I haven't even combed my hair or washed my face this morning. You're all shaved and showered and smell as good as you look.''

"Do I look good to you, Avery?" he asked.

"You *know* you do.''

"It isn't nearly obvious enough to me.''

"I'll spell it out for you, if you want,'' she said. "I think you're the best-looking, most virile man I've ever known. I thought you were handsome with a frown on your face. It's a wonder you aren't vain, being as attractive as you are.''

"You helped to take away the frown, Avery,'' he told her, eager to bestow his own compliments. "You're the most beautiful person I've ever known. You're also a pretty, sexy woman, in case I need to spell out my appreciation of your physical attributes.''

"You really mean that?'' she queried wistfully. "You find me pretty and sexy?''

"Can't you feel the evidence?'' Clark demanded. Holding her with one arm, he wrapped the other arm lower, around her hips, and welded their lower bodies together even more intimately. The pleasure and frustration of the contact made him groan. "I've wanted to make love to you for weeks now, Avery. The need keeps building up until I'm afraid I'm going to *explode.*''

She moaned softly. "I'm in a similar condition, Clark. Only with me it's a constant ache that gets worse. I've never had erotic dreams before! Last night—'' She broke off.

"Tell me,'' he insisted.

"I'm ashamed.''

"You shouldn't be. Tell me your dream.''

"I was out by the pond, waiting for you. It was during the day. You came through the woods. We took off all our clothes and started kissing on the grass. In broad daylight,'' she added in a shocked tone.

"Did we make love?'' he asked.

"I woke up as we were just on the verge of it." Her answer conveyed her physical frustration and disappointment.

"I'm sorry I didn't satisfy you in your dream," Clark apologized gently. He set her down on her feet and hugged her in a less sexual embrace.

She hugged him around his waist, her face against his shoulder. "I wish I could satisfy your sexual needs, Clark. I know that if I don't, some other woman will."

He didn't reply because her sigh of regret was lifting and swelling her breasts, making him that much more aware of their roundness pressing against his chest.

Clark had never wrestled with any more powerful temptation than the urge to let his hands roam up under her loose garment. But he knew he didn't dare get either of them any more aroused or he would end up taking her right there in the kitchen, with Elizabeth upstairs. The fact that it was up to him to maintain control thrilled him and made control that much more difficult.

The coffee had been brewing. He summoned all his willpower and patted her back. "That coffee sure smells good," he said. "Why don't I fill a couple of mugs while you go upstairs and get dressed?"

"It does smell good, doesn't it?" she said, pulling away from him. "Just pour yourself a mug. Mine might get cold before I come down. I'll wake up Elizabeth and help her get dressed."

"Don't wake her. Let her sleep," he objected. "I'll see her at noon."

"Whatever you say. The mugs are here." She opened the same cabinet door.

"Avery, you aren't miffed at me?" Clark grazed his knuckles across her cheek.

"I'm embarrassed. Also self-conscious that you caught me looking my most unglamorous." She made a little self-deprecating face. "And, yes, I guess 'miffed' to be sent off with a pat on the back to get dressed."

"Surely you don't think that drinking coffee with you is what I would like to do now?"

"My reaction isn't reasonable, Clark. I realize that. Now if you don't mind, I'll excuse myself."

"Avery, can you appreciate how it affects me to know you're not wearing a stitch underneath this?" He fingered the sleeve of the nightshirt. "It's taken every bit of my self-control not to have my hands all over you."

"Especially with me being so willing. I should have asked you to step outside for a minute and give me a chance to make a modest exit. At this belated stage of the game, I'll just ask you to turn around."

Clark leaned on the counter, mildly provoked by the lack of communication. "I wasn't blaming you."

"I know you weren't. I'm blaming myself."

"You don't ever make any conscious effort to be provocative, Avery. I just find you very desirable."

"You need to go to bed with a woman, Clark."

"Any woman, you mean."

"Maybe not *any* woman," she conceded glumly.

"Just one woman in particular—*you,*" he said, straightening up. He framed her face in both hands, tilted it up and kissed her on the mouth. Her lips clung sweetly to his and parted when he applied pressure to deepen the kiss. She clutched his waist with both hands, responding and kissing him back.

Clark was breathing raggedly when he lifted his head. "The next time we kiss like this, you're going to have to stop kissing me first," he informed her. "The next time things can get out of control between us, you're going to be the one to have to put on the brakes."

"I understand," she murmured dazedly. "It isn't fair for you to have to be the one with self-control. Then you find yourself in the position of having to apologize for making me feel slighted because you kept your head."

"It's the part about making you feel slighted that I can't handle." Clark dropped a tender kiss on the tip of her nose. "Now I'll turn around and pour those mugs of coffee. Make it quick, will you?"

"I'm going." The assurance was reluctant.

He hooked a finger through the handles of two mugs and set them down with a clatter. But instead of pouring the coffee, he turned to watch her leaving the room. Avery had reached the very spot where she'd confronted him last night. She turned her head and sneaked a look back at him. Clark grinned sheepishly.

"You caught me in the act," he admitted.

"I sure did! You cheated!" She sounded more amused and flustered than indignant. "And I thought you were a man of your word."

"I said I'd turn around. I didn't promise not to peek."

The grin stayed on his lips after she'd escaped his view, turning into the stairwell. Her bare feet made no noise on the wooden treads. Clark waited several seconds, as though allowing her time to reach the upstairs hallway. He was gazing in the direction of the bookshelves. As he focused on the assortment of framed snapshots and photographs of Avery's sons, his mood became sober.

The scene this morning between them didn't change a thing. Her first priority was being a mother to those two boys. Clark couldn't even disapprove, as much as he wanted to be of at least equal importance to her.

He wanted her to be his wife, but he wanted her to be happy. She wouldn't be happy, separated from her children. They weren't little human pawns or Clark would propose the obvious, that Avery take them away from their father and bring them back to Louisiana to live with her and Clark and Elizabeth. Would that be in their best interest? Would Avery's ex-husband agree without a custody fight? That was another unknown.

The only known factor for Clark was that he wasn't going to give Avery up. There *had* to be a workable solution.

Avery paused in the upstairs hallway, breathless. She'd hurried up the stairs, but her heart wasn't beating fast just from the exertion. She felt giddy and buoyant. *She felt the way a woman feels when she's newly, romantically in love.*

"I love him," she whispered, dismayed over the admission that came as no great surprise.

It was so foolish of her to fall in love with Clark. She would have been so much wiser just to be friends and neighbors with him. Loving him was no magic prescription for happiness. Just the opposite was true, if anything. Avery hadn't needed this complication in her life.

She *wouldn't* let her judgment be affected. This kind of love wasn't lasting or dependable, as experience had taught her. This giddiness and intoxicating gladness were transient emotions. She'd felt them before when she fell in love with John.

A faint sound from the bedroom where Elizabeth had slept intruded on Avery's thoughts. She went to the door and looked in. The little girl had kicked off the sheet and turned on her opposite side since Avery had checked on her earlier before going downstairs.

Clark had said not to wake her, but Avery decided that she would disobey those instructions. If Elizabeth woke up in the strange room, she might be frightened. Plus she would be disappointed not to see her father this morning. It would be selfish of Avery to let the little girl sleep while she had breakfast with Clark.

"Are you ready to wake up, sunshine?" Avery went over to sit on the side of the bed and rubbed Elizabeth's shoulders and back.

Elizabeth smiled and inquired sleepily, "Did you rub my back all night, Ms. Avery?"

"No, darling. I slept in my bed and I've already been downstairs this morning. Your daddy is here. He came over to visit us."

"My daddy's here?" The little girl's eyes had popped open at the mention of her father. She sat up, all eager.

"Why don't you go on down in your nightie and keep him company while I get dressed?" Avery suggested. "We'll get you dressed later."

Elizabeth was already climbing out of bed.

Avery delayed the adorable little girl long enough to give her a warm hug and kiss. She'd been right to follow her maternal instinct instead of her woman's instinct.

Clark's voice, deep and loving, floated up the stairwell into her bedroom where she stood getting underwear out of a drawer. "Good morning, baby." After that, she couldn't make out his words as he carried on conversation with his daughter. Avery had known that he would respond with genuine delight to the appearance of his small daughter.

She could depend on the father in him taking precedence over the man.

Elizabeth was sitting on his lap when Avery joined them in the kitchen. Clark looked around and smiled at her. She blushed at the frank male approval in his gaze as he noted her freshly combed hair, freshly washed face and simple attire, a sleeveless blouse tucked into pleated knee-length shorts.

"Will you stay for breakfast?" she inquired, walking over to the refrigerator. "I was planning to make French toast."

"Oh, goody!" Elizabeth exclaimed. "Stay and eat with us, Daddy."

"I don't need to have my arm twisted," Clark said. "All I need is a halfhearted invitation."

"Elizabeth and I both insist," Avery stated with brisk friendliness.

"Can I help?" he wanted to know.

"Can I help?" Elizabeth echoed.

"You both can help."

Having him moving around the kitchen seemed preferable to having him watch her with that intimate gleam in his dark brown eyes.

During the breakfast preparations Avery wasn't sure that she wouldn't have been less distracted with him seated at the table. She had to concentrate on mixing up the batter for the French toast. His casual touch and his nearness wreaked havoc with her normal efficiency. Avery recognized all the classic symptoms of being lovestruck: a speeding pulse, a shivery sensation down her spine, an almost-uncontrollable urge to smile.

Her distraction didn't cause her to ignore Elizabeth. Nor did Clark pay his small daughter any less attention than usual. She was included and adored by them both, her presence adding to the element of domestic harmony.

This could be a typical morning in my life, Avery thought. Clark was offering her the chance to have breakfast with him and Elizabeth on a daily basis. *If only that offer could include her two boys, she would risk leaving herself open to hurt and devastation a second time.*

She would speak wedding vows again, not believing in them, knowing that someday Clark might come back and ask for a divorce, just as John had.

All her instincts said that she could trust Clark to keep his word and stick to his bargain, but her instincts had been wrong before....

Following breakfast, Clark got up to go. "What do you two have planned for this morning?" he inquired.

Elizabeth automatically looked at Avery.

"I think we may drive into Covington, if that's okay, and go to the library there." Avery expanded on plans for her impromptu outing. "Maybe we'll also do a little shopping and have lunch."

"Of course, it's okay," Clark replied, his expression becoming a little downcast at the news that they wouldn't be back by lunchtime. "You and Elizabeth have fun."

"Could we do any errands for you in Covington?" she offered.

He thought a moment. "Actually you could pick up a couple of items for me. And bring them by the nursery when you get back."

"If you need them as soon as possible, we can get them and come straight back."

"No, there's no rush. Having you deliver them is actually just an excuse to see you both," he added candidly.

Before today he hadn't ever encouraged Avery and Elizabeth to visit him at the nursery.

His goodbye hug and kiss destroyed Avery's self-protective impulse to spend a day away from Felton and get some breathing room.

"On second thought, why don't Elizabeth and I pick up hamburgers and French fries and be back in time for lunch?" she suggested.

Elizabeth enthusiastically elaborated on this revised plan. "We could have a picnic outside in our yard. Or outside in Ms. Avery's yard. By her pond would be a good place. We could spread a blanket."

Avery and Clark exchanged glances. She knew that he was thinking, too, about her erotic dream.

"Why don't you two just play it by ear and do whatever you want to do?" he said. "If you're back at noon, we'll have a picnic or whatever. If you're not, I can fend for myself."

Elizabeth was agreeable to being flexible, which meant that Avery was going to be the one to decide whether Clark had a solitary lunch.

"The weather may play a role," she pointed out. "It could be pouring down rain by lunchtime."

The weather didn't play a role. The sun shone brightly at midday, but Avery and Elizabeth ended up having lunch in Covington.

After picking up the items Clark needed from a hardware store, they paid a visit to the library. There in the large children's area, they met a mother and daughter who were also from Felton. The other little girl, Melissa, was Elizabeth's age. Melissa's mom, Karen, a vivacious brunette in her late twenties, was several months pregnant.

Avery was pleased for Elizabeth to have the opportunity to make the acquaintance of another child who might become a playmate.

The four of them left the library about the same time, Elizabeth and Melissa walking together and chattering.

"Melissa and I are going to her favorite burger place for lunch. Would you and Elizabeth like to come with us?" Karen Tollison invited spontaneously.

"It's up to Elizabeth," Avery replied. "We could, if she would like to."

Elizabeth nodded eagerly in response to her smiling look of inquiry.

"We'll just make a quick call to your daddy and tell him," Avery said.

There was a pay telephone located conveniently outside the library. She and Elizabeth stopped to use it while Elizabeth's new little friend and her mother walked on to the parking lot.

A phone call wasn't necessary, but Avery knew that Clark would appreciate her calling and touching base with him. Also, she simply wanted to hear his voice.

His reaction to her brief summary of events was just what she was expecting. "That's great that Elizabeth has made a friend," he declared. "She needs to be around other children more." His voice softened. "Thanks for calling."

"You're welcome. Elizabeth wants to say hi to you." Avery turned the phone over to his daughter, thinking that her conversation with him had ended.

"Daddy wants to talk to you some more," the little girl said, handing the phone back after she'd told him goodbye.

"Hi," Avery said uncertainly.

"I just wanted to thank you again for taking the time to call. It was very considerate." His tone was warm and intimate.

"I knew you'd be interested in what was going on with Elizabeth."

"See you in a couple of hours or so?"

"An hour and a half probably."

"It's just as well that the picnic idea fell through."

Avery blushed as she agreed, "Yes, probably so. Elizabeth is waiting patiently for me to hang up."

"I'm being selfish, aren't I?" He said goodbye with the same intimate undertone.

Avery hung up, flushed with the giddy pleasure she'd felt that morning. He'd kept her on the phone just to hear her voice.

Clark was acting like a man who was smitten.

The lunch had been a complete success, Avery reflected with satisfaction as she and Elizabeth and Karen and Melissa Tollison gathered up the debris from the table. Elizabeth and Melissa had gotten better acquainted, sharing information about one another while they munched on hamburgers and dipped French fries in little paper cups of ketchup and sipped their soft drinks through straws.

Though Avery had nothing to hide, it suited her fine that the children had dominated the conversation. Karen Tollison had seemed to be of the same opinion. She had listened with interest, but not with avid curiosity, to the explanation that Elizabeth had come to live with her father because her mother was ill while Avery herself was house-sitting for Larry Wade for a year, having lost her job with the same big oil company that had previously employed him. Avery had mentioned in passing that she had eleven-year-old twin boys who were living with their father in California, and Karen didn't press her for details.

Avery was able to surmise that the Tollisons were fairly affluent. Karen's husband, Ray, was an airline pilot. Their home was located on ten acres, and they had a swimming pool and a stable for their riding horses. Melissa had her own pony.

Leaving the restaurant, Avery had every intention of inviting Melissa to play with Elizabeth that afternoon. Before she could issue the invitation, Karen spoke up, "Can Elizabeth spend the afternoon with us? She and Melissa can ride Smokey and swim in the pool. I'll keep a close eye on them. I've been accused of being an overprotective mother."

"*Please,* Ms. Avery!" Elizabeth begged.

"*Please* let her!" Melissa implored.

Both little girls were jumping up and down with eagerness. Avery hadn't ever seen Elizabeth display such animation.

"We would have to get permission from Elizabeth's father," she answered sympathetically but noncommittally. "I'm just her sitter, not her mother."

"He'll say it's okay if you tell him it's okay," Elizabeth stated with complete confidence. "Will you tell him, Ms. Avery?"

Avery assured her that she would vote in favor of the visit, if asked for her opinion.

It was decided that Karen and Melissa would go by the nursery so that Clark could meet them. Avery suspected that Karen wanted to meet Elizabeth's father anyway, an understandable attitude for a parent to have.

Clark would meet with Karen's approval. Avery didn't have any doubt about that. She wasn't quite so sure that he would let Elizabeth go to the Tollisons, but she thought he probably would yield to his little daughter's persuasion. If he didn't, Avery was ready to propose that Melissa stay at Elizabeth's house and play.

"I think she'll be fine." Avery uttered the reassurance standing next to Clark and gazing after the Tollisons' sporty four-wheel-drive vehicle. "Karen impressed me as a very good mother."

It had come down to Avery's vote. Clark had looked to her, asking silently, *What do you think?* He'd read her answer, that she condoned letting Elizabeth go.

He sighed. "She'll be starting school in the fall. I can't have the constant peace of mind of knowing she's with you."

"Today was the first day that she really acted like a normal child," Avery mused. "If you'd said no, she might have even misbehaved for a change and thrown a little temper tantrum. Then what would you have done?"

"I don't know," he admitted. "I haven't had any experience with being a disciplinarian. Frankly, I was glad that you approved and I didn't have to disappoint her."

"Now I have the afternoon free. I guess I'll go home and let you get back to work," Avery said.

Clark didn't answer, and suddenly her words didn't seem as innocent as they'd actually been.

"What will you do?" he asked finally.

"Oh, I can do a number of things . . . work in the garden, clean house . . ."

"But you'll definitely be at home?"

Her throat was too dry for her to speak. She nodded.

"Why don't I take a break in about a half an hour and come over? Maybe you could make us some lemonade?"

Avery met his gaze. "Clark, I hope you don't think that there was even any subconscious wish on my part to get rid of Elizabeth for the afternoon."

"That thought never entered my mind. I hope you don't think that I wanted to have her out of the way."

"Of course, I don't."

"We didn't create this chance to be alone together, Avery."

Nor did they have to take advantage of it.

Avery tried to summon the willpower to ask him not to visit her. She simply couldn't bring herself to say the words.

"We'll have our lemonade outdoors," she said instead. Her erotic dream to the contrary, she couldn't imagine herself losing all sense of propriety outside in the open air.

The shadiest, most inviting spot in her yard at this time of the afternoon was the grove of trees at the far end of the pond. Avery felt a little embarrassed about the location as she set down a large pitcher of lemonade and two plastic glasses and then sat down on the grass.

Clark hadn't indicated whether he would drive to her house or park his van at his place and walk over. For some reason she assumed that he would do the latter. Sure enough, after she'd been waiting only a few minutes, he appeared, emerging from the end of the path.

Avery waved as he glanced and saw her, having headed for the grove of trees without pausing. Evidently he was expecting her to be in that general vicinity.

As he took the last few steps, she busied herself pouring the glasses of lemonade. He sat down beside her on the grass and took his glass. They both sipped lemonade.

"Hmm. This tastes good," Clark said appreciatively. He sprawled back, resting on his elbow.

Avery changed her position so that she could look at him. Pleasure seeped through her. "It didn't occur to me that I was suggesting having lemonade out by the pond," she remarked.

"I figured you hadn't stopped to realize that Wade's yard doesn't have much shade early in the afternoon," he replied.

Putting aside his glass, he reached out his hand and caressed Avery's face with his fingertips. She closed her eyes, delicate shivers of delight running through her.

"Remember our conversation this morning?" he inquired huskily. "I didn't bring my self-control with me, Avery."

"I remember our conversation," she murmured, clasping his big hand and pressing a kiss on his knuckles. Her whole being was brimming with the knowledge that she loved him.

He lay on his back. Avery opened her eyes, but could summon no resistance when he took her forgotten glass of lemonade from her. It was only after he'd put the glass a long arm's length away beside his that she protested weakly, "We really should drink our lemonade. The ice will melt and make it watery."

"That whole pitcher of lemonade won't quench my thirst or cool me off," he said softly, circling her neck with his free hand and exerting gentle pressure. Avery let him draw her closer to him, feeling the heat and vitality pulsating in his hand. When she couldn't bend any farther, he grasped her by the waist with both hands, lifted her and brought her half on top of him, so that her chest rested on his.

"Clark, you're so incredibly strong!" she gasped.

He hugged her tight and groaned. "It feels so good to have your breasts pressing against me."

"I know...." It felt just as good to her to be crushed against him, his heartbeat a mighty thud beneath the muscular hardness of his chest.

"I won't be satisfied, Avery, until I feel your nipples against my bare skin."

"I've seen you without a shirt. Your skin isn't bare," she pointed out, able to imagine so vividly the sensation of nestling the hard peaks of her breasts in his tangle of dark, wiry body hair. Excitement curled through her.

With a powerful movement, Clark turned on his side, laying her on her back. Leaning over her, he brought his mouth to hers. Instinctively she put her arms up around his neck. He kissed her hungrily, with urgency. She kissed him back with an answering hunger, an answering urgency. His passion was like a fire burning hot in him and igniting passion in her.

He pulled her blouse loose and thrust his hand up under it. His palm rubbed her midriff. Avery arched her back, using body language to tell him that her breasts ached with the need for him to move higher. His hand immediately claimed one breast, gathering the soft fullness. She moaned with the exquisite pleasure when he squeezed hard.

"Help me take off your blouse and your bra," he urged against her mouth, and Avery responded with a feverish haste, undoing the buttons and the clasp for him while he deepened the kiss again, branding her lips and searing her tongue with his.

He bared her breasts, lifting his head to look down. Avery sucked in her breath with anticipation as he bent and kissed one sensitive peak and then the other. She clutched his shoulders and stroked them in her wild pleasure as he tasted and suckled her with his mouth and caressed and squeezed her with his hands.

Avery assisted him when he began unfastening her shorts. She gazed back at him when he raised his head to look into her eyes as he slipped his hand beneath the elastic of her panties. They shared the intensely intimate moment when he laid sure claim to her womanhood.

Without speaking a word, Avery communicated to him that she desperately needed for him to be inside her, and he conveyed to her how urgently he wanted to bury himself in her.

"Let me touch you first," Avery said, caressing his face.

Clark stripped off his clothes with a few abrupt motions. Fully naked and fully aroused, he finished removing her clothes with more gentleness.

It was just like Avery's dream. She felt like Eve must have felt with Adam. There was too much shameless pleasure in being nude with him for her to be self-conscious. She was captivated by the sight of his body and wanted to gaze at him, touch him, kiss him, absorb his raw masculinity and ruggedness.

Avery almost wished that her need and his need to make love weren't so urgent and consuming. Kissing and touching were an agonizing pleasure with restraint cast aside along with their clothes. When she combed her fingers down Clark's chest, he caught her hands and brought them down lower. He clutched Avery's shoulders, his whole body rigid, during the mere seconds that he could withstand the intimate fondling and stroking that he'd wanted.

Suddenly there was no waiting any longer. Moving together and of one frenzied mind, Avery lay on her back and he bent over her. They cried out in unison, ecstasy in their voices, as he drove deep inside her.

Avery was merged with his physical strength, with his emotional intensity, with his passionate nature. In the midst of her wild joy, she thought of how she'd known that first day they met that Clark could take her into a sublime realm of passion, to a higher plane of ecstasy than she'd ever reached before.

What she hadn't known was how thrilling it would be to sheathe him, to sense that she was woman enough to satisfy his pent-up sexual need. His explosive climax followed hers within seconds and rocketed his big body, rendering him helpless. Avery hugged him tight, her love for him welling up and making her satisfaction total and sweet.

Chapter Eleven

"She was out like a light before I finished the third page of the storybook she wanted me to read tonight," Clark said, entering the living room from the hallway just as Avery was entering from the kitchen.

"She had a marvelous time today."

"And came home with her heart set on having a pony."

"So I gathered."

They had reached each other, with Clark covering more than half of the distance. He put his arms around her and hugged her. "What were you doing?" he asked curiously.

"Just making myself useful. The dryer had finished its cycle, so I took the clothes out." *His clothes.*

"Thank you." He gave her a hard squeeze. "You didn't have to do that."

"I didn't mind."

The truth was that she'd enjoyed hanging his shirts on hangers, folding his jeans and his underwear.

"You'll spoil me if you're not careful."

He guided her to the sofa, his arm around her shoulders. Instead of letting her sit beside him, he pulled her down onto his lap.

"Clark, I'm too big to sit on your lap!" Avery protested.

"You aren't big everywhere, but you're generously endowed above the waist," he replied. His possessive tone affected her as much as his gaze of male appreciation, directed at her chest. "I have to admit I noticed your measurements the first day we met."

"As scared as I was that day, I noticed that you had a good physique. It came as quite a surprise to discover that you weren't a crotchety old bachelor, as I'd imagined you."

"Why did you imagine me to be crotchety and old?"

Avery was distracted because he was touching her breasts while she answered him.

"Clark, you can't expect me to carry on conversation while you're doing that!" she finally broke off to say.

"If I have to keep my hands off you for us to have conversation when we're alone, we may be a silent couple," he answered, smiling. "I'm showing remarkable restraint not taking your blouse off out here."

"We made love all afternoon. Surely you're not feeling in a sexual mood tonight?"

"Why don't I carry you into my bedroom and let you find out for yourself?" With a forefinger, he worried her hardened nipple through the layers of her clothing. "Your body seems to be giving me the go-ahead."

"I suspect you can always get the go-ahead signal from my body. My conscience questions whether we should go to your bedroom tonight or any other night. Remember, we agreed that we shouldn't carry on an affair in front of Elizabeth."

"When I told you that I didn't want an affair, I knew then that what I wanted was to marry you. I was willing to be patient. I certainly didn't think that we could be around each other indefinitely and not have a physical relationship. Did you?" he asked.

He had stopped fondling her, but his hand clasped her upper thigh, the tips of his fingers mere inches away from the juncture of her legs and pelvis.

"No," she admitted. "Deep down I knew that it was a matter of time before nature won out."

"Nature is going to keep winning out."

"So why fight it? Isn't that rationalizing away right and wrong?"

"Not for me, it isn't. We could go tomorrow and apply for a marriage license, as far as I'm concerned. So in my mind there's nothing immoral about our sleeping together. I don't feel any sense of guilt," Clark explained.

"If things were simpler, if there was only myself to consider, I would be all in favor of our getting married right away."

"That's some source of consolation for now." His hand squeezed her thigh and then slipped up inside the loose leg of her shorts. "Avery, I can't give up being able to do this when we're alone together. That doesn't mean that I don't admire and respect you for your qualms." He was easing one finger beneath the elastic of her panties, awakening delicious anticipation.

"When you touch me like that, my qualms don't have a chance," she said. Lifting her hands to his broad shoulders, Avery was aware that it wasn't guilt that she was suppressing, but disappointment that he hadn't been interested in continuing the discussion of marriage obstacles.

Their communication became intimate and intense, both of them speaking a silent language of lovers that left no room for misunderstanding. Clark tilted back his head, conveying his desire for her to kiss him. Avery gazed into his eyes, telling him with her loving smile that she wouldn't willingly deny him any request, certainly not that one.

His lips were firm and responsive against the softness of hers. His tongue was ardent, his breath warm on her face. Kissing him was sheer sensual delight with her fingers combing through his hair and touching his hard cheekbones and strong jawline. Her excitement built up as his passion ignited and burned hot in him.

Clark carried her in his arms to his bedroom, and they undressed one another and made love in his bed.

"This is really shameful," Avery muttered afterward, completely sated. "No two people need this much sex in one day." His only answer was a deep contented sigh. "You must be exhausted," she said after a few moments. "I should get dressed and go home."

"Don't go home tonight," he objected, holding her closer against him. "Sleep with me."

"Clark, I can't sleep here!" she protested with not nearly enough conviction.

"We'll wake up early. You can go home and feed your animals and come back and have breakfast with us. Please."

"Just tonight," she gave in.

He rubbed his cheek against her hair. "I'll sleep better having you here safely in bed with me. I never have liked your being over there by yourself at night."

"Not even with my faithful watchdog, Sam?"

"Old Sam doesn't do much for my peace of mind. I've thought about lending you Shep as a watchdog, but he'd bark at your chickens."

Avery was touched that he'd worried about her. "You don't actually think I'm in danger?"

"Well, no," he admitted. "Or I wouldn't have agreed to letting Elizabeth stay overnight with you. I might as well warn you, in case you haven't detected the signs. I'm one of those men who can be overbearing about protecting their womenfolk."

"I had detected the signs, as a matter of fact."

There was wistfulness in her lightly ironic reply. She couldn't think of any more wonderful fate than a lifetime of putting up with his protectiveness.

"Time to wake up, sweetheart."

"I'm awake," Avery murmured. Her sleepy voice conveyed her pleasure in waking up to find her body nesting snugly against his big frame. Her shoulders and back were against his chest and stomach, her hips and legs fitted to his lower body.

"Did you sleep well?" he inquired in the same low, tender voice.

"Very well."

He was rubbing his palm just below her breasts. She waited in delicate suspense, feeling her nipples tingling and contracting. He moved higher and began to caress her breasts.

"I love the way you touch me," she confided in a whisper.

"I love touching you," he answered. "Your skin is soft and smooth. You're all curves."

"Shouldn't we get up?" she inquired with the utmost reluctance. "You have to go to work."

His hand stilled its delightful fondling and squeezing. "Unfortunately, I do. I can't stay here in bed and make love to you all day."

"When you get dressed, aren't you going to have trouble zipping up your jeans?" She could feel his hard, aroused condition.

"Since I met you, that's been a chronic problem." He patted her hip and eased apart from her.

Avery turned over on her back as he got out of the bed. She gazed at him with female admiration, coping with her own less-visible awakened sexuality.

"Join me in the shower?" he invited, smiling and holding out his hand.

"A shower sounds wonderful, but is that a wise idea?" Even as she expressed her reservations, she was letting him assist her in climbing out of bed. "We might forget to be cautious."

Clark picked up a packet from the bedside table. "Without this, it would be very foolhardy."

They showered together and made love under the cleansing, pelting spray.

Both of them wearing towels, Clark shaved while Avery kept him company, perched on the toilet seat. She'd used his spare toothbrush and his comb. The spacious master bathroom had a long vanity with his and hers sinks.

When she left to go home, he hugged and kissed her and sent her out the kitchen door with instructions to hurry back and eat breakfast with him and Elizabeth. Avery did as she was told because she really didn't want to argue.

She had no incentive to refuse when Clark included her in his lunch plans before departing for work, suggesting that she buy shrimp po-boys in the village for the three of them. He grinned as he said, "Weather permitting, we'll have that picnic that didn't materialize yesterday."

Threatening rumbles and an ominous sky discouraged eating out-of-doors at noon. Instead they set up a card table on her front porch overlooking the pond. Avery was prepared for some mention of supper plans that she'd decided in advance she should not agree to, just to exercise some independence and enforce a code of moderation. To her disappointment, there was no reference to an evening meal. Then during the afternoon Clark called and asked her to take steaks out of his freezer.

"How do grilled steaks sound?" he added, plainly assuming that she would share his evening meal as she had shared breakfast and lunch.

She replied truthfully, "Grilled steaks sound marvelous. But after supper, I really must go home, Clark. I want to write the boys a letter tonight."

"Can't you write them a letter at my house? Or better still, call them and talk to them on the phone while I'm putting Elizabeth to bed? You can just dial direct."

"I can't run up your phone bill making a long-distance call," she protested.

"With all the competition among long-distance companies, the rates are ridiculously low. Don't worry about it," he chided. "Now don't forget the steaks."

"I won't."

After she hung up, Avery thought about his words, *better still, call them*. Better for whom? Was he being thoughtful by suggesting that she call instead of write or did he want her to do the most expedient thing and have a telephone conversation with her sons while he was otherwise occupied?

Whatever the answer was, it didn't alter the fact that she wouldn't feel right calling her sons from Clark's house and charging the call to him. She was going to write a letter to Bret and Bart, and that was that. If Clark wanted her to stay after dinner, she would, but with the understanding that he couldn't totally monopolize her attention.

Not now. Not ever. Falling in love with him didn't make her any less a mother. Clark had to realize that.

Avery brought her stationery tablet and box of envelopes to his house when she made the trip over with Elizabeth to take out the steaks.

Passing through the living room on his way to his bathroom to shower and change, Clark saw Avery's correspondence paraphernalia arranged prominently on the coffee table. Evidently she meant to write a letter to her sons tonight rather than take his suggestion and call them.

If it were simply a matter of economics, he would press the issue, but Clark suspected that more was involved than dollars and cents. Avery was telling him in a subtle way that her children came first with her. He would rather not hear her spell it out openly that he didn't matter nearly as much as they did. Knowing his status was difficult enough.

Clark would rather have her in the same room, with or without her thoughts focused on him, than be by himself tonight or any other night while she was next door. In his relationship with her, he simply had no choice but to take what she could give him of herself and count himself fortunate, something being far better than nothing.

Still he couldn't help wishing for an ideal state of things that would exist if he and Avery were man and wife. They wouldn't have to observe the rules of propriety in front of Elizabeth. It hampered him not to be able to send a message to Avery to follow him to his bedroom. Clark had no need for privacy where she was concerned. His idea of space was to have her in kissing range.

Maybe she required more privacy and needed more space than he did. Maybe she was giving him a signal when she brought up going home tonight after dinner and writing a letter to her sons. He would have to be aware that he should not crowd her.

Clark put aside this cautionary advice to himself until later when he and Avery would be alone. Elizabeth's presence established a family atmosphere that made it unnecessary for him to consciously avoid being overly attentive to Avery.

The three of them cohered so well as a small family, *his* family. At the heart of Clark's enjoyment during the dinner preparations and during the hearty, tasty meal was the conviction that the bonds that had formed, connecting them into a happy unit, shouldn't be broken.

Before he picked up his fork to eat when they sat down at the table, he reached for Avery's hand and his little daughter's hand, his state of mind one of thanksgiving.

Avery settled herself at one end of the sofa so that the lamplight shone on her tablet, which rested on her lap. After writing the date and the salutation, *Dear boys,* she sat and waited for Clark to come into the living room.

When he saw her, pen in hand, she expected him to insist that she telephone the twins. She meant to make her position clear.

It was pointless to try to concentrate on her letter until they'd had the discussion. She was tense and nervous. This might well develop into a serious confrontation.

"Can I get you anything?" Clark's low-pitched inquiry came as a relief.

Avery looked around as he came to stand behind the sofa. "No, thank you."

"Is that enough light?" he asked, his tone solicitous.

"I can see fine," she assured him.

"Would you like a large book to use as a lap desk?"

"That isn't necessary. I'm all set."

"In that case I'll catch up on some reading." He walked around the opposite end of the sofa and went to sit in an armchair with a hassock. A stack of trade magazines sat on the lamp table near the chair. After thumbing through them, he selected one and stretched out comfortably, propping his feet on the hassock.

Avery had been braced for some physical contact. She was used to his touching her every time he came close enough.

"Feel free to turn on the television," she offered. "It won't bother me."

He smiled at her warmly. "Don't worry about me. I'm in good shape."

She watched, frustrated, as he opened the magazine to an article and began to read. He glanced up and raised his eyebrows inquiringly.

"There isn't a lot that's happened the last couple of days that I can write about to my children," she said. "It's more the material for a diary."

"That's right. You talked to the boys a couple of nights ago," Clark recalled.

"Yes, they've called several times. Apparently John gives them permission."

"That's decent of him."

"I suppose. It's wonderful to hear their voices, but I always feel upset afterward." She sighed, thinking of the most recent phone conversation with the twins. "I'd really like to get your unbiased view about the way John is going about trying to make them into rough, rowdy boys."

"He's giving them more rein than you did?"

"He's allowing them to fight with one another! They both ended up with bloody noses!"

"Roughhousing is natural for boys that age," he pointed out reasonably. "I doubt your ex-husband would condone his sons' seriously trying to do injury to one another."

"He's brainwashed them into believing that they were sissies before, just because they weren't bullies."

"Isn't it possible that they saw themselves as sissies before?" he suggested in the same reasonable tone. "I'm no psychologist, but the problems they had may have done damage to their self-esteem. It could be that it's healthy for them to express some ridicule about their former behavior."

"Just because John is a father, you don't have to side with him," Avery commented.

"I'm not siding with John. I'm trying to be objective, something that's difficult under the circumstances. Knowing you, I'm certain that you wouldn't have sent your boys to John if you hadn't been terribly anxious about them. If they'd been more resilient, secure youngsters, you'd have kept them with you, despite financial hardship."

"That's true. I would have," she agreed unhappily. "It wasn't not being able to give the twins material things that made me come to my decision. It was worry about whether I could erase their fears and build up their self-confidence as well as their father could. He emphasized time and again in our telephone conversations the experience and the special insight he has in relating to boys because his job—selling sports equipment—takes him into schools. He reminded me over and over that he had been a little boy himself." Avery sighed. "You think I'm trying to find fault because I want to believe I'm the better parent, don't you?"

"I'm sure you're the best mother those boys could have had," he replied earnestly. "And I've no doubt whatever that you put one hundred percent into bringing them up by yourself. But kids need two parents."

"So I was remiss not to remarry and give them a stepfather? That's a good theory, but finding a husband requires a working mother to schedule in a social life. It means extra expense for sitters and evenings spent away from her children. I chose to devote every penny I earned and every minute of free time to Bret and Bart.''

"From a purely selfish standpoint, I'm awfully glad you didn't remarry,'' Clark reflected honestly.

Avery felt a wave of sick dread. Without realizing it before now, she'd been steering the conversation in this very direction. This was the discussion she'd needed to have with him.

"Is it possible that you would rather give John the benefit of the doubt as a father?'' she asked. "Wouldn't you feel better marrying me and knowing that the twins already had a good home and you wouldn't find yourself faced with being a stepfather?''

"Those are a couple of loaded questions,'' he protested. "There isn't a simple yes or no answer to either one of them. If you and I were married, I would be the twins' stepfather, whether or not they lived with us.''

"But the ideal situation for you would be that the twins were happy and well adjusted with their father, you had custody of Elizabeth and I was your wife and her stepmother, content to keep in touch with my sons and have them come for visits here to Felton.''

"In *close* touch with your sons. I know they mean the world to you. This house could be their second home.''

Avery was filled with anguish by his earnest, hopeful words. "Your ideal situation isn't ideal for me, Clark,'' she managed to say after a moment.

He sighed heavily. "I know it isn't.''

"I'm put in the position of having to choose—'' She broke off. The telephone in the kitchen was ringing.

"That must be either news of Marilyn or my attorney,'' Clark said tersely, getting up and going quickly out of the room.

Fifteen minutes passed. Avery fidgeted with her pen, wanting to get up herself and go to the kitchen and lend her support, if it was needed.

When he returned, one glance at his face made her heart sink. The seething anger had been rekindled in him. His big hands were clenched into fists, and he radiated that same restrained violence that had made her quake with fear the day she met him. Now her fear was for him.

"Was it your attorney calling with some discouraging news?" she asked gently.

He shook his head abruptly. "No, it was Marilyn. She was calling Elizabeth at this hour. After I hung up from talking to her, I called the Lairds and then made a call to Faith Willis at home."

Avery was hoping that he would sit on the sofa near her, but he sat down again in the armchair. She cringed when he smashed one fist into his open palm. "*Damn* her!" He shook his head, the muscles of his jaw standing out in hard ridges.

"Where was Marilyn calling from, Clark?"

"From her private room at the sanatorium. I don't want her talking to Elizabeth when I'm not here, Avery. There's just no predicting what damaging things Marilyn will say to her. Be sure that you answer the phone from now on during the day."

"Don't worry. I will." Avery ached with sympathy for him. "What kind of reaction did you get from Elizabeth's grandparents?"

"They swear that they have no intention of helping Marilyn retain custody, but I just know they will, when it comes down to brass tacks," he said bleakly.

"Maybe they won't this time." She got up and went over to sit on the hassock at his feet. Placing her hand on his knee, she urged, "Try not to be pessimistic."

"I can't give her back to Marilyn and let Marilyn totally screw up her life."

Avery leaned forward and covered one of his clenched fists with both her hands. "No, you can't. You're a wonderful father, Clark."

He caught her hands in his and held them tight. "I'm glad you didn't go home tonight. When I was out there in the kitchen, it helped just knowing you were in here. I know that's damned selfish of me wanting to share my problems with you."

"I'm glad I'm here." She moved to sit on the arm of his chair. Pulling her hands free, she hugged him around his shoulders. Clark's arms circled her, and they held one another in a close embrace, his head cradled against her chest. Avery's love for him overflowed her heart.

She wished that she could say the words that would give him more hope than any other words of reassurance. *I'll marry you, Clark, and stand beside you in court and help you get custody of your little girl.*

But how could she make a lifetime commitment that didn't take into consideration her children's claim on her?

"What have you told Bret and Bart about me?" Clark asked.

Avery had just stuck her letter to the twins into the envelope and was licking the flap. She grimaced at the taste of glue.

"I've told them that you're the man who lives on the adjacent property, you own a nursery, you have a German shepherd dog. I described you as having a bad temper and not liking trespassers when I wrote them an account of Billy and the chickens escaping from the pen. In my letter telling about my accident, I praised you as my kind rescuer. Of course, you've gotten mention as Elizabeth's father." Avery summed up, "I've downplayed you."

"Why?" Clark rose from his chair and came over to sit beside her on the sofa. Earlier he'd been firm about her following through with her intention to write the twins.

"Part of the reason at first was that I was trying to downplay you in my mind and keep my distance. Also, you have to understand that it would be a strange idea for Bret and Bart for their mother to be interested in a man. Somehow I doubt that they would like the notion very much."

"Don't you think it might be better to prepare them? They'll be visiting you in a few weeks."

Avery nodded. "I know. I can hardly wait."

"You haven't answered my question."

"While they're here, I won't be sleeping with you, Clark. The twins are older than Elizabeth. They would catch on to the fact that something was going on between us."

"It goes without saying that we won't be spending nights together. But you and I can't put on an act for two weeks, Avery. I assume that you do intend to spend some time with Elizabeth and me while they're here visiting."

"Of course, I want the boys to make friends with Elizabeth and have a chance to get to know you. I'm a little nervous over the whole prospect, though," she confessed.

"Just think about the point I've tried to make," Clark said, putting his arm around her. "It will be a lot easier on Bret and Bart if they come here expecting to see me show affection to their mother."

"They've had so much upheaval in their lives, Clark. It's terribly important to me that their visit be a good experience for them in every way."

He pressed a tender kiss to her forehead and held her close in his arms. A moment later he asked, "Are you staying with me tonight?"

Avery answered, "Yes."

Chapter Twelve

"Daddy, why can't I go to the airport tomorrow with Ms. Avery to pick up Bret and Bart? I would be good."

"I know you would, baby."

"I don't *want* to stay here and have Ms. Hano take care of me."

Clark smoothed back his little girl's soft dark hair from her forehead. Her puzzled, unhappy expression reflected some of his own mood tonight, which he was trying to cover up. "It's been all arranged. Try to understand that tomorrow is a very exciting day for Ms. Avery. Let's not you and I do anything to spoil it for her. She's been so generous and kind to us."

It was the same reminder he kept making to himself.

"Why would it spoil tomorrow for her if I went, too? I want to see Bret and Bart."

"You'll get to see them. But give Ms. Avery a chance to have them to herself for a while. Now are you ready for me to read you a story?"

Elizabeth shook her head no. Tears welled up in her eyes, and her lip trembled. *"Please,* Daddy. Ms. Avery would take me if you asked her to."

Clark's helpless frustration welled up in him. "Daddy isn't going to ask Ms. Avery to take you, baby," he stated gently, but firmly. "She's driving her pickup truck. There wouldn't even be room for you."

He'd offered her the use of his van, but she'd refused, saying that she hadn't driven it before and wouldn't feel comfortable. Clark had suggested tentatively that he might take off from work and act as chauffeur, but she'd shown lukewarm enthusiasm for that arrangement. Therefore, it hadn't materialized. He understood completely his daughter's disappointment and sense of rejection at being excluded from tomorrow's trip to the airport.

"Will we all have supper tomorrow night here at our house or at Ms. Avery's house?"

Clark smothered a sigh. "Baby, I just don't know. Ms. Avery hasn't suggested it. Things may be different while her boys are here. We may not be having supper with Ms. Avery every night."

"Or breakfast or lunch, either?"

"Or breakfast or lunch," he confirmed. "If you don't want to hear a story, turn over on your tummy, and I'll rub your back." She silently complied and lay there, awake and inconsolable. "Baby, you like Ms. Hano. I'll bet she'll let you help her cook. I'll tell her how much you enjoy helping in the kitchen. And you can still invite Melissa over to play with you while Ms. Hano is looking after you the next couple of weeks. Melissa's mommy is sure to have you over to their house several times. So cheer up," he cajoled, giving her some tender pats on the back.

Elizabeth sighed. Her eyelashes dropped and her eyes stayed closed. She'd fallen asleep. Clark could only hope that she didn't have unhappy dreams. He sat on the side of her bed several minutes longer, massaging her little back and shoulders.

How could he cheer himself up? What words of consolation could he speak to himself before he joined Avery? Tonight was his last night alone with her before her boys arrived. He faced two long weeks of sleeping apart from her and not having private evenings with her. Just the prospect made him miss her in advance.

Clark knew that he should be glad for Avery that her long-awaited visit from her children was finally here. He was honestly trying to feel glad. It might be easier if he knew exactly what his role was supposed to be during the next couple of weeks. What did Avery expect of him?

His efforts to determine how he and Elizabeth figured into her plans hadn't given him any clear idea. Tonight he would make another attempt.

"Here you are. I searched the whole house for you." Clark closed the kitchen door behind him. He'd finally found Avery out on his back porch, sitting in a wicker chair and petting Shep, who sat upright beside her.

"I was telling Shep that Bret and Bart are dying to meet him," she said.

"Are they?" That was news to him. Clark dropped down into the chair that was a mate to hers. He couldn't hitch it closer because Shep sat between them. "Your boys like German shepherds?"

"They've always wanted a big dog. I didn't think it was fair to coop a large dog up in an apartment, but I probably would have gone along if we'd lived in apartment buildings where pets were allowed." She stroked Shep's head, making Clark envy his dog for the affectionate attention he was getting.

"Maybe they can talk their father into a large dog," he suggested. "Now they have a yard, don't they?"

Avery's hand stopped, and she didn't look at him. Shep whined, and she resumed petting him as she answered, "Apparently Cindy isn't a dog person. She has two Persian cats. I hadn't realized before that I might be a dog person. Now I can't imagine not having a dog around."

I can't imagine living without you, Clark thought. "Shep could be your dog," he said. "He would come in the bargain if you married me."

"Of course, he would. He's a member of the family," she replied.

The regret in her voice was Clark's cue that he should save himself some pain on this eve of her sons' arrival and not propose to her a second time. She would only say no a second time, for the same reasons. Those reasons were named Bret and Bart.

Avery went on. "You've considered the possibility that you might get the twins in the bargain at some point, if I married you?"

"Of course, I have," he assured her. "Unforeseen things can happen. Whatever happened, whatever problems or crises cropped up, we could face them together. Nothing could split us up," Clark declared earnestly. "I'm not cut out of the same cloth as your ex-husband, Avery. I believe marriage is forever. Marilyn divorced me. I didn't divorce her."

"You're a fine man, Clark. You would make me a good husband and the twins a good stepfather." She sighed. "If only I'd known I would meet you, I wouldn't have made the decision I did. I would have kept Bret and Bart with me."

He wasn't a fine enough man that she wouldn't uproot herself when her year in Felton was up and leave him. That was the unstated message in her words. As much as he understood her conflict, Clark felt anew a deep sense of rejection.

"It was the right decision, given the circumstances," he said. After a slight pause, he added what he knew she didn't want to hear. "It might have been the right decision regardless of what the future held."

"But it might *not* have been the right decision!" Avery argued. "What if it *wasn't?* We're talking about my children's lives and about what kind of people they grow up to be. I can't abandon my responsibility as a mother, Clark."

"I would never expect you to," he told her. "At the end of a year's time, you should be able to make some judgment about John's abilities as a father. You have to give him a chance."

"You're hoping he measures up."

"What kind of person would I be to hope that any man failed as a father?" Clark asked.

"You wouldn't be you." She reached out her hand across the space separating them. Clark took it.

"Move, Shep." He nudged the German shepherd's haunch with his foot. The dog obeyed, making room for Clark to slide his chair close to hers.

"I'm already missing you," he said.

"I'll be right next door. It's not as though I were going away."

They sat, holding hands. The porch faced west. A vivid sunset was fading as night fell. There was enough light to read the temperature on an oversize thermometer.

"It's still eighty-five degrees out here," he remarked. "We didn't get a thunder shower this afternoon to cool things off today."

"Do you want to go inside?"

"No, I'm comfortable with the ceiling fan stirring some air." Clark glanced overhead. "Actually I was thinking about your trip to the airport tomorrow. There's more than a fifty percent chance that you'll have to drive in a downpour. The boy's luggage will have to go in the back of the truck."

"I guess I should pick up a plastic tarp at the hardware store and be prepared, shouldn't I?"

A plastic tarp wasn't what Clark had in mind.

"You're welcome to use my van. And I can drive you, for that matter."

"It's nice of you to offer, but I hate to take you away from the nursery. You're having that new sprinkling system installed."

"I don't have to be on hand to supervise."

"No, but you would rather be there, seeing that it's done properly, wouldn't you?"

"If nothing more important was requiring my attention. You're more important than a sprinkling system. But if you prefer not to have me tagging along, just say so."

"We would have to take Elizabeth, if you drove. You haven't seemed to be in favour of her going along."

"I've wanted to give you the option of not taking her. And she wouldn't necessarily have to be included just because I was driving you. It all depends on whether you want to meet the boys' plane with a whole welcoming committee."

"They're expecting just me to meet them and for me to be driving Larry's pickup. You've already made arrangements for Billie to take care of Elizabeth. At this point, we should probably just stick with the plan that's most convenient for everybody."

"Okay." Clark tried to sound calmly resigned and not offended.

A few minutes later he broached the subject of whether he and Elizabeth were included in her plans for celebrating the twins' arrival. Did she intend for the five of them to get together tomorrow afternoon? What about supper plans? He'd kept waiting for her to tell him something definite, and so far she hadn't.

"The twins' plane arrives at two o'clock. Are you bringing them straight home to your place?" he inquired.

"I thought I would," she replied.

"I didn't know whether you might take them somewhere in the city, some favorite place."

"One day while they're here, we'll make a trip to New Orleans, if they're interested in doing that."

Clark nodded, giving her a chance to say more. When she didn't, he ventured, "Are you planning to cook them a favorite meal tomorrow night? Or take them out to eat at the Barbecue Pit?" Given the slightest encouragement, he would suggest that the five of them go out to eat with him paying, of course.

"For their first night, I thought I would cook hamburgers. Tomorrow morning I'm making a potato salad."

No mention of him or Elizabeth being invited. Clark swatted dejectedly at a mosquito buzzing around his head. It was fully dark now. He was glad that they'd stayed outside. He didn't have to keep his emotions from showing in his expression.

"I guess Billie will cook a big meal for your supper," she said tentatively. "I know how much you like her country cooking."

Clark squeezed her hand. No food was likely to taste good to him tomorrow night, not when he was sitting at the table with a little daughter who wasn't going to be at all happy with just his company.

He couldn't speak his thoughts. It wasn't fair to Avery. Nor was it fair for him to be down in the dumps tonight. Remembering the bottle of champagne he'd bought for this occasion, Clark stood up.

"I almost forgot the champagne," he declared. "You sit here and relax. I'll bring out the bottle and a couple of glasses."

"Would you rather go inside where it's cooler?"

"No, let's stay out here."

He welcomed the screen of darkness and sensed that she did, too.

Avery leaned back her head on the back of her wicker chair and closed her eyes. Clark was trying hard to hide his feelings. Still it was apparent to her that he wasn't looking forward to the twins' visit at all.

How she wished that he could share her excitement, her anticipation. Obviously he was just going through the motions. His offers to drive her to the airport had come across as halfhearted. He was acting out of a sense of obligation, not any real desire.

Whatever she asked him to do, he would do. She had no doubt of that. He would put forth any amount of effort the next two weeks to help her entertain her sons. But the whole time he would be counting the days until they were gone.

Clark's world was complete with Elizabeth and Avery. Although he hadn't said as much, Avery knew that he was hoping she would change her mind about going to California. He was hoping that she would have reconciled herself to being separated from the twins when the time came. But

Avery knew she *wouldn't* be reconciled, not even if John were a marvelous father.

She had been trying hard not to resent Clark these past few days and not succeeding much better than he was succeeding at being glad over the twins' visit.

He was doing his best to be thoughtful, a good example being his buying champagne for tonight. Avery would hold her resentment in and pray that it went away without ever being aired.

She turned her head as the kitchen door opened and Clark's tall, broad-shouldered body was framed in the rectangle of light. *When he met her boys, he couldn't help but like them,* she thought, her love for him welling up. *He would surely become fond of them while they were here, and they fond of him.*

The five of them, Bret and Bart and herself and Clark and Elizabeth, would have such a good time together, once the ice was broken. For now, that was all Avery asked.

The day started off wrong. Avery woke, feeling groggy and headachy from the champagne. Clark wasn't in the bed, she realized. This was the first morning he'd gotten up and left her asleep. She'd grown so used to waking up with her body curled against his.

In the morning when he was drowsy, he used endearments such as *sweetheart* and *darling*. Avery had missed that today. Raising up on her elbows, she gazed bleary-eyed at the open bathroom door. The light wasn't on in the bathroom, and there was no sound coming from the shower. Had Clark already showered and shaved and gotten dressed?

As if in answer to her question, he entered the bedroom, clean-shaven and fully dressed, a mug in one hand.

"I brought you some coffee," he said. Coming over to the bed, he set the mug down. Bending, he kissed her on the forehead and walked back to the door, leaving her with her lungs full of his clean, masculine scent.

"Why didn't you wake me?" Avery asked, sounding as peevish as she felt.

"You were dead to the world. Today being a big day for you, I decided you might need a few extra minutes of sleep."

"It was the champagne," she grumbled instead of telling him that she would much rather have missed the sleep and spent those extra few minutes with him this morning.

"Billie will be arriving in about thirty minutes."

"I'd better put on my clothes and go home then." Avery sat up, the sheet falling away.

Clark's gaze dropped to her bared breasts. "I'd better get back to the kitchen," he said.

When the bedroom door had closed, Avery got up and dressed hurriedly. Despite her slight hangover, her body tingled with needs he'd brought to life with that lingering glance.

Before leaving the room, she took time to make up the bed and remove the evidence that he hadn't slept alone.

Clark was standing at the stove, turning strips of bacon. Avery set her cup in the sink and went over to him. He set down the fork and put his arms around her and hugged her.

"I hate to miss having breakfast with you and Elizabeth, but my stomach is a little queasy. It's a combination of nerves and champagne," she explained regretfully.

"Coming back here for breakfast this morning probably wouldn't be a good idea, anyway," he replied. "It'll be better for Elizabeth not to see you. When you left, she might make a scene, and that would make you feel bad."

"Yes, it would make me feel bad. I hope she isn't unhappy all day today."

"She'll be fine. Drive safely." He kissed her goodbye and walked her to the door.

Shep accompanied her across the backyard to the path that led through the woods. Then he trotted back to the porch. Avery paused and gazed over her shoulder at Clark's house. *Today was such a special day, and everything felt wrong.*

She wished that Clark and Elizabeth were going with her to the airport to pick up Bret and Bart. She wished that Clark had *wanted* to drive her in his van and not just been willing.

Avery had paid her dollar toll and was southbound to New Orleans on the Lake Pontchartrain Causeway when she remembered she had to buy a plastic tarp, in case it rained. The weather forecast was for an eighty percent chance of afternoon showers. She would just have to keep her fingers crossed. The sun was shining brightly. Maybe she would get lucky, and the forecast would prove to be wrong.

The causeway was twenty-four miles long without a bend or a curve. Actually it was two parallel two-lane bridges with only a few turnaround points located miles apart. Accidents could cause horrendous pileups with fatalities and automobiles plunging through the railings into the lake. Such disasters were always reported in the news with all the gory details.

In the middle of the day traffic wasn't heavy, but the fifty-five-mile speed limit obviously wasn't being enforced. Cars and other types of vehicles breezed past Avery. She sped up and then slowed down again. The higher rate of speed made the ride bumpier in Larry's lightweight pickup. Emergency call boxes located at mile intervals blinked an ominous reminder that tire blowouts and mechanical breakdowns occurred on the bridge.

Belatedly Avery began to worry about whether she should have had a mechanic service the pickup. All summer she hadn't thought about having the oil filter changed. Were the tires on the truck in good condition or was the bumpiness a warning signal?

It wasn't just getting to the airport safely and on time that was making her anxious, but transporting her two boys safely back to the country.

I wish Clark had insisted on coming with me. He should have known that I would be in a nervous state. If he really cared about me, he wouldn't have taken no for an answer.

Avery's anxiety fed the hurt and resentment that she'd carefully hidden from him. He didn't care deeply enough. If he did care, he would be lending her his support today, not letting her go off alone to the city on such an important mission.

With the toll booths in sight at the end of the causeway, Avery relaxed her grip on the wheel, some of her tension easing. In just an hour, she would see her sons after long months of separation. The thought sent her spirits soaring.

It was strange and unpleasant to be back in the urban congestion. Cars everywhere, horns blowing, no one smiling and waving. She'd gotten used to waving to strangers as she drove along the country roads of Felton at a leisurely speed.

If the twins didn't show any particular desire to come back to the city for a day, that would suit Avery fine. She was completely out of tune with this frenetic pace, this sense of everything being so crowded and impersonal.

Interstate 10 took her to the airport exit. Traffic slowed to a crawl with the airport terminal in sight. Avery's excitement mounted as did her nervous tension.

At long last she'd reached the airport and then the parking garage. On an upper level she finally spotted an empty gap between cars and squeezed the pickup into it. Heart pounding, she rushed to locate the elevator and made her way along with throngs of other people into the terminal.

Inside she learned that the twins' flight was delayed. The airline personnel could offer her no explanation. Avery found a waiting area where she could sit and worry. Why wouldn't a jet leave on time and arrive on time in this space age of technology? Had something been wrong with the engine or equipment prior to takeoff?

She wished that Clark were there with her to give some reassurance and calm her fears. He would be, if he loved her. But he didn't love her. He was deeply fond of her and physically attracted to her, but when her year in Felton was over, he would let her leave, just as he'd let her go off on her own today.

That knowledge kept Avery from finding a phone and calling Clark long distance.

An hour passed. Another hour passed. She was drained of all emotion except relief when the flight finally arrived. Standing with a crowd of people near the concourse gate, she was dependent on her first glimpse of the twins to kindle her joy. But even this eagerly awaited moment wasn't quite right today.

Avery couldn't help feeling that Clark was at least partly to blame for the fact that her sons' visit was starting off on a wrong note.

Catching sight of two blond-headed boys walking side by side, she felt the expected surge of delight and an automatic pride. A wide smile spread across her face. The two boys, both with California tans, were Bret and Bart, though someone meeting them after just seeing their pictures in her living room might not easily identify them.

Her sons were much changed in appearance, starting with their hairstyles, which were sightly different on each boy.

Bret's head was shaved to above his ears, leaving a blond stubble on top of his head. On the nap of his neck his hair grew long and straggly. Bart's hair was shaved high all around his head with a cap of hair on top.

Their clothes were new and didn't match. She would never have put them on a plane dressed that way. Both boys wore baggy cotton shorts that came to the knee. Bret wore an oversize tank top and Bart a T-shirt that was sizes too large. The colors were bright and clashing. On their feet were high-top black sneakers left untied and worn without socks. Around their wrists were braided bracelets.

Avery's rush of love didn't block out her opinion that she wasn't crazy about their new look. They were certain to attract attention in the rural environs of Felton, where the fashion for boys was more conservative and Western. She'd been planning on buying them each a Stetson hat and a pair of cowboy boots.

They saw her, and their faces lighted up, grins breaking out. Avery disregarded the superficial changes as she held out her arms and enveloped both her children in a welcoming embrace.

It wasn't as easy to overlook changes in behavior that were immediately evident. Though they'd had their minor squabbles, Bret and Bart had always been confederates and gotten along well together. Avery was taken aback by the way they spoke to each other now in a jeering tone of voice and made belittling remarks.

Their abuse of one another wasn't just verbal. There was punching and shoving. She was aware of disapproving glances from strangers.

Was this a preteen phase they'd entered? Avery wondered, hating that she was forced to scold them right away.

"Aw, Mom," Bart said after being admonished not to call his brother stupid. "We're just acting like boys."

"Yeah, Mom," Bret chimed in. "You'll get used to it."

"Your father lets you treat one another this way?" she couldn't keep herself from asking sternly. They were down in the baggage claims area waiting for the boys' luggage.

"He acts rough with us," Bart explained.

"All three of us wrestle and stuff," Bret elaborated. "Cindy doesn't like it, either. You should have seen how upset she got when Dad and Bart and I were fooling around the other night and knocked over a lamp and broke it. She said she'd be glad for some peace and quiet during the two weeks we were gone."

"Dad got mad and said maybe she'd like it if he went somewhere, too," his twin elaborated. Avery found the story very disturbing.

The boys elbowed one another, snickering.

Avery pressed her hand to her head, feeling the dull throb of a headache. The day that was supposed to be so wonderful was continuing to unfold in a disappointingly wrong way.

Lugging her sons' heavy duffel bags, new acquisitions to replace the "sissy" suitcases they'd taken to California, she thought about how easily Clark could have carried the bags, if he'd come along.

Bret and Bart weren't overly impressed with Larry's pickup truck. They inspected it critically and remarked on its small tires while Avery was hefting their luggage into the exposed back.

Their attitude wasn't her main worry at this juncture. Crossing the glass-walled walkway from the terminal to the parking garage, she'd seen how threatening the skies outside were.

Sure enough, she hadn't gotten onto the interstate before a great crash of thunder made all three of them flinch. Huge drops of rain spattered the windshield, and within seconds a heavy downpour began with blinding flashes of lightning followed by jarring reverberations of thunder.

The twins huddled together, their bravado deserting them. Avery took her hand away from the wheel long enough to give them each a reassuring pat on the leg.

"It's just a summer rainstorm," she said soothingly. "In a few minutes it will be over, and the sun will probably pop out."

The going was slow and hazardous on the interstate, the torrential rain making visibility very poor. Contrary to Avery's optimistic prediction, the deluge showed no sign of lessening.

"You said it would be over in a few minutes, Mom," Bart reminded her with a scared voice.

"Yeah, Mom. What if we get in a bad wreck?"

"I'm being very careful, boys. Try not to be nervous."

The rain had slackened to a steady downpour by the time she'd reached the exit taking her to the causeway.

"Maybe we're leaving the bad weather behind us," Avery suggested hopefully, approaching the toll booths minutes later.

Before they'd gone two miles, they were driving in a downpour as heavy as the one on the interstate. The rain drummed loudly on the cab of the little truck. Hard gusts of wind made it necessary for her to grip the wheel hard to keep from serving.

"At least it's not thundering—" A great booming clap cut her off in the middle of her sentence.

"What if we hit the railing and drive off into the lake, Mom?" Bart asked.

"Yeah, we could get blown off, Mom."

"Please, you two, just relax. Your mom is a good driver."

The twenty-four-mile trip was grueling. There was hardly any letup from the weather, and her sons expressed their fear by complaining and comparing Louisiana unfavorably to California. Avery's nerves were stretched to the snapping point when they finally reached the end of the causeway.

Still the rain continued coming down in sheets.

"How far is this place where you live?" Bart asked.

"Yeah, how many more miles is it?" Bret asked.

"We'll be there in less than an hour," she assured them. "The worst is over now that we've gotten this far."

Once outside the city limits of Covington, Avery began to relax. Thank heaven, they would be safely home in another thirty minutes, she reflected. Tomorrow this whole dismal experience would be in the past.

Five minutes later she was parked on the shoulder of the road with a flat tire, her windshield wipers slapping at the steady flow of rain. She didn't even have the luxury of resting her head on the steering wheel and breaking down into tears, not with her sons regarding her anxiously and telling her what she already knew. There wasn't a house or a service station anywhere close.

Avery was going to have to attempt to change the tire herself and get soaked to the skin.

"A car's pulling up by us, Mom."

"Roll down your window, Mom."

The car was a Mercedes, the driver a middle-aged woman. "I have a car phone. Is there someone you'd like me to call?" she inquired.

"Yes, please," Avery answered gratefully. She hesitated ever so briefly, overcoming pride, and gave the woman Clark's name and number and the message that she'd had a flat tire.

Fifteen minutes later a tow truck with two men in yellow slickers arrived from a garage in Covington. They explained that they'd been dispatched by Clark to change her tire, but had come prepared for any eventuality. Using their own power jack, they made short work of putting on the spare, not nearly time enough for Avery to fully grasp that Clark hadn't come himself. Evidently he hadn't wanted to bring Elizabeth out in the rain.

When she asked the two men for their bill, they waved aside the inquiry, saying that it had already been charged to Clark on his credit card.

Now wasn't the time to mull over how he'd responded to her summons for help. She had to put aside her feelings and deal with her children's needs and emotions. The boys were quiet and tense as the journey was resumed.

"Are you hungry?" she asked, wanting to dispel the sense of impending disaster. "I had planned to cook hamburgers tonight, but there's a restaurant where we could stop and eat."

They both claimed to be hungry. Avery suspected that they would have agreed to stopping anywhere to get out of the truck. Their trip from the airport probably seemed like an endless, claustrophobic journey into the unknown. She almost regretted that their bratty behavior had been cast aside, leaving them vulnerable and insecure.

Only one other vehicle was parked in front of the Barbecue Pit. Evidently the driver was the grizzled older man sitting alone at a table, also the only other customer. The twins glanced around dubiously at the Western decor, which looked shabbier tonight than it had on other occasions when the restaurant was noisy and crowded and cheerful, the way Avery had been hoping it would be tonight.

If Clark had brought Elizabeth in his van instead of calling a garage, the five of them could have been trooping inside instead of just her and the boys. Why hadn't he sensed that she desperately needed him to come to her rescue and not just to change a flat tire?

The twins picked at their food. Avery herself didn't have much appetite. Her voice sounded strained as she sought to find a topic that would draw them into an animated conversation.

"Do you eat at restaurants often with your dad and Cindy?"

Their answers revealed that they had frequent meals at fast-food restaurants. Avery hadn't been prying, but she couldn't help inquiring further about their diet. She learned that they got their own breakfast in the mornings. Cindy got up early with John and the two of them had breakfast together. For lunch the boys were mostly left to their own devices, too. Cindy apparently went shopping a lot with women friends and didn't feel obligated to be home at noontime.

Here Avery had been thinking that Bret and Bart had the benefit of a stepmother who didn't work outside the home. She'd been led to believe that Cindy was wholly in favor of the twins' moving to California to live with their father. It didn't sound to her as if John's wife was showing much maternal interest in his children.

Avery didn't like the picture she was getting. She changed the subject to school and inadvertently gleaned another bit of disturbing information.

"Cindy's signed up for real-estate school," Bart volunteered. "She's going to be a real-estate agent and sell houses."

Bret elaborated, "She wanted to hire a maid, and Dad said he couldn't afford it. So she told him that she'd earn her own money and pay for it herself."

Had having two boys around the house prompted the desire for housecleaning help? Avery could guess that it had. The transition from a childless household to one with two eleven-year-olds would require some adjustment for Cindy.

It didn't sound as though she was adjusting too happily. With the kind of personality change that John was cultivating in the twins, Avery wasn't surprised. She herself wouldn't be thrilled with roughhousing that resulted in broken lamps.

How she wished that she could discuss the whole disturbing matter with Clark later on tonight, but she wouldn't bring it up when she called him to thank him. He wasn't vitally interested in the twins or he would have been with her today.

Avery was as much alone now as she had been when John left her eight years ago. The burden of worry about her children's future rested solely on her shoulders, just as it had months ago when she made her difficult decision.

Chapter Thirteen

"Daddy, can I call Ms. Avery's house and find out if she and Bret and Bart got home yet?" Elizabeth asked plaintively.

"No, baby. We shouldn't bother Ms. Avery," Clark answered. "She knows we're here. It's your turn," he reminded her. They were playing a board game, and she wasn't concentrating.

Fortunately, her mind seemed to be more on the house next door than on the telephone call from her mother that afternoon, which had turned her back into the troubled child she'd been at the beginning of the summer. He'd forgotten to instruct Billie Hano not to let his daughter answer the phone. Weeks had gone by since Marilyn's one other call from the sanatorium, and his vigilance had relaxed.

"Daddy, this isn't any fun with just you and me." Elizabeth sighed. "I liked it better with Ms. Avery and you and me."

"I liked it, too, baby," he admitted. "But we're just going to have to make the best of things while Ms. Avery's boys are here."

"I wish they hadn't come if I can't have her take care of me. I didn't see her all day."

Clark was in complete empathy.

"Hopefully we'll see her tomorrow," he said.

Surely Avery knew he was waiting for her to call and let him know she'd arrived home safely. He expected her to figure out that something major must have prevented him from going himself and changing her tire. When the woman, a Mrs. Anderson, relayed the news that Avery was stopped on the side of the highway, he'd just arrived home fifteen minutes earlier to find Elizabeth in an upset state. He'd had his hands full trying to soothe the guilt feelings Marilyn had aroused and also ease his little daughter's despair that rose out of the belief that she had to go back to her mother.

Clark couldn't help thinking that if Avery had only included him and Elizabeth in her plans today, Elizabeth would have been spared some unnecessary emotional and mental anguish. He would have been along on the trip to and from the airport to take care of any emergencies such as a flat tire.

What if she'd had the damned flat tire on the causeway? The thought gave Clark nightmares.

"You look mad, Daddy."

"Do I? I don't mean to look mad." Clark smoothed the frown from his face. "Is it my turn now?"

"We don't have to play this game." Elizabeth began to pack up the board game. When she'd finished, she climbed up in his lap and wrapped her arms around his neck. "I love you, Daddy."

He hugged her close. "I love you, baby."

"Do you love Ms. Avery?"

"Yes, I love Ms. Avery a lot."

"Me, too." She was quiet a moment. "You say 'I love you' to me, but I don't ever hear you say it to her."

"No, I haven't said it out loud to her."

"How come?"

"It's hard to explain, baby. Grown people aren't always free to say what they feel."

"Ms. Avery loves you and me both." She patted his shoulder with a small hand, making Clark wonder if he was comforting her or vice versa.

"She's very fond of us both, I know." He kissed the top of her head. "Why don't you and I have a snack, huh? How about a glass of milk and some cookies?"

"Okay, Daddy," she agreed.

He carried her out to the kitchen.

"There aren't any houses around, Mom."

"This is a spooky place, Mom. You can't even see a light anywhere."

"Mr. Strong and his little girl actually don't live very far through the woods," Avery wearily assured her nervous sons. She turned off the engine, leaving the headlights trained on the back porch. "Let's make a run for it. I'll come back and get your bags."

Opening the door into the kitchen, she was hit by an awful odor. Poor old Sam had been closed in all day and had had an accident.

It certainly wasn't Clark's fault, and yet he'd been right here close by today, not out battling the elements, like she had. He could have thought about Sam. He could have saved the old dog this humiliation and prevented their homecoming from being one more unpleasant experience.

Avery folded the last garment from the dryer and carried the heaped laundry basket upstairs. She'd put the boys' wet clothes through a rinse cycle before drying them. The last batch was done and now she could go to bed.

In their bedroom she set the basket down and tiptoed over to the bed to gaze down at her sleeping sons. They both lay curled up on their sides facing outward, their backs touching.

Poor darlings, what a miserable beginning for your visit, Avery thought, sighing. She bent and kissed Bret on the cheek and walked around to the other side to kiss Bart.

Leaving the door open and the hall light on, she walked tiredly to her bedroom, got undressed and slipped on one of the nightshirts that she hadn't worn all summer. Removing her watch, she glanced at it, noting the hour. Ten-thirty. Clark was probably just going to bed.

He hadn't called. For all he knew, she might never have arrived home safely. How much trouble would it have been for him to pick up the phone and dial her number?

Her hurt and resentment welling up anew, Avery sat down on the edge of her bed. She was reaching to pick up her phone when it rang shrilly, startling her.

"Hello."

"Where have you been?" Clark demanded, sounding terse and angry. "I've been waiting all evening for you to call me."

"You know my phone number. Why were you waiting for me to call?" she asked.

"I guess I thought it was your place to call."

"I suppose it was my place since I'm in your debt. Thank you for sending help," she said thickly, tears suddenly clogging her throat. "Of course, I'll reimburse you."

"For heaven's sake, Avery, you're not in my debt. I'm in your debt. You've taken care of my daughter all summer and done a hundred and one kind, considerate acts. I sure as hell am not going to let you reimburse me."

"Why are you so furious?" He was the one who had let her down, not vice versa.

"I'm *not* furious," he denied. "Or I guess I am furious at myself. I should have my butt kicked for not taking it upon myself to go with you today, whether I was welcome or not. You risked your life and your boys' lives driving in all that bad weather. I have more sense, even if you don't."

"You make it sound as though I didn't want you to drive. That's not true. I would gladly have agreed. I can't tell you how many times today I wished you had been more insistent."

"Avery, I offered not once, but three or four times!"

"I thought you merely felt obligated to offer."

"You thought wrong." He tempered his tone. "I'm just thankful that no harm came to you or your boys. What time did you get home?"

"It was about eight-thirty. We stopped at the Barbecue Pit for supper since we were running so late. When I got here, I had a mess waiting for me. I'd forgotten all about poor Sam."

"Damn! I forgot about him, too," Clark said disgustedly. "I could have gone over and let him out."

"I wished you had. Anyway, I had to clean that up. I felt so bad for him. He was terribly ashamed. The boys came on upstairs and got their baths without any mishap, thank goodness. I retrieved their duffel bags, which were practically afloat in the back of the truck. Even if I'd had a plastic tarp, which I'd forgotten to buy, it would have blown away in all the wind."

"Their clothes got wet, I take it."

"Soaked. A few minutes ago, I finished rinsing and drying everything. All in all it's been a horrible day," she summed up. "The best thing about it is that it's over, and I have Bret and Bart with me."

"I'm sorry. You deserved for it to be a good day."

His gentle tone made tears threaten again. "Don't be sympathetic," she warned thickly. "I'll break down and cry."

"I wish I could put my arms around you."

Avery wished that, too.

"How did Elizabeth and Billie get along today?" she asked.

"They got through the morning well enough. But then this afternoon Marilyn called and Elizabeth answered the phone and talked to her."

"Oh, no, Clark! I didn't think to remind you about cautioning Billie!"

"It slipped my mind entirely. Anyway, the damage was done. When I got home, Elizabeth was in her room crying and trying to decide what things she would take back to Shreveport with her. Her mother had told her that she had to go and live with her grandparents so that she could visit her every day and make her well."

"Poor little girl!" Avery murmured. "What kind of mother could put that kind of guilt trip on a seven-year-old child! Did you call the Lairds tonight and tell them?"

"Yes. They weren't aware that Marilyn had called again. They assured me that they weren't at all in favor of Elizabeth's coming to live with them, as much as they love her. It's all just a crazy, selfish scheme that Marilyn has cooked up in her head."

"What terrible luck that she chose today, of all days, to phone."

He went on. "In the midst of trying to dry up Elizabeth's tears, I got the S.O.S. from you. I figured you would know that nothing short of an emergency would keep me from coming to take care of your problem myself."

"I suppose I should have known, but I didn't." Honesty forced her to admit the truth.

"That's why you didn't call when you reached the Barbecue Pit? You thought that my actions showed I didn't care enough to come out in the rain?" He sounded both wounded and incredulous.

"You would have had to bring Elizabeth out. I thought that might be the reason."

"I don't know what to say," he said quietly. "At this point in our relationship, I would expect you to know beyond a doubt that making sure you're safe is of the utmost importance to me."

"My thinking wasn't very rational by the time I had the flat tire, Clark. The drive across the causeway was really frightening. Bret and Bart were terrified. I'm sorry—now that I know the reason—that I didn't call. I was about to, just now," she added apologetically. "If you'd waited fifteen seconds, your phone would have rung."

"Where are you?" he asked.

"Sitting on the side of my bed. Where are you?"

"The same place."

"It's been so long since I slept here. I felt strange tonight putting on a nightgown," she confided. "Do you realize that I never slept in the nude with John? I always wore a nightgown to bed. When we had sex, I always got up afterward and put it back on."

"I normally sleep in my underwear," he said.

"That's all that you have on now?"

"Yes."

She could visualize him, and the image intensified her loneliness for him. It was disturbing that she felt lonely tonight with her sons in the house.

"We should say good-night," she said. "Tomorrow will come early for me."

"Elizabeth and I want to see you tomorrow and meet Bret and Bart." His voice was sober.

"When?"

"Whenever we're invited. I'm taking off from work to look after her myself."

"Come over for breakfast."

"What time?"

"Eight o'clock?"

"We'll be there."

There was a pause.

"Sleep well," Clark said.

"You, too. Good night now." *I love you,* Avery told him silently as she hung up.

Rain still pattered on the tin roof. Lying in her bed in the darkness, she wrapped herself in the awareness that her children were asleep in the room down the hallway. Their presence didn't keep her from needing Clark's body next to hers.

The sky was gray and overcast, but at least it wasn't raining when Avery awoke the next morning.

Please let the sun come out, she prayed. How she was hoping for a day of fun and harmony to make up for yesterday. If breakfast went well and the five of them all got along, plans should develop naturally including Clark and Elizabeth. Avery would gladly turn over to him the role of director of activities.

After she'd gotten dressed, she went into the boys' room to rouse them. "Wake up, fellas. We have to do our farm chores this morning before our company comes."

They both burrowed their blond heads deeper into their pillows, tugging the sheet higher. Avery smiled with maternal indulgence. "I'll give you fifteen more minutes and then I'll be back up."

Downstairs she let Sam out, put the coffee on to brew and mixed up a bowl of batter for French toast. Then she went back upstairs. The twins weren't any more responsive to her second wake-up call. Avery decided to let them sleep longer their first morning.

It was silly to feel disappointed, she told herself as she went outside to feed Billy and the chickens by herself. Today was *not* starting off on a wrong note just because the boys weren't up, bright and eager and ready to experience country life. They would soon get into the routine.

On her return to the house, she set the table for breakfast, then poured herself a cup of coffee and went outside to sit in the swing on the back porch. The thought that Clark was probably having a cup of coffee by himself this very moment brought a pang of the same loneliness she'd felt last night.

Having her sons with her was no longer enough to make Avery a complete person. She needed not only to be their full-time mother, but also to be Clark's wife. Could those separate needs both be fulfilled?

Not unless Clark could take her sons to his heart the way she had taken Elizabeth to hers.

At ten minutes to eight, Avery made another trip upstairs, this time shaking the boys and staying long enough to make sure they were getting up. They came trooping down the stairs just as Clark walked up onto the back porch, carrying Elizabeth in his arms. She opened the door for him, seeing that he wore rubber boots. He'd taken the path through the woods.

"Good morning, you two," she greeted them.

"Hi, Ms. Avery." Elizabeth smiled sweetly and held out her arms.

Avery stepped up close so that the little girl could hug her around the neck and kiss her cheek. Bret and Bart had come up and were standing, observing the scene. She glanced back at them and then up at Clark's face.

"Aren't you going to kiss Ms. Avery, too, Daddy?" Elizabeth asked.

Avery gazed at him helplessly, torn between wanting him to kiss her and hoping that he wouldn't in front of the boys.

"I need to take off my wet boots," he said.

She backed away to make room, and he set Elizabeth down. The little girl slipped her hand confidently in Avery's and surveyed the twins with shy interest.

"Elizabeth, I want you meet my boys, Bret and Bart. Fellas, this is Elizabeth, who lives next door."

"Hi," Elizabeth said. "Which one of you is Bret and which one is Bart?"

"I'm Bart." Bart tersely identified himself first and gestured abruptly at his brother. "He's Bret."

Bret scowled at Bart. "I can talk, stupid. I can tell her my own name."

"Boys, I told you not to call each other names," Avery scolded.

"It will be easy to tell them apart," Elizabeth remarked to her. "Because their hair is different." She addressed the two boys with an innocent candor. "Your hair is kind of funny-looking. And your clothes are too big for you."

By now Clark had removed his boots and stepped inside in his sock feet, closing the door. "That's not a polite thing to say to Bret and Bart, Elizabeth," he reprimanded her sternly.

Elizabeth's face clouded up. "They don't look like their pictures, Daddy," she said in a chastened voice.

"You didn't mean any harm, sweetie. The boys aren't insulted, are you, boys?" Avery held out her hand, but Bret and Bart didn't come closer. Nor did they answer. They were eyeing Clark, taking in his height and size. "Say hello to Mr. Strong, Elizabeth's father," she prompted.

They both mumbled hellos.

"Hi, Bart. Hi, Bret," Clark greeted them in turn. "It's nice to meet you after hearing so much about you from your mother."

They made no response.

"Now that the four of you have met, you can all sit down at the table and keep me company while I cook our breakfast," Avery directed cheerfully. "Elizabeth and Bret and Bart can have some orange juice, and Mr. Strong can have a cup of coffee."

"Why are you calling my daddy that, Ms. Avery?" Elizabeth asked uncertainly. "You always call him Clark."

"I'll still call him Clark," Avery explained. "But the boys will call him Mr. Strong. Or Mr. Clark. Whatever he and they are comfortable with. Okay?"

Bret and Bart hadn't made a move toward the table.

"I'm not hungry, Mom," Bart announced. "I don't want any breakfast."

"I'm not hungry, either, Mom," his twin said. "I don't want any breakfast, either."

"Of course, you're going to have breakfast," she declared. "I'm cooking French toast. Wait until you smell it. You'll realize you are hungry." Avery smiled at them beseechingly.

"It's your favorite breakfast," Elizabeth piped up. "And my favorite, too. Ms. Avery fixes it for me all the time."

The twins scowled up at her, jealous resentment on their faces.

Clark spoke up. "Perhaps this wasn't a good idea, Avery. Elizabeth and I could take a rain check on breakfast and come over later and visit."

"No, Daddy, I want to stay!" Elizabeth implored. "I want to have breakfast with Bret and Bart."

"Of course, you're staying," Avery stated firmly. "And Bret and Bart will sit down at the table with us, whether they're hungry or not. They've been taught better manners than this."

Sullenly the twins took places side by side. Elizabeth climbed up in a chair, and Clark went over to help himself to a mug of coffee. Avery smothered a sigh of discouragement, getting her bowl of batter out of the refrigerator. This initial get-together could hardly be going any worse. Her sons seemed to be bent on making a poor impression on Clark.

Glancing out of the window, she saw that it had started misting rain.

"Can I help you?" Clark inquired, his tone personal.

Avery wanted to answer in the same kind of tone, but she was aware that the boys' eyes were trained on them and that they were listening. "Thank you, but I have everything under control," she refused pleasantly. "You're a guest."

"Then I'll get out of your way," he replied, turning away and going to sit down at the table.

"Your mom tells me that you have a swimming pool at your dad's house in California." He addressed Bret and Bart. They mumbled answers to that question and to the others he asked them in the effort to engage them in conversation.

Avery's spirits sank lower as she set about preparing the breakfast that obviously none of them was going to enjoy. Why did Clark have to sound like he was conducting an interrogation? And why did her sons have to show themselves in the worst possible light?

"Where does Elizabeth's mom live?"

Out of the blue, Bart had blurted out the question to Clark. Before Clark could respond, Bret followed up with a companion question. "Why does she live with you and not with her mom?"

"You shouldn't be so inquisitive, boys!" Avery protested, taking a step away from the stove.

"Sure, they should," Clark corrected her. "It's natural that they should want to know answers to questions like that." His note of rebuke was for her. Clasping Elizabeth's little shoulder lightly with one big hand, he replied to her sons, "Elizabeth's mother is in a hospital in northern Louisiana. She has a mental illness and isn't able to take care of Elizabeth anymore." He squeezed his daughter's shoulder. "I plan to keep her with me permanently."

Elizabeth nodded solemnly, otherwise not intervening in the conversation.

"Our dad wants to get custody of us, too," Bart said to Clark.

"Yeah, he wants us to live with him from now on," Bret added.

"And how do you feel about that?" Clark asked.

"Clark! Don't put them on the spot like that!" Avery objected. "That's not fair to them!"

"They brought up the subject, Avery," he pointed out quietly to her. "It's undoubtedly something that's on their minds."

Her sons were looking at her as though waiting for her permission to continue the sensitive discussion.

"How do you feel about living permanently with your dad?" she asked tightly. "And I want to hear the truth."

"We like California better than New Orleans, Mom," Bart said apologetically. "We can ride our bicycles and nobody jumps on us and bothers us."

"We'd like California a whole lot if you lived there, too, Mom," his brother contributed earnestly.

"Yeah, we could live with you and go swimming over at Dad's house and see him on weekends and stuff."

Elizabeth had slumped in her chair. She put in tearfully, "I don't want you to move to California, Ms. Avery. I want you to stay here with my daddy and me."

"It doesn't matter what *you* want," Bart informed the little girl fiercely.

"She's *our* mom," Bret stated, glaring at Elizabeth, who began to cry.

Avery gazed at Clark accusingly, asking him silently, *Now that we're all at each other's throats, are you satisfied?* "Don't cry, Elizabeth. I'm not going away soon, honey," she soothed.

Clark took a napkin and tenderly wiped his daughter's wet cheeks. The talk of her moving to California hadn't noticeably upset him at all.

"Let's all eat our breakfasts," he instructed in a no-nonsense tone when Avery put the food on the table. The twins obeyed as well as Elizabeth. Apparently the only one in the group whose appetite had been ruined by the hostile interaction was Avery herself. The others had reached a truce.

"We'll pitch in and help clean up," Clark said when breakfast was over. "Then if you boys are game, we'll try our hands at doing some fishing in the pond."

"It's raining," Avery pointed out.

"It's not really raining. It's just drizzling. This is perfect weather for fly-fishing. The boys have rain slickers, don't they?"

Bart spoke up before she could answer. "We don't know how to fly-fish."

Bret added, "We haven't ever been fishing. Our dad is going to take us deep-sea fishing sometime."

Clark was undeterred by their lack of enthusiasm. "I can teach you how to use a casting rod in about five minutes. It isn't difficult."

"Can I fish, too, Daddy?" Elizabeth asked eagerly.

The twins scowled at her.

"No, you and Ms. Avery can watch. You're not old enough to fly-fish."

His answer pleased her sons as much as it surprised them, Avery noted. They'd been expecting him to humor Elizabeth.

Clark got up from the table and carried his plate over to the sink. The three children followed suit. Avery was the last to rise. When she brought her plate over, Clark took it from her.

"Thank you. The breakfast was very good," he said and bent and kissed her on the mouth.

"Thank you, Ms. Avery," Elizabeth piped up sweetly.

Bret and Bart mumbled in sequence a shocked, "Thank you, Mom." Their glances at Clark were hostile, and she read reproach in their blue eyes when they looked at her.

The rest of the cleanup was performed in silence.

Avery was expecting her sons to balk when it came time for them to accompany Clark outside to the pond. Judging from their attitude toward him, they wouldn't want to put themselves in his hands as students of the art of catching fish.

But they didn't balk, surprisingly. Clark organized his small expedition like a Boy Scout troop master, first selecting fishing gear. Larry Wade was a fisherman and had given Avery permission to make use of his various rods and reels and tackle boxes of lures.

She gathered that Clark had some knowledge and expertise himself.

Any hopes that he and the boys would make friends went the way of her other hopes as she and Elizabeth watched from the porch. Bret and Bart treated him with the wary respect they might have shown their school principal, and he didn't seem to be putting himself out at all to win their affection. His whole purpose in the outing might have been to teach them skills, not see that they were having fun.

To her delight—and theirs—each boy caught several fish. They held up their catches for her to admire, calling in thrilled voices, "Look, Mom!" She fetched her camera and took some snapshots, despite the dreary weather conditions.

The boys didn't suggest that they pose with Clark, and neither did he.

Avery suspected that Clark deliberately wasn't competing with her sons to land a prize fish and outdo them. Several times his fishing rod was bent almost double, but the fish got away.

At noon she and Elizabeth made sandwiches and served lunch on the porch. After the meal, Clark asked Bret and Bart if they'd had enough fishing, and they answered, "No, sir."

"Have you had enough?" Avery asked him.

He evaded her question, remarking that a fisherman never gets tired when the fish are biting.

Late in the afternoon Clark went home to shower and change clothes. Then he returned and he and Elizabeth had supper with them. Avery cooked the hamburgers she'd planned for last night's supper.

The twins had become more resigned to Elizabeth's presence, but still shunned her, and she'd grown more peevish toward them as a result of their unfriendliness. Clark calmly overlooked the friction and ignored the twins' disapproval of his affectionate treatment of their mother. They glowered at him when he made any physical contact with her, put his arm around her waist and hugged her, squeezed her shoulder or patted her on the hip.

He didn't touch her any more or any less than he would have if they hadn't been there. Avery surmised that he'd decided the twins had to adjust. Being sensitive to their feelings, it was impossible for her to respond naturally, without any self-consciousness.

The main improvement in the group dynamics since that morning at breakfast was a spirit of tolerance. The twins apparently accepted that Clark and Elizabeth weren't going to go away for the duration of their visit, and Clark and Elizabeth apparently accepted that being with her for these two weeks meant being around Bret and Bart, too.

At the supper table Clark proposed a trip to a global wildlife preserve the next day. An hour's drive was involved, and they would go in his van. The twins and Elizabeth were intrigued when they learned that the tour of the preserve was by covered wagon.

For all the lack of harmony, there was unanimous agreement to a plan that included all five of them.

The trip was a success and yet it didn't accomplish any miracle. At the end of the day, the four people she loved dearly were simply willing to continue the truce and spend more days together because she was important to them.

Before Avery knew it, a week of the boys' visit had gone past. As much as she appreciated Clark's efforts to entertain them, she couldn't blind herself to the truth: he wasn't developing any deep fondness for them. He wasn't taking them to his heart as she'd so hoped he would.

For Clark not to find her sons lovable hurt unbearably. While they hadn't really opened up to him or been as endearing toward him as they were capable of being, he still should have felt drawn to them because they were her children.

There wasn't any doubt in her mind how he would react if she told him she wanted to keep Bret and Bart here with her and enroll them in school rather than send them back to California. He would be opposed.

If Avery could only count on his support, there wouldn't be any decision to make. But he wouldn't support her. In good conscience he would argue John's rights as a father. The twins had been well behaved around Clark thanks to his influence, and hadn't exhibited the brashness and rudeness that she found so objectionable on their arrival at the airport. From conversations with him, she knew that Clark gave John credit for doing a good job of parenting.

Maybe John *was* doing a good job. Maybe Avery was looking for an excuse to find fault. The one thing she was certain about was that it was asking too much of her to put her children on a plane in another week.

When they were gone, she wouldn't be able to resume the same relationship with Clark. Something vital would have died in her.

Chapter Fourteen

Clark's phone was busy. Who was he talking to at this hour? Avery wondered as she cradled her phone and got into bed.

He'd gone home an hour earlier after dropping her and the boys off. They'd visited a llama farm this afternoon and then driven into Covington to see a movie and have supper at a fast-food restaurant of the twins' choosing.

It was Friday. Their flight was on Sunday. She hadn't been able to enjoy today, thinking about how soon the precious time with them would be over.

If he didn't call her, she wouldn't call tonight, Avery decided. Almost immediately the phone rang. Assuming that the person on the other end was Clark, she was all the more unprepared to hear her ex-husband's voice.

"John, it's after ten o'clock here," she said. "The boys are asleep."

"I called late on purpose," he replied. "I need to have a serious talk with you. It isn't working out, Avery. Cindy is going to leave me if I keep the kids. It's a helluva fix to be in. I don't want to lose her, and I can't raise those two little guys by myself anyway."

Avery had sat up in bed. She was clutching her night-gown over her heart, almost afraid to believe the implications of his words. *He wanted her to take the twins back.*

"This arrangement wasn't working out for me, either, John. Just box up their clothes and things and send it all here."

"Wait a minute, Avery. Let's discuss some options," he urged. "Why stay in Louisiana? Come out here to California and get a fresh start. I'll give you all the financial help I can during the transition period while you look for a job and so forth. This is a great climate, a good place to live. The boys like it here. Ask them about what I'm suggesting and let them have some input. They'll be teenagers before you know it. That's a difficult phase. Let me help you get them through it. They could have two parents, even though we're divorced. There's nothing tying you to that place in the country, is there?"

"I'll give some serious thought to moving to California, John. The boys have told me that they like it out there."

Whether or not she stayed in Louisiana would depend on Clark, but she wasn't going to explain that to John.

He applied more selling pressure. Then Cindy came on the line and assured Avery that she was supportive of the idea of Avery's relocating. The discussion lasted until well past eleven o'clock. By the time Avery hung up, the reality was sinking in: *she was getting her children back.*

It was late to be calling Clark, but she wanted to tell him this incredible development. He picked up immediately.

"I have unbelievable news," she said.

"So do I," he replied, a ring of gladness in his voice. "I just got off the phone with Faith Willis. She'd been trying to reach me since this afternoon. Marilyn's parents have agreed to give their affidavits, stating that they fully support my having custody of Elizabeth."

"That's wonderful, Clark. Faith thinks that their support will greatly increase your chances?"

"She feels that my getting custody is almost a sure thing. Her confidence level is such that she didn't even pressure me tonight to hurry up and marry you."

"I didn't realize she was pressuring you."

"She hasn't let up since the day I interviewed her."

The same day that he'd come from the city and proposed to Avery.

"What's your good news?" he asked.

"It has to do with the twins, naturally. Tonight I had a phone call from John. He's decided that he can't give the twins a home after all."

"Why on earth not?" Clark demanded.

"Because Cindy has threatened to leave him. She's not happy with having Bret and Bart living with them."

"So he's shuttling his kids back to you, like they were excess baggage? What kind of a man is he?" There was indignation and contempt in his voice.

"As far as I'm concerned, it was like the answer to a prayer," Avery said. "The closer Sunday came, the more depressed I got."

"So they won't be going back to California on Sunday? Is that what you and John decided between you?"

"Cindy was involved in the discussion, too. Both of them are in favor of my moving out there so that the boys can spend time with their father. Their suggestion was to go ahead and put the boys on the plane and make plans immediately to relocate."

"I see," he said heavily. "Did you bring up my name at all? Or do they have any inkling that I might have a say in your plans? Do they know I exist?"

"I didn't bring up your name," Avery admitted. "They aren't aware that we're closely involved."

"And you didn't think it important to tell them?"

"I didn't feel that I had to fill them in on my personal life over the telephone. You could act a little glad for me," she burst out. "You must realize how much it means to have my children back."

"Of course, I realize how much it means. I know that they mean everything to you. It's late. I think we should say good-night," he said in a weary tone.

"Yes, it is late," Avery concurred miserably.

"Good night, and I truly am glad for you."

"I'm glad for you." She bade him an unhappy good-night.

I wish we were both glad for us as a couple, she thought, hanging up. Tears slid down her cheeks, wetting her pillow, as she lay in bed.

If Clark didn't want her to stay in Louisiana with Bret and and Bart, what choice did she have but to move to California for her children's sake? There she would have some support in setting up a household. She would need to get as good a job as she could find if she was to resume life as a single working mother.

Evidently that was her only option.

"Mom, you need to wake up."

"You let us sleep too late, Mom. Today's our next-to-last day here."

The reproachful voices of her sons woke Avery. "What time is it?" she asked groggily.

"It's eight o'clock."

"Yeah, Mom, eight o'clock. Are you sick or something?"

"No, I'm not sick," Avery denied. "I just had a bad night and didn't sleep well. Would you boys go on down and let Sam out, please?"

"Sure, Mom. And we'll go ahead and feed Billy and the chickens."

"We know how much feed to give them."

"I would appreciate it. Be sure the gate's closed securely when you're leaving the pen," she cautioned sadly.

They trooped noisily down the stairs, talking to one another in the tones of normal, happy eleven-year-olds.

Avery dragged herself up and got dressed. Downstairs in the kitchen she glanced out and then stood there, gazing at her two towheaded sons scattering chicken feed in the pen.

Minutes later, they came dashing inside, emanating boyish energy and wanting to know what was for breakfast. Her inquiry as to their preference brought, not surprisingly, eager requests for their favorite breakfast food, French toast.

"French toast, it is," Avery said. "You boys can help speed things up by setting the table."

"Should we set places for Mr. Clark and Elizabeth?" Bart asked.

"Are they coming over to eat with us?" Bret asked.

"No, it will just be the three of us," she replied.

"How come?"

"Yeah, why don't you call them up? Elizabeth likes French toast."

"Mr. Clark has probably already made breakfast for them. I would have thought you'd be pleased that you didn't have to share your French toast with Elizabeth," she added.

Both boys shrugged.

"You would just make extra for her and Mr. Clark."

"You would make plenty enough for us."

Avery might have persisted in pinning them down on their feelings about Clark and his daughter, but there seemed little point in it.

After her sons had finished breakfast, she kept them sitting at the table. It was time for the talk she needed to have with them.

"Your dad and I had a long discussion on the phone last night. We've agreed that for the good of all concerned, you should live with me and not with him. I haven't been happy being separated from you boys. And Cindy doesn't feel that she's capable of being a full-time stepmother."

The news wasn't coming as a shock to them. If anything, they seemed to accepting it with relief.

"So we aren't leaving Sunday?" Bart asked.

"We'll be staying longer?"

"It all depends," Avery said. "If you do fly back to California on Sunday, you would be returning to your dad's house temporarily. One of the plans under consideration is for us to make our home out there."

"You mean you would move to California soon?"

"In just a week or two?"

"Not any longer than that," she confirmed. She interpreted their uncertain note as insecurity.

"But what about Sam? Who would take care of him?"

"And Billy and the chickens?"

Hearing his name, the old Lab had whined. The piteous sound tightened Avery's emotions.

"I would have to make arrangements to see that they were all taken care of," she explained.

"What about Mr. Clark and Elizabeth?" Bart asked hesitantly.

"And Shep?" His twin added to the list of complicating factors.

"They'll stay here in Felton, of course. Whatever we decide to do."

Her sons nodded solemnly.

"I was expecting a little more excitement when I mentioned the possibility of making our home in California," Avery remarked.

"We're having fun here."

"There's lots of stuff to do, like fishing in the pond."

"You don't want to leave on Sunday?" she asked, verifying the message she was getting from them.

"No, we'd rather wait and go with you."

"Yeah, Mom, that way we could help you pack up and all."

Perhaps they didn't trust her to follow them if they went without her, Avery reflected.

"What are we going to do today, Mom?"

"Is Mr. Clark taking us all somewhere?"

Her sons' main concern was the present, not the future. They seemed free of any anxiety. Avery wondered if they wouldn't adjust fairly easily to the idea of making their home in Felton, the alternative that she hadn't brought up.

She'd even gotten a glimmer of a readiness on their part to accept Clark and Elizabeth as permanent fixtures in their lives. The intuition only deepened her depression.

"I doubt that Mr. Clark will be taking us anywhere today," she told them. "I suspect we're on our own."

That information caused downcast expressions and inquiries that she couldn't answer about what Clark and Elizabeth were doing on their own.

The kitchen was a scene of gloom as the three of them cleaned up. Avery had just switched on the dishwasher when the phone rang. Both twins raced to answer it, making excited predictions that Mr. Clark was calling and arranging an outing.

The caller was Elizabeth, they reported disgustedly, holding the phone out to her.

"Hi, Ms. Avery." The little girl spoke in a tone barely above a whisper. "My daddy won't let me come over today. He says you probably won't want company. You'll be busy packing Bret and Bart's things."

Clark evidently assumed that she would be putting the twins on their plane to California Sunday, as John and Cindy had suggested, freeing herself to make arrangements for an immediate move.

"Did he give you permission to call?" Avery asked gently, fairly sure of the answer.

"No, ma'am," Elizabeth admitted guiltily.

"Where is your daddy?"

"He's in the kitchen sitting at the table. He's working on his res-a-may." She sounded out the syllables of the last word.

"His résumé, did you say?"

"Yes, ma'am. He told me what it is, but I don't remember. It's papers."

"I understand what a résumé is, dear." What she didn't understand was why Clark would be updating his.

Had he suddenly decided to send it out and see what kind of offers he might get in landscape architecture, his former field?

"Could you and Bret and Bart come over and visit us, Ms. Avery? I know my daddy would want you to."

"Is your daddy in a happy mood today, Elizabeth?"

The little girl's sigh came over the line. "No, ma'am. But you could make him be happy."

Avery wasn't at all sure that she could raise Clark's spirits, but she wanted to get to the bottom of the business about the résumé.

"The boys and I will walk over. You meet us outside in the yard with Shep so that he won't bark. I'll go in and surprise your daddy. Okay?"

"Okay, Ms. Avery." She agreed with alacrity, a lilt in her voice.

It didn't take any persuasion getting the twins to accompany her over to Clark's house. They didn't even object when she instructed them to keep Elizabeth with them outside while she went inside and saw Mr. Clark.

He was rising from the table when she opened the door into the kitchen. "Avery. I thought I heard voices."

"The boys are keeping an eye on Elizabeth. Can we talk?" she asked.

"You have dark circles under your eyes," he noted with concern, coming over toward her.

"I didn't sleep very well last night after our phone conversation."

"That makes two of us." He touched her on the cheek.

Avery turned her face into his hand. "Please hold me, Clark," she pleaded. "Make everything right."

His arms came around her immediately, enveloping her in his strength. She hugged him tight around his waist. They held each other for long seconds while discord and uncertainty were melted away by their emotion. Words were for the purpose of clarification when they began to speak.

"I love you," she told him.

"I love you. I want you to be my wife."

"I want to be your wife, 'til death do us part."

She pulled back and looked into his face. He gazed at her, sharing the thrill of loving and being loved in return.

"You'll marry me right away?" Clark said.

"At the earliest possible moment."

He kissed her tenderly.

"If we're going to get the kids enrolled in school in California, there isn't any time to lose. We'll have to find a house and get you settled. I'll put the nursery and this house and property up for sale. I've been bringing my résumé up-to-date this morning so that I can have copies printed to send out to landscape-architect firms." He gave an explanatory glance over at the kitchen table.

Avery put her arms up around his neck and brought his head down for another kiss. "You can put your résumé back in its folder. I'm marrying the owner of a nursery who will come home to lunch every day."

"But will the boys be happy here? We have to consider them."

"I think they'll be. We can give ourselves and them a year to find out, can't we?"

"You aren't just trying to accommodate me? A man does what is best for his family."

"A man like you does," Avery said softly. "I love you that much more for being willing to change your whole life for a couple of eleven-year-old boys you haven't known two weeks."

"They're your kids. It may take awhile, but I'll win their affection once they get over their resentment and distrust," he assured her.

"And they'll win your affection?"

"They've already done that. They won me over when they looked at me out of your blue eyes."

"I would never have known. You're so demonstrative with Elizabeth. And with me. I kept waiting for you to pat them or tweak their ears or do something that showed you liked them."

"They're boys, and they've been very standoffish. I think because there's two of them, it doubles their resistance to being friendly to a man they undoubtedly view as a threat."

He went on, amusement warming his voice. "I get the biggest kick out of the way they operate on the same wavelength. Without even looking at each other, they know how the other one is reacting."

"I guess I've gotten used to it."

"Bart always takes the lead when they have something to say. Bret follows up and expands on Bart's statement."

"That's true."

"Shall we go out now and get their reaction to the news that Elizabeth's father is marrying their mom?"

"First, their mom would like a real kiss from Elizabeth's father."

Clark didn't need any urging. He kissed her deeply, with love and passion and commitment.

Then they went outside where his daughter and her sons were romping on the lawn with Shep, soon to become the pet of a family of five.

Epilogue

"Boys! It's time to go!" Avery called to her sons. "You don't want to miss your flight."

"Coming, Mom!"

"Just a minute, Mom!"

Their voices, deeper than a year ago, came to her from the stable. It had been constructed in December to house their two horses and Elizabeth's pony, their Christmas presents.

"Elizabeth, come back here!" Avery held out her hand helplessly as her stepdaughter flew past, headed toward the stable. "You've already said goodbye to Miss Priss."

Clark came out of the house, loaded down with luggage.

"Relax, darling," he said in the loving, proprietorial tone of voice that was reserved for her. His gaze slid down her figure, resting briefly on her full breasts and coming to her slightly curved abdomen. "We're on schedule. We'll get the boys on their plane and then head north to Shreveport. Tomorrow we'll drop Elizabeth off at her grandparents."

He stowed the luggage in the van and then came over to take her in his arms and hug her as he resumed reviewing the itinerary, a ring of anticipation in his voice. "Once we've dispatched our kids, we can set out on our delayed honeymoon. I'll have you all to myself for a change."

"Next summer we won't be dispatching all our kids," she reminded, fussing with his collar.

He grinned. "That's why I intend to make the most of these next two weeks. I plan to keep you captive in that cabin we're renting in the mountains of North Carolina. We'll make love—morning, noon and night."

"I like that plan," she said, smiling at him. "But what's different about it except the captive part?"

They kissed, and then Clark helped her into the passenger seat of the van. Taking a step back, he glanced at his watch and commented ruefully, "You'd think these kids of ours were being sent away to prison instead of on vacation, the way they're dragging their heels."

"I know. That's a compliment to us, I guess. They're happy being at home."

"I know I'm happy."

"I couldn't be happier. Especially now that I'm pregnant with our baby."

They exchanged a warm, intimate look.

"I love you," he told her softly, words she never tired of hearing.

"I love you."

She held out her hand. Clark took it and squeezed it gently in his big, strong hand.

"We need to get this show on the road," he said, glancing toward the stable. "Bret. Bart. Elizabeth. Let's load up, kids. On the double."

They all three came running in response to his authorita-tive summons. As they passed him, Clark gave each one of them a playful swat on the rear.

He slid the van door securely closed after they'd hopped in. Before he closed Avery's door, he leaned in and kissed her, resting his palm on her abdomen.

"I thought we were in a big hurry to leave," Bart jeered.

"Yeah, so did I," Bret sang out with feigned irritation.

"Me, too," Elizabeth piped up.

"There wasn't time for us to say goodbye to our horses, but Clark has time to kiss Mom."

"Clark always has time to kiss Mom."

"You've got that right," Clark said good-naturedly. With a broad smile he came around and got behind the wheel.

"Shep's gonna miss us," Bart lamented as they drove off.

"It's gonna be a long two weeks for him," Bret predicted morosely.

"Your dad is taking you deep-sea fishing," Avery re-minded.

"Yeah, that should be fun."

"Yeah, lots of fun."

"Elizabeth, you know you're looking forward to seeing your mother. And your grandparents are taking you to Dis-ney World in Florida. You're going to have a wonderful time, darling." Avery addressed her stepdaughter, trying to cheer her up.

"I know I'll have fun," Elizabeth concurred. "And I do want to see Mommy. I just feel bad about leaving Miss Priss. I'm afraid she'll think I've gone away and won't come back."

"Just think how excited she'll be when you return from your vacation."

Among the year's blessings had been Marilyn's im-proved mental health. A new drug had done wonders in combatting her depression. Plus her psychiatrists believed that losing custody of Elizabeth had actually had a positive effect, freeing her of responsibility she'd never actually wanted. She had a job and was dating a man. She and Elizabeth corresponded and talked occasionally on the phone. Elizabeth shared the letters with Clark and Avery and voluntarily related the conversations.

Thank heaven, the little girl's summer visit to Shreveport wasn't the disturbing or threatening event it could have been. Clark's relaxed attitude was proof of that.

He spoke up, adding his reassurances, "Hey, we're all coming back. This is strictly a temporary separation. And there are telephones, remember. We'll be calling and talking to all three of you."

"You promise?"

Elizabeth was serving as the mouthpiece for her two stepbrothers.

"We promise," she and Clark said in unison.

The general morale was improved for the duration of the trip to the New Orleans airport. There the parting scene was touchingly poignant, underlining what Avery already knew: in a year's time they'd bonded into a close family.

Elizabeth kissed each of her stepbrothers goodbye and they embraced her awkwardly. Next it was Avery's turn. She hugged and kissed each boy, urging, "Now have a wonderful time." Then she stepped back, making way for Clark. He squatted down on his haunches and gathered both boys to him, one in either arm.

"We'll miss you, sons," he said huskily.

"We'll miss you and Mom and Elizabeth," they mumbled, hugging him.

When Clark rose, he had tears in his eyes, too, she saw. Avery thought her heart would burst with her love for him.

It was a special moment, as emotional and significant as those first seconds after the minister had pronounced them man and wife a year ago. Speaking her wedding vows, Avery had felt a tiny chafing fear at the emotional scar left by John's desertion. That fear was now gone. The scar was nonexistent. She trusted completely in Clark's devotion to her and to his family.

Later when they were alone, she would express all of this in words, not rely on their unspoken communication, as eloquent as it was. One of the rules they'd agreed upon was never to assume that he could read her mind and she could read his. Communication was simply too important to rely on perceptiveness. They'd learned that lesson the hard way earlier in their relationship.

Several times the twins turned and waved.

"Well, two down and one to go, Mom," Clark said to her when they'd disappeared from sight.

"Then it will just be you and me, Dad," she replied, hugging him around the waist.

"More or less," he remarked. "It's too late for a completely private honeymoon."

They smiled at each other, reveling in the expansion of their family, news that they hadn't shared with their other three children yet.

The little new member on the way would be much loved, but not any more loved or special than the twins or Elizabeth. There would simply be four children that came under the category of "ours."

* * * * *

A Note from the Author

My heroines always become real people to me within the pages of my books. They take on life and refuse to have wrong words put into their mouths. They balk sometimes at playing roles I've outlined for them. Avery Payton was more independent than most, but a delight to me. There was never any doubt about Avery's responses or her behavior. From Chapter One, she was candid and straightforward to a fault, following the dictates of her heart and conscience.

I like her very much and admire her honesty, her strength of character, her generous and loving spirit. To me, she is the best possible mother—a mother who truly puts her children's best interests first. Avery deserved finding a wonderful man like Clark Strong.

One of the pleasures of writing romance novels is playing matchmaker and bringing together people who are perfect for one another.

I'm thrilled that *More Than He Bargained For* is a featured selection in Silhouette's That Special Woman! series.

We women *are* special in today's world. We make a great contribution in every facet of modern society—in the business world, in education, in the professions, as well as in the home. Yet we retain our womanliness. With all our freedoms, all our independence, we revel in being female, in being different from men.

I'm proud to be a woman in the 1990s, proud to be a Silhouette author, a wife and a homemaker. It's nice being my husband's "special woman"!

It takes a very
special man to win
That
Special Woman!

She's friend, wife, mother—she's you! And beside each Special
Woman stands a wonderfully special man. It's a celebration of
our heroines—and the men who become part of their lives.

Look for these exciting titles from Silhouette Special Edition:

August   MORE THAN HE BARGAINED FOR by Carole Halston
Heroine: Avery Payton—a woman struggling for independence
falls for the man next door.

September   A HUSBAND TO REMEMBER by Lisa Jackson
Heroine: Nikki Carrothers—a woman without memories meets the
man she should never have forgotten...her husband.

October   ON HER OWN by Pat Warren
Heroine: Sara Shepard—a woman returns to her hometown and
confronts the hero of her childhood dreams.

November   GRAND PRIZE WINNER! by Tracy Sinclair
Heroine: Kelley McCormick—a woman takes the trip of a lifetime
and wins the greatest prize of all...love!

**December   POINT OF DEPARTURE by Lindsay McKenna
(Women of Glory)**
Heroine: Lt. Callie Donovan—a woman takes on the system and
must accept the help of a kind and sexy stranger.

Don't miss THAT SPECIAL WOMAN! each month—from some
of your special authors! Only from Silhouette Special Edition!

TSW3

MEN MADE IN AMERICA

Fifty red-blooded, white-hot, true-blue hunks from every State in the Union!

Beginning in May, look for MEN MADE IN AMERICA! Written by some of our most popular authors, these stories feature fifty of the strongest, sexiest men, each from a different state in the union!

Two titles available every other month at your favorite retail outlet.

In September, look for:

DECEPTIONS by Annette Broadrick (California)
STORMWALKER by Dallas Schulze (Colorado)

In November, look for:

STRAIGHT FROM THE HEART by Barbara Delinsky (Connecticut)
AUTHOR'S CHOICE by Elizabeth August (Delaware)

You won't be able to resist MEN MADE IN AMERICA!

Silhouette®

SPECIAL EDITION®

MORGAN'S MERCENARIES

by Lindsay McKenna

Morgan Trayhern has returned and he's set up a company full of best pals in adventure. Three men who've been to hell and back are about to fight the toughest battle of all...love!

You loved Wolf Harding in HEART OF THE WOLF (SE #817) and Sean Killian in THE ROGUE (SE #824). Don't miss Jake Randolph in COMMANDO (SE #830), the final story in this exciting trilogy, available in August.

These are men you'll love and stories you'll treasure...only from Silhouette Special Edition!

Silhouette®

SPECIAL EDITION®

WILD RIVER TRILOGY

by Laurie Paige

Come meet the wild McPherson men and see how these three sexy bachelors are tamed!

In HOME FOR A WILD HEART (SE #828) you got to know Kerrigan McPherson. Now meet the rest of the family:

A PLACE FOR EAGLES, September 1993—
Keegan McPherson gets the surprise of his life.

THE WAY OF A MAN, November 1993—
Paul McPherson finally meets his match.

Don't miss any of these exciting titles—only for our readers and only from Silhouette Special Edition!

Silhouette Books has done it again!

Opening night in October has never been as exciting! Come watch as the curtain rises and romance flourishes when the stars of tomorrow make their debuts today!

Revel in Jodi O'Donnell's STILL SWEET ON HIM—
Silhouette Romance #969
...as Callie Farrell's renovation of the family homestead leads her straight into the arms of teenage crush Drew Barnett!

Tingle with Carol Devine's BEAUTY AND THE BEASTMASTER—
Silhouette Desire #816
...as legal eagle Amanda Tarkington is carried off by wrestler Bram Masterson!

Thrill to Elyn Day's A BED OF ROSES—
Silhouette Special Edition #846
...as Dana Whitaker's body and soul are healed by sexy physical therapist Michael Gordon!

Believe when Kylie Brant's McLAIN'S LAW —
Silhouette Intimate Moments #528
...takes you into detective Connor McLain's life as he falls for psychic—and suspect—Michele Easton!

Catch the classics of tomorrow—*premiering* today—
only from ♥ Silhouette

Silhouette Books
is proud to present
our best authors,
their best books...
and the best in
your reading pleasure!

Throughout 1993, look for exciting
books by these top names in
contemporary romance:

DIANA PALMER—
Fire and Ice in June

ELIZABETH LOWELL—
Fever in July

CATHERINE COULTER—
Afterglow in August

LINDA HOWARD—
Come Lie With Me in September

When it comes to passion,
we wrote the book.

B0BT2